Healing Lily

HEALING LILY

a novel of hope

D. Stephenson Bond

Manufactured in the United States of America
ISBN: 978-0-9823079-0-8
Cover Photo: Molly Bond

9 8 7 6 5 4 3 2 1

First Edition

The characters and events in this book are fictitious. Any similarity to real persons (living or dead), businesses, or landmarks is coincidental and is intended only as fictional verisimilitude.

Library of Congress Cataloging-in-Publication Data

Bond. D. Stephenson
Healing Lily : a novel of hope /
by D. Stephenson Bond.
p. cm.

ISBN: 978-0-9823079-0-8 (pbk.)
1. Grief and loss (psychology)—Fiction
2. Psychoanalysis and psychotherapy (psychology)—Fiction
3. Francis Hodgson Burnett and The Secret Garden (literature)—Fiction
1. Title

2009941400

Alternative Views Publishing
Web site: http://www.alternativeviewspublishing.com

For Terry Bryan Bond
July 29, 1959 — October 8, 2009
because you never give up on the dream

CHAPTER ONE

A Bit Of Earth

HARACTER IS DESTINY," WROTE FREUD. "THE SUPREME and only lasting limitation on a man is the wall that ensures he cannot in the end go beyond himself." Daniel hoped devoutly that this were true. For if it were not true, then he would most certainly fail.

Dr. Daniel Osgood laid the book aside. He no longer had time for Freud. Or Jung. Or Winnicott, Kohut, Klein, Bion, and even Lacan, although he wasn't sure he should waste his time there. No, all these gentlemen would have to wait their turn.

He had now to line up his shot. Turning out the lights, it was difficult to get it sighted properly in the dark. He had to work by touch alone with no way of accurately predicting whether his shot might be wide left or right. With a long sigh he closed one eye to focus, wishing, not the first time, that he had had a bit more practice.

There was a small explosion of light and a clacking sound as the old projector complained, hesitated, then snapped into rhythm. The beam of light illuminated tiny little dust motes in the air that made him wonder, somewhat disconcertingly, if they were always floating there in the room or merely thrown out from this 1950's variety 8 millimeter he had tracked down at a yard sale.

Presently an image flickered to life on his screen. He noticed how he automatically gripped the film between his thumb and index finger, feeling the slick emulsion side gliding through the pads of his fingers so that he could detect even the smallest defect in the film, a single torn sprocket hole, every splice of glue or of tape. The touch of the film was familiar and comforting. It dawned on him in that moment that without thinking about it he knew exactly what to do with a hundred feet of film.

This is how psychoanalysts think about things; observing how people react to new situations through the lens of the past. And he was reacting to his situation in a rather clever way, it could be argued. What is an analyst to do when he is no longer analyzing?

Daniel had probably run his first film in health class in the seventh grade, a film about the blood system with wonderful cartoon animation if he were remembering correctly. In that film he had learned for the first time that one shouldn't dance too soon after eating because the blood was absorbing nutrients in the stomach to carry to the cells, whereas dancing required increased oxygenation out in the muscles. It would give you an upset stomach, the film insisted. His hematology course in med school had corrected him of that opinion much later, but still, in the seventh grade he had been far more concerned with the upcoming dance and any advice was welcome, if in the long run unsuccessful at improving his dancing skills, which in and of themselves were probably not the problem all along, but rather, his skills in approaching girls.

Those girls in Jr. High School were as strange to him as a German-built optical 8 millimeter projector. Nothing worked in the way one would predict. *Most likely as a result of the lack of a sister*. Perhaps that was the single key to seventh grade confidence, having the easy familiarity with a well-endowed sister that made crossing the Maginot Line of the boys and the girls in the darkened gym on Friday nights seem less suicidal. He did marvel at those fearless boys, every one of them with sisters as a matter of fact. It's the incomprehensibility that robs confidence.

Elementary school was a known quantity. The girls there seemed more approachable. Had he feared to approach Emily O'Donnell on the swing sets? *No.* They met every day at fifth-grade lunch recess to swing side by side and talk. That part was easy. Daniel could even give her the very best of his Valentine cards without embarrassment.

Talking to himself as he would have talked to his training analyst several years back, he remembered now. There was a strange situation in which his school was overcrowded and so the school day was split in two, with the southern neighborhood children attending in the morning and the northern neighborhood children in the late afternoon.

That was when he lost her in the sixth grade. How bizarre. But stranger still, he found a math book in his desk one day with a couple of graded papers. He could not believe his eyes when he saw her name on the papers plain as day: *Emily O'Donnell.*

You've got to be kidding. This was too good to be true, even for a sixth grader. And yet later research confirmed this uncanny coincidence of sitting at the very same desk in a split shift school with his first love from the fifth grade as she continued to leave tantalizing clues to her lost life there for him to find—a spelling quiz, a brown bag lunch, chewed pencils, various hairclips, and once a comb. He was tempted to keep the comb, frankly. This was, without doubt, the world's sexiest comb.

Ah yes, the voyeuristic thrill of close contact at a safe distance. Should he keep it? When the princess returned, not finding her comb where she left it, she would surely cry out "Someone's been sleeping in my bed!" And hence his dilemma, whether to break the enchantment by communication with her across separate worlds.

He might easily have preferred the enchantment. However, as he had later learned from Piaget, pure concrete operational thinking is a thing of joy to a boy. He could transform matters of the heart into a more manageable mathematics of probability and outcome. It was a problem of finite numbers. Since they had recently been learning about rounding off numbers, it occurred to him that February 14th was the single most clever way to announce his presence to her. So it was settled. He put the comb back where he had found it.

Such happiness he knew in those five months leading up to Valentine's Day. Elementary school was such a perfect place. The plan unfolded flawlessly, her messiness a source of constant delight. Candy wrappers. Half-eaten lunches. Hair ribbons. Notes from others kids. Sherlock Holmes himself could not have been more pleased with these clues.

The fateful day approached. Utterly un-self-conscious, he chose the Valentine card he liked best from the pack of fifty cards as they used to come in those days. It said: *You are the queen of my heart.* There was a wonderful picture of a queenly girl with a gold embossed crown. Perfect.

He wrote: This is Daniel. I sit in your desk. Do you remember me?

The day passed quickly. All of the children had spent time with glue and cardboard making their mailboxes for Valentine's Day and in a frenzy of fun had been let loose *en masse* to stuff their Valentines in the correct pockets hanging from the wall with each of their names scrawled in Crayola. Normally it would have been a matter of great import to decipher precisely who had left whom the best cards. It would fill the whispers of playground time for weeks to come. Daniel did not even notice whether Jane, or Sarah, or Paula had left him the best card that year, no doubt a cause of heartache all around. He had higher business.

After cupcakes and Kool-Aid, the school day wore down. The moment came and he silently blessed the envelope with a thousand blessings before depositing it middle ways into the desk where she would surely find it. *Oh no!* In his excitement he had forgotten to write anything on the envelope at all, so in a rush he had to debate whether it would be better to find an unsigned envelope appearing seemingly out of nowhere in your own private desk or more inviting to find an envelope with your name on it. He feared unsigned she would give it to the teacher without ever opening it. *To Emily*, then, and he shoved it back in the desk just as the bell rang.

Yes, the human psyche is the most amazing thing, thought Daniel nodding his head. To think that so much of our emotional landscape is a map laid down from the dizzying heights and the crushing lows of long forgotten experience that we traverse again and again with only dim awareness of the familiarity of this place that we can sense but seldom name as it floats on the tip of the tongue just out of reach. Is it cruel, then, or beneficently gracious that everything should hang in the balance of that single moment on the shoulders of a sixth grade girl who could not have known, of course, that she had become a queen of hearts and rendering her queenly judgment decree whether in that kingdom love would rule or else be exiled with no hope of return?

And so he waited, quietly and patiently. When the morning came and with it his desk at the front of the class, the children streamed into the room loudly, books flopping, feet stomping, voices chattering. Amid all the routine confusion he carefully placed his things on the top of the desk as he always did and then, shielded by the noise and clatter, glanced below. From that angle he could only see the lip of the shelf below the desktop so he let his hand explore the dark interior, feeling along the smooth polished wood.

Empty. The envelope was gone. She had left no response. Not so much as a candy wrapper from the Valentine's Day party. To understand this, Daniel reminded himself, you had to think like a sixth grade boy. Probability and outcome. That is why there were no tears, no self recriminations. He had made a calculation, that was all. If he had worked out this equation incorrectly, then perhaps he could get it right on the next quiz. And yet, as the simple math of fractions and decimals, multiplication and division, was the foundation of the algebra that would come later, and that algebra the precursor of trigonometry and advanced calculus, so this first lesson in love was at the bottom of what he knew about women.

On the second day he hoped again. He let his fingers enjoy the hard polished feel of the wood in the empty desk all through Mrs. Van Dussen's lessons, reading aloud to them from Caesar's *Gallic Wars* as she often did before the final bell. To be a hero like Caesar, he half thought, would be a wonderful thing.

At the opening of the third day he attended to his heavy books, laid on by the night's homework, and was delayed. So it came as a surprise. Her note on ruled paper. She had written in the pretty cursive script that only elementary school girls can master:

I remember you.

That was all. That was all there ever was to be with Emily from that day forward. But it was enough.

When he was moved to Boston unexpectedly at the end of that school year, his family following his father to a new position at Massachusetts General Hospital, Daniel had a dream that was the first dream he could remember in his entire life. He dreamed that he saw an elegant staircase as one would only see in a formal mansion with two stringers left and right above him descending to a wide landing set with a magnificent stain-glassed window. The lower staircase opened before him. And there was Emily, descending from above, until she was framed in streaming white light pouring through the window on the landing. It was absolutely real. Though he had not seen her since the final day of fifth grade she was captured in every detail more perfectly than if she had been filmed for the occasion.

The birth of the anima, Daniel had been taught. The end of childhood. The beginning of being pulled and allured and tempted with tender promises into the world that on account of her would seem to offer so much; a fickle mistress, granting ruin and triumph in equal measure for reasons of her own.

THERE ARE THINGS YOU NOTICE IN FILMS. *Little things.* Daniel couldn't help it. The way a child holds back, or turns away from a toy. The way the bride looks down or to the side. Even the way two hours of home movies in someone's old shoe boxes, films from the Fifties, are somehow always films of things—Disney Land, purple mountains, beaches in Hawaii, Niagara Falls—but seldom films of people, of your own family.

There are things only the camera sees. That little girl, clinging to her mother's skirt, did she grow up with that same basic insecurity and always hold back from life, shying away from challenges and opportunities just as she did in the film? And that bride at her wedding, when she looked down was she merely gathering herself to face her nervousness or did she know, even then, that she had made a mistake and could not find the strength to stop it? And what must it have been like to grow up with a father like that, the unseen father behind the camera, who overlooked his children and always found something more important to film than the people right in front of him?

He really couldn't help it. He was a psychoanalyst and these were the things a psychoanalyst notices. Daniel wasn't analyzing, he was just observing, concerned only with getting a good image down on digital tape; with cutting the dead spots, leader film, overexposed stretches so that you wouldn't see the mistakes; with laying down the sound track underneath old films that had never had any sound, any emotion, any expression. Just kids opening presents, Christmas after Christmas. Mothers holding babies and squinting into the bright lights as they waved for the camera. A thousand nameless grandmothers and grandfathers, there in virtually every film. Old, even then, as it said on the original yellow Kodak box, still intact, still impressed with the postmark of August 20, 1962, from the Kodak Processing Laboratory, 343 State Street, Rochester, New York, 14650 where you could send your films off to be processed and returned for fifty cents a roll. These people, the dead from another century, he could digitally remaster with a clarity they could never have comprehended, so that if they were to have seen themselves as they looked now on someone's flat panel wide-screen television screen with full surround sound swelling at the most tender moment they would have thought that heaven must be a movie.

He was selling nostalgia DVD's. He was selling story, a way for people to see their lives flashing frame by frame before their eyes, forty years edited, sequenced, composed, and cross-faded together into a one hour whole. Your very own personal Ken Burns video of your life story. He could digitally scan a box of old photos, pan and zoom across the images in the software, add guitar and cello playing period music, even cut in grandma's voice from the reel-to-reel Walenzak someone had made forty years ago, so that when you saw it all come together it would make you cry. It would make you believe that from this perspective, from this distance, a human life is comprehensible.

A little like psychoanalysis. A little like the way people get so lost and confused that their life resembles those yellow film boxes thrown randomly in the shoe box and they need someone to look through them and make sense of it. They really need to know *what do you see when you look at me?* Because sometimes we become so unfamiliar to ourselves we need someone with a good eye to take a look. *"Is that really me? Did I really look like that?"* we used say in the dark as the film rolled by, half-joking, but not really joking at all.

His good eye noticed something about her without him being able to stop himself. When she reached across his desk with the shoe box full of fifty Super8's, already apologetic, even though she held his eye with a quick toss of her blond hair, as Daniel extended his hands to receive them it was as if there were a space around her, an untouchable space that proclaimed itself in just a slight hesitation that even with his hands and her hands on opposite ends of the box spoke quietly that he was too close.

"Just wondering if there's anything here worth saving," she said.

"I can run one film through the projector and see if there's an image. That way you can decide if you want to do the rest."

He noticed it a second time. Even with his desk between them she had to wait until he took his hands from the box; and even then her small fingers, delicate as she was, seemed to hide as she flipped through the yellow boxes.

"This one."

"It says *Lilly, 11th Birthday Party*," Daniel offered, holding the film up to the light. "There is a little water damage on the front of the film, but I can fix that. Seems well preserved."

"I was just cleaning out my mother's old things."

"Okay. Come back tomorrow and I'll have something to show you."

She seemed surprised, and smiled a bigger smile than you would thought a little thing like that was worth. Yet somehow it was worth it to her for reasons he could not guess.

"Who's Lilly, by the way?" He risked in spite of himself as she turned to the door. He couldn't help himself. He was a psychoanalyst still.

"That's me."

AS IT TURNS OUT, in spite of long years of training in the art of observing people closely enough to get even a basic idea of what makes them tick, it remains difficult to get enough perspective just to see yourself. An analyst, for instance, often has problems interpreting his own dreams. So it was not obvious to Daniel, at first, why the humiliation of having his medical license suspended had by some strange inner logic returned him to film and video.

A memory is like a thread on the shoulder of a comfortable old sweater. You can pull the whole damn thing out if you pick at it long enough, and sitting there by the projector with *Lilly, 11th Birthday Party* running through his fingers Daniel was glad the day was warm and he'd left his cardigan on the couch at home so that Lilly hadn't seen he was that type of fifty year-old man who still wore cardigans because there was no woman in his life to tell him not to do that sort of thing in this day and age and make him break down and actually going shopping for something a little more stylish.

The thread of memory was that film on the blood system in the seventh grade and the bright red cardigan he'd gotten that Christmas and rather liked to wear as he tromped the halls with projectors and film from class to class now that the teachers had found out he could be useful. He could be competent. As a matter of fact, running the films gave him the chance to do something that made him feel competent at a time when in every other area of his life he was feeling pretty incompetent.

Now that's a start, he thought, lining up the video camera for the transfer. *Maybe I am feeling a little incompetent when it comes to losing my license.*

All through high school he had run the films, set up the microphones, recorded the musicals and the Glee Club concerts, filmed the football games to run on Monday mornings. The first thing he did when arriving at Brown was to report to the library and sign himself up as an Audio-Visual assistant, trotting off to various places across campus with AV carts loaded with projectors, XLR cables, powered speakers, and the occasional Kodak Ektagraphic or closed doublet head 3M overhead. And arriving at med school he found he could not tolerate the sound quality of poorly set up demonstrations and more often than not intervened with what his classmates assumed was an inherited surgeon's swagger. But they were wrong. They didn't know his father.

For all of that, from the day he graduated from med school, he had never touched a projector again. Never owned a video camera. Never took a single photograph. It didn't interest him. He had entirely forgotten about having been an AV geek.

Until the day they suspended his license to practice medicine and he was left to figure out some way to earn an income while his fate hung in the balance.

"I am so confused about you," Lilly said, plopping her shoe box down on the desk the next day. Her eyes drifted to his floor-to-ceiling bookshelves filled with hundreds of obscure volumes on mythology, philosophy, anthropology, psychology, and the imposing black volumes of Jung's *Collected Works* in the hardbound Bollingen series, flanked by the dark green and gold of the 4th Edition of Freud's *Collected Papers*. The paneled walls were hung with sophisticated and colorful, if strange, paintings by his patients of the images cascading out of their unconscious like amateur Chagalls. Taking two steps, Lilly's fingers nuzzled his miniature figures of animals, fairy-book characters, and other symbols that represented the menagerie of the human imagination by his sandtray tucked by the door somewhat incongruously, he would admit, against the hard-core intellectualism of his library collection. Not a single projector or camera was to be seen in the entire place.

Hence his video clients were perplexed from time to time, as Lilly was now. They were expecting a retail operation, he quickly surmised. He didn't even own a cash register. Giving in to the exigency of the moment Daniel had simply used his analytic office so that his video clients were confronted with two overstuffed chairs strategically positioned by an open window (he had forsworn the couch long ago) looking back on his desk nestled in the corner. In this role he was not, of course, their analyst; but he struggled at first to find a new persona, his own impersonation of a shopkeeper. He had to practice. He had to learn his lines. He had to remind himself that all they really needed was a place to drop off their home movies, old 8 millimeter and Super8 film, slides and family photos, and rapidly demagnetizing video tape from the early Eighties onward.

"Your sign on the door says VIDEO PRO and the sign right under it says PSYCHOANALYST," she offered.

"Must be the guy next door."

"The guy next door is Daniel too?"

"By a very odd coincidence, two guys with the same name ended up side by side in the very same office building in a city the size of Boston. Imagine the odds of that."

"Must be a conspiracy then."

"I grew up in a television studio."

"Your father was a star?"

"No, definitely not a star. Well, some people might think so. But I mean my mother. She was a weather girl, once. Back when they had weather girls."

"Oh, that explains it."

"Explains what?"

"Explains why you would be into video."

"And films."

"What's a psychoanalyst?"

"Umm,…difficult to explain. I have never come up with a good way of describing it."

"That's like a shrink, right?"

"Yes. Like a shrink."

"Great. Maybe you can give me some advice while I am picking up my films. Sort of a two for one deal."

"Not really."

"Could you get anything off that old thing?"

"Of course." He loaded the DVD into his computer and pulled the screen around for her to see it. Standing back with arms folded, they watched together. She was half a foot shorter than he, her hair still naturally blond.

"There's music!" she said enthusiastically, delighted.

"I think it makes the old films easier to watch."

For any other AV geek, it would have been like watching laundry. It would have been like waiting for the dryer to finish as mothers snapped at the children and single guys folded their socks, a hundred little things that spell the story of a human life that no one takes the time to read. Daniel couldn't help it. He couldn't help himself from seeing the person behind the image so that as *Lilly, 11th Birthday Party* rolled by already he was curious about the shy and quiet child, who would have been a good ten years younger than himself, as she sat alone with her pointed hat and paper noisemaker while the other children capered all around her. And being curious about the child, he was curious about the woman.

Daniel couldn't help but notice just how unhappy this birthday girl seemed. The other children at the party roughhoused and played. They pulled her hair and turned somersaults. They wore their hats and ate their cake with gusto. But the birthday girl, obviously clothed for the occasion in a special flowered sun dress, did not join in. She seemed to sit patiently while gaiety unfolded around her, looking away from her cake when it was presented to her and halfheartedly blew out the candles.

She was so unenthusiastic that her mother had to unwrap her presents for her, smiling nervously, and holding up the gifts for the camera to see. More dresses. More Barbies. More toys. And then her mother brought out a large box, the last present. Eyeing it suspiciously, the girl watched while other mothers jumped in to clear a space in front of her as the box was hoisted on the table. When the camera found the girl had disappeared, it tilted and turned to another angle, just wide enough to get the mother shooing the girl towards the box with encouragement. The girl looked to the mother. The mother waved her hands. There was no way out. She had to open the box herself.

Several layers of wrapping paper later, she carefully pulled back the flaps, standing on her chair to peer down into the box. Her expression changed. It was as if the cloud across her face was turned inside out to reveal blinding white sunshine. The girl had seen an angel. In awe and disbelief she drew from the box the long and slender figure of a woman. Goddess-like, the wood had been carved into a shape with generous hips, rounding at the top, then curving again to sumptuous breasts. A slender, elongated neck, inlaid with mother-of-pearl, rose above the figure to a smallish, out of proportion head. In the hard light of the movie camera, six strings glinted and shone near as bright as the girl's eyes as she lifted the guitar from the box and wrapped her arms around it in happy tears.

He was happy for that. Happy to see the transformation of the girl in the film. Daniel had watched it five times trying to get the exposure right, again transferring the digital image through the firewire cable to the computer, twice more loading it up in the editor and trimming the leader and tail on the film. By the time he was ready to set it to music— a quiet, instrumental guitar piece he thought appropriate—he had narrowed the film to watch it frame by frame so that he could match the swell of the song where the music strained in the minor key, aching upward towards resolution. The box appeared. The music rose back to the major key out of a minor subdominant interlude just to that spot where her face had changed as she looked in the box, crescendo-ing as she pulled out her new guitar in triumph.

"Oh…Oh…" Lilly's eyes filled with tears. "This is the birthday when I got my first guitar."

Daniel watched her gently, giving space to the moment. He could not tell from the outside quite how the older Lilly was regarding the image of her younger self. The last image of her holding the guitar like a lost mother faded to black as the music ended.

She turned away. He returned behind his desk and retrieved the DVD without looking at her. The temptation was overpowering. Normally, just at that moment he would have been a good therapist, helping her understand what had happened to her on that primal day in her childhood. But, no. She was there for her film. It was a line he should not cross.

"I'm sorry," she said finally, waving a Kleenex from her purse. "I had no idea what these old films were about."

"It said *Lilly, 11th Birthday Party*, on the box."

"I didn't read it. Well, I did, but I didn't know. I had forgotten. I had forgotten about that guitar."

"I would say the films were all about you. And if they are in as good a shape as this one, you've got two hours of video there."

"Yes, we'll have to do them all. When can you start?"

"Soon, but it will take a while. A month, at least, with the other projects I have going. Was the music appropriate? I never quite know."

"I have another CD with music for the other films. Maybe you could use that one."

She handed Daniel a home-burned CD, with a computer printed liner that had her picture on it, holding a guitar. The title hid her pretty face: *Lilly Summers: Thoughts in A Musical Language.*

"This…This is yours? The music, I mean."

"Aah…yes. I burned it. It isn't really very good, you know." She had wrestled all week with whether or not to put her own music behind the films. "You don't have to listen to it, do you? When you put the music on the films, I mean."

"I certainly do."

"Oh, well, try to cover your ears then."

"I'm sure it's fine."

"I am a folk singer," she blurted out, as if she were saying it out loud for the very first time. But she quickly backed away. "Not a professional. No. I couldn't be like that. I am a hair stylist, but I like to sing. They have a coffee house over at the Church of the Covenant. I play there sometimes. Anyway…"

"Looks like you learned to play your guitar then."

"Yes, a little."

"I like folk music. I'll look forward to hearing this."

Daniel didn't really like folk music. At least he thought he didn't. He had never bought an album or gone to a concert, usually more interested in hearing Mahler at the Boston Symphony.

"At the Jade Den," she said abruptly.

"Is that a folk music club?"

"No. A salon. Huntington Avenue behind the Prudential Building. That's where I work. You should come. We have a new wellness area. Aromatherapy."

"Yes. New Age, huh? I should get my hair cut sometime. But, I won't be ready for a month. Your films. Remember what I said about needing some time. I want to get it right."

THE HUMAN PSYCHE IS THE MOST AMAZING THING if one could stop and think of the sheer elegance required to so conspire after nearly forty years to bring him right back around to where he had found himself initially—grasping at film to make himself feel better. So it was all there in a nicely wrapped package on the very day he volunteered to run the film in Mrs. Johnson's class—the film on blood, presaging his medical career and, deeply unconscious to him at that age, reaching back to his great grandmother's genetic blood disease that put three generations of Osgood men on the path to medicine, balanced by the compensating love of film and the gadgets to make them come alive. Daniel was once again, as in the seventh grade, suddenly and incomprehensibly miserable. He had been happy working with his patients; their lives, their dreams, their lonely struggles. Now and then he taught the trainees at the Jung Institute, carefully preparing his lectures. He had even written a few articles that had been well received.

And now his license to practice medicine was suspended, provoking, he realized in that moment, the very same loss of face he had felt in junior high school. The same anger, panic, and humiliation.

He shook his head. It had always seemed a strange choice to open a video shop. His friends were perplexed. A little bit too blue-collar for a doctor they might have thought, but would never have said. His patients were the most perplexed of all. They were grief stricken when he told them he could no longer see them and it broke his heart.

Damn it all. It wasn't even as if David had been one of his regular patients. Daniel had been working on a per diem basis at Arbour Hospital to earn a little extra money. It was purely medical, just good doctoring, not a case for psychoanalysis at all. When he answered the phone that morning he was already suspicious of the Memphis drawl of the police detective.

"Dr. Osgood?"

"Yes?"

"Dr. Daniel Osgood, Boston, Massachusetts?"

"Yes. What?"

"Did you prescribe medication to a Mr. David Stankiewicz?"

"I'm sorry, you are calling in regard to what, exactly?"

"My name is Detective Howard Manozzi, Memphis Police Department. Mr. Stankiewicz was found dead this morning in the Meditation Garden here at Graceland Mansion, apparently from an overdose according to the initial M.E. report. If Mr. Stankiewicz was your patient, we need your help in finding next of kin. We'll also be needing the medical records and anything you know about the circumstances of his visit to Memphis."

But he wasn't supposed to be in Memphis. He was supposed to be home with his parents in St. Louis. And he wasn't supposed to be dead from an overdose on the sixty day supply of lithium prescribed by Daniel at his discharge. They had put him on the bus at South Station with a ticket straight through to St. Louis. Later they discovered he had gotten off the bus already in Springfield and somehow made his way south to Graceland.

That was all three months ago now. Three months of relentless downward sliding calamity. Daniel had called the family, *a mistake*, his lawyer later told him. In trying to comfort them he had made himself a target. He should have talked to the lawyer first, immediately after he received the phone call. He should have known this was going to be a problem. Didn't he understand how this looked on paper? He had discharged a patient from the hospital, an implicit judgment that David was no longer a threat to himself or others. Obviously if he overdosed three days later in Memphis he was still sick. Beyond that they had put him on a bus unescorted when he did not have the mental capacity or impulse control to get himself from Point A to Point B. The lawyer was apoplectic. How could Daniel have left himself so exposed?

That it was an act of kindness was no defense, he realized. If anybody really wanted to know, patients were often discharged when their insurance expired. In David's case it was either put him on the bus or put him on the streets. The parents could not afford to come to Boston, so Daniel had paid for the bus ticket himself. Besides, David's mood had stabilized, his thoughts had cleared from the manic episode, and at age 21 he had a history of higher functioning when he stayed on his meds, enough to complete his third year at Harvard. Such a smart kid. The entire treatment team had agreed he was medically cleared. Daniel found himself ruminating on these facts incessantly.

They made no difference. The only defense was the age-old truth that no matter how far our medical science might progress there remains no way of predicting human behavior.

When the civil papers from the distraught parents arrived in his office by special courier, he realized the family intended to really play hardball by reporting the civil claim to the Board of Registration of Medicine in the Commonwealth of Massachusetts.

"I don't understand," said a bewildered Daniel sitting in his lawyer's office. "Summary action?"

"I was afraid of this, Daniel. That's why I wanted you to let me make a settlement offer. The Board can make a suspension prior to the hearing if someone convinces them you've done something that represents an immediate and serious threat. They pulled your license."

His malpractice insurance carrier wanted him to settle quickly. The lawyer agreed. Daniel was dubious. It was a *technicality*, his colleagues assured him. It was just that in the Commonwealth of Massachusetts, beset by a few astounding cases of psychiatric ineptitude over the last decade, the medical board was compelled to be overly cautious. Prior to the Complaint Committee hearing there was no official blemish on his record. It would go away in six months or a year if he would just walk himself through the process. Every one knew someone who had been in a similar situation. These things always worked themselves out. No one assumed he was guilty of anything more than making himself the target of a grieving family. The sympathy of his colleagues was seductive.

"Character is destiny," wrote Freud. "The supreme and only lasting limitation on a man is the wall that ensures he cannot in the end go beyond himself." In the give and take of common events there are a thousand causes, but that can never forgive what is more deeply known. The things that happen in life appear out of ourselves as from a dark dream to test whether we deny or whether in the end accept what we see of ourselves.

That was the trick. That was the test, not to become so bogged down in the minutiae that he lost track of the real human being in the process.

CHAPTER TWO

THE STRANGEST HOUSE

I N THE SWIRL OF LEAVES THAT FALL WHEN THE COLORS are more intense than the red and orange Duck boats at the Public Garden, Daniel walked down Newbury Street after crossing Arlington. The great advantage of living on Beacon Hill was the walking and Daniel lived for the walking. Living alone for so long his interior space had grown into quite a house, rambling, in New England fashion, from the original building on a fieldstone foundation to the lean-to kitchen one hundred years later, connected crazily to a covered walkway out to the carriage house that in modern times would have been converted into a garage and attached family room.

In reality, his Beacon Hill brownstone was nothing like a New England farmhouse, of course. His personality had been stuffed in there since the move in 1965 from Indianapolis. Limited by the basic design, only four rooms per floor could be achieved, with a hallway down the middle. Up and down the block they were all the same: living room in the back with an elegant fireplace sometimes flanked by a great shelved wall and a pocket door sliding back to reveal the sitting room or parlor; kitchen in the back opening to the dining room with its window at street level two feet away from the passersby on the sidewalk. Hence the noted Beacon Hill ostentation of competing window treatments, great wide swaths of elegant drapes, curtains, valances, portieres, and lambrequins. It was a competition he had long since lost, his windows remaining exactly as they were when his mother died years ago. Window dressing did not interest him. He had spent a lot of time taking window dressings apart with his patients.

Upstairs, three bedrooms and a single bath, all certainly considered small by modern standards. Lately the gentrified rehabs were in the habit opening up the back two rooms to create imposing master bedrooms with marble baths. He had considered this many times but somehow never got around to it, as he seldom had guests in his bedrooms. But he needed to keep up the place, he told himself. It must be worth a small fortune by now. People up and down Mt. Vernon Street who had rushed to sell in the mid 80's were so pleased with themselves to have missed the housing bust of the early 90's, only to kick themselves for what they could have gotten for the very same houses after the turn of the millennium. Through all of that he did what he did best. He contemplated what he might do, while the economic cycles washed up and down around him like the tide.

In previous times the third floor, such as it was, would have been the servants quarters, or a safe house on the underground railroad. His family had never used it, but his accountant had convinced him to do two things: "Oh my God, you are sitting on a gold mine!" when he finally agreed to convert the third floor into a tiny apartment charging ridiculous rent like all the other nook and cranny apartments on Beacon Hill; followed shortly thereafter by, "Oh my God you have got to have some expenses to put against your income!" when he had let himself be talked into giving up the parlor as his analytic consulting room (European style) and taking a ridiculously high rent office on Newbury Street.

So it was all a wash financially, which was pretty much his opinion of what happened when you followed your accountant's advice.

The only difference was that he got to walk to work across the Public Garden every morning. Since he had an indoor personality, this change of pace turned out to be the perfect compensation. For Daniel, it was like the curtains had been pulled aside on a sunny morning, allowing people to see, for once, what one of those Beacon Hill brownstones looked like on the inside, at least as far as the parlor where a hundred years ago guests would have been welcomed.

And he was, turning fifty, more welcoming himself nowadays. Prior to that you always had the sense you were talking to someone greeting you cheerfully at the door, leaning on the frame and talking with his free hand, without ever quite inviting you in.

There are certain benefits to psychoanalysis. In the seventh and final year of his second analysis Frau Cardia Delarosa, Zurich-trained and in her eighties by then, looked him square in the face.

"Daniel, how old are you?"

"Forty-two, as you very well know."

"And how long do you plan to live?"

"What do you mean?"

"Answer the question."

"I don't know. Seventy-Five, Eighty-Five. I don't know."

"Hmmm. Maybe thirty years then. *Ganz gut*. Is that a long time?"

"Is this a test?"

"No. Thirty years goes quickly. *Nicht*? Faster than your previous thirty?"

"I suppose so."

"So, when are you going to let go? What are you waiting for?"

"I don't understand."

"Yes, you do. Do you plan on letting go of what has happened when you are fifty-two, then? Sixty-two? Seventy-two?"

She seldom showed him her Swiss sternness. But when she did, it always put him at a loss for words.

"I...I don't know what to say."

"Do not wait. Life is short, *nicht*? You are alive, if you want to be. Remember what Jung has said."

"*Jung hat gesagt*, as always. No, I do not remember."

"Often I have felt as if I were on a battlefield, saying, Now you have fallen, my good comrade, but I must go on..."

"That is cruel."

"Life is cruel, Herr Osgood."

"What...do you memorize these every morning from a little calendar?"

"You will remember them too when they mean something to you. Do not wait, Daniel."

"You know very well that it is not a decision the ego can make."

"I believe no such thing. In fact, it is a decision only your ego can make. Your dreams will not serve you here. They wait for you to make up your mind."

"Fine. I let it go. I let it all go. From this day I will not let the past hold me back."

"You mock me?"

"There. You see how little effect it has just to whistle past the cemetery."

"We shall see, next week, shall we not?"

And for all of that, to his amazement, somehow she had induced the desired effect. Only later, two or three years later, did he realize that shortly following that conversation he had agreed to that cockamamie plan to take up an office on Newbury street and by doing so open himself up to the world, both literally and figuratively. He began to actually use his dining room for dinner parties with selected friends. He took up the symphony. He made his way down Commonwealth Avenue for the occasional Red Sox game. He frequented the theater district, ventured over the South End, signed up for sailing lessons on the Charles River. Daniel was enjoying Boston again for the first time in fifteen years.

Something had changed that day, in spite of himself. Sometimes things have to be prepared in the inner life long before they are ready to bear the weight of living them in outer life. Frau Cardia Delarosa had warned him. She had pushed him. As a matter of fact, how prepared does a man have to be? Eight years now out of his training that totaled twelve long years of analysis Daniel was as prepared as a man can be to face his deepest fear: *fear of love is fear of life.*

SO WHEN TWO NEW WOMEN WALKED INTO HIS LIFE he was not unprepared. And still he stumbled because he wasn't ready yet. He still had things to learn.

That glorious autumn evening, when the colors were as crisp as the Canadian air, he was not on his way back to the office to finish up a video, but on his way to the opening reception of the C. G. Jung Institute, Boston. Classes for the semester would begin the following day. In his self-imposed exile he had wondered if this were an appropriate public appearance. Carla Greer, who was serving as President of the Training Board that term, was hesitant when he told her of his situation.

"Aaah, I'm not really sure it's necessary for you to be telling me all this. It's a private matter." She was a good sort, someone he had trained with at the Institute.

"Not so private, Carla. There are court papers."

"It doesn't seem fair."

"Fair is not the rule."

"It's bad enough you feel you shouldn't teach. I can't believe you stopped your practice."

"I can't quite believe it either."

"But what will you do?"

"Videos."

"What?" *There it was again*, that same bewildered, out of context expression of having confounded someone's expectations.

"I make videos. Long story. Talk to me sometime about your old home movies."

"Videos about psychology?"

"No, not really. You know…weddings, soccer games, high school plays. That sort of thing." *More faltering expressions from an old friend who couldn't think of what to say.* "So, do you think it's kosher for me to show up for the reception in my current condition?"

"It's temporary, Daniel. Of course, please come."

"I wonder."

A party at the Jung Institute is a strange thing to behold. In the first place, unlike virtually any other gathering in the United States, the vast majority of the analysts and trainees are introverted. Now, it isn't that introverts don't like to talk, as Daniel taught the trainees at the Institute. An introvert will talk your head off for hours. But it's a soliloquy. Introverts love to talk as long as the script can be adequately delivered and received, like Shakespeare in a summer session. That's the life of an introvert—long bouts of listening followed by brief bursts of intense talking. The life of a psychoanalyst, in other words. Hence the skewing of the bell curve of general personality types in the population to put a thin slice of people all more than two standard deviations from the norm in the same room at the same time, all committed to listening intently to the other people in the room while waiting to deliver their own soliloquy. So a party at the Jung Institute is a bit quiet.

And then there is the problem of being in a room full of psychoanalysts. People do have the wrong idea. When they come across an analyst at a party, people like to joke *Oh! I-had-the-strangest-dream-the-other-night!* Happens every time. And, no, psychoanalysts do not somehow magically know what your dream says about you just by hearing it at a dinner party. *Is it just the extraverts who think this is entertaining?* Daniel wondered.

On the other hand, actually they do. A little bit. Enough to make them uncomfortable at sharing something so private as a dream at a party.

But at a party of psychoanalysts, the stakes are raised. Of course you wouldn't talk about your dreams. Impolite. And then, unlike people working in virtually every other profession, you can't really talk about your work. You don't talk about your patients at a party.

All of this narrows the topic of conversation down to a tiny circle. It's easy to miss the mark. Daniel had found that travel was the preferred conversation starter. These analysts were a traveling bunch — Arizona and New Mexico were popular, if predictable, Europe safe and stimulating. Then there was Australia, always a winner, topped only by New Zealand. *Say, did you hear how well the analysts in New Zealand are doing? Everyone is interested in Jung there.* Fascinating. Sprinkled into the mix were trips to Africa or China or Russia where hundreds of people might show up for one of your lectures. Unfortunately, Daniel was not much a traveler and was reduced to commenting on visits to the Cape.

Now, you might think a little alcohol was in order here. Maybe something to loosen things up. Jung himself used to give some wild parties during the early days in Zurich, according to what the first generation analysts said in the films. They all got drunk and chased each other around a bit. But that was Europe. That was sixty or seventy years ago. This was Boston, where the puritanical streak ran deep. Only Brahmins and Boston College kids could get drunk. So at the Institute they served only strong mineral water. There was no chasing (or chasers) involved.

Every fall, then, at the opening reception of the Jung Institute you have a small group of introverted analysts and trainees, listening avidly, in groupings of two for about thirty minutes at a time quietly taking their turn giving soliloquies about travel that dare not talk about their work or about themselves; then they glacially move to the next little grouping, drained of energy like empty water bottles, so that at the end of an hour and a half every single person has talked to only three other people at the party who were just as drop dead tired as they were. Quite the party.

Daniel loved it. He found it kooky fun. The analysts in the New England Society were a kooky lot, no doubt. Jung himself had visited Boston as early as 1909 on his way to that thriving intellectual center of Worchester, where he and Freud had introduced psychoanalysis to Americans at Clark University. Yet Jung seemed to prefer Maine to Boston, arriving for sailing trips with Ester Harding off Bailey Island.

Even with all of that classic Jungian history for some reason the first analysts didn't come over from Zurich until the 1970's, getting word back to Switzerland about the fact that Boston was short of analysts. Then they came in droves right through the 80's, Boston becoming the New Zealand of its time. The New England Society was populated with Zurich-trained analysts, ex-patriots returning to the States for the most part, Frau Delarosa excepted, who was pure Swiss right down to her sturdy black shoes.

The kookiness resulted from the difficulties of trying to go home again. Fresh off the plane from Zurich, they were faced with the cultural shock that happens to anyone who has been out of the country for a while. After all, they had left during Jimmy Carter's America and returned to Ronald Reagan. Great swaths of pop culture were missing from their vocabulary.

"I dreamed that Michael Jackson was fixing my breakfast…"

"Please tell me, who is this Michael Jackson?" Frau Delarosa had asked Daniel during the early years of his time with her, gathering the associations to the dream.

"You don't know who Michael Jackson is? Well…let's see, I guess you'd say maybe Michael Jackson is sexually androgynous, racially androgynous, somewhat childlike."

"Ah, the hermaphrodite!"

"Actually, he is a singer."

"A tenor?"

"Um, I guess so."

"Wagnerian or Italian?"

"Motown."

"Motown?"

"Motown Records. Mo-tor town. Detroit?"

And on it went. Television references were often lost—characters, names and gossip column lives of the stars, commercials, sport teams, sport heroes, local news stories. From Big Bird to Bill Buckner, these things did not exist. Even for the repatriated Americans, they seemed never quite at home back home. The smell of Europe hung over everything; their living room offices with European furniture; their style of dress and hair cuts; their tastes in film and cigarettes. Yes, back then the first thing that happened when Daniel sat down with Frau Delarosa was her offering him a try of some dark brown Dunhill's.

How wonderful! He loved the smell. The European flavor of it all made analysis seem quite exotic, the perfect vehicle for stepping outside of yourself. The atmosphere of sitting in someone's house while her cats and dog surveyed you tinted everything with a warm Swiss *gemutlichkeit* that made it easier to toss aside American consumer culture for an hour.

His psychiatric training had been all business. The differences could not have been more stark. Daniel was a big believer in the analytic principle that the analyst must be analyzed. Completely oblivious to the implications of delving into yourself, most of his medical colleagues were in dire need of analysis.

Daniel understood. The single most typical attitude of the doctors he knew was the chip on their shoulder that came from the appalling treatment they were subjected to during their internship and residency. It was appalling and inhumane. He knew it from his own experience. Following the dictates of the great medical myth American medical supervisors inflict brutal recriminations and humiliations on their students always under the mantra that when you take a human life in your hands you better be tough. Socialized bullying was a way of life.

Now Daniel could debate the value of the enforced objectification of the patients that was required to immerse yourself in blood and death, but it was clear to him even as an intern that more often than not the intimidation was about power, pure and simple. Power and retribution resulting from the trauma of training, and not so seldom emotional trauma reaching further back than medical school.

Be that as it may, the irritating thing about his unanalyzed medical colleagues was simply the unending air of entitlement that came from believing that no one else had sacrificed so much, endured so much, suffered as much as they had done in order to become doctors. Well, he wanted to tell them but never did, *other people suffer too*. Other people suffer too. Your suffering is not so special as you believe.

And then the money, of course. The unanalyzed doctor is entitled to the money, and the privileges, and the house on Beacon Hill, and the summer house at the Vineyard because he has sacrificed so much, endured so much, worked so hard. Well, you know, *other people work hard too*. And they have none of those things.

In all of his anger about the medical profession Daniel was talking to his father, which would be obvious enough to anyone else and yet it took him well into the third year of his first analysis with Dr. Stanley Marcowitz to really grasp that at a gut level himself.

"Tell me, what brings you here today?" said Marcowitz, not even looking up from his notepad. A short, dark man with a black, bushy beard, his Europeanism was expressed in a more north-German, Scandinavian minimalist chic. Looking out over the Charles River through the back window, the sixth floor office was set with an expansive teak desk on a polished black tiled floor, a black Ekornes recliner flanked by delicate chrome floor lamps, and the slender black leather couch where Daniel found himself leaning forward more nervously than he had anticipated.

"I wanted to begin a training analysis. When I asked for the literature at the Jung Institute, I read that one hundred hours of analysis is required to even begin the training, so I wanted to start right away."

"I see," said the unreadable Marcowitz, who had yet to even make eye contact. "And for what purpose do you seek training?"

"I am a psychiatrist."

"That is a good reason to be analyzed," replied Marcowitz with a slight ironic smile in his voice, in spite of himself.

"No, it isn't that I have any problems," Daniel countered. "I wouldn't want you to get the wrong idea. I have no symptoms. No complaints of any kind. It is simply that one hundred hours are required."

"No symptoms? As you say. Tell me, why did you select my name?"

"From the list of analysts at the Jung Institute. Your office is on Beacon Street, so it was convenient for me."

"There are several analysts in the Back Bay. Surely there was more to it."

"Well, you were the only doctor on the list. I feel that one should start with the best."

"Ah. Perhaps that is your symptom. That only doctors can be the best."

"A symptom of what?"

"That is the question. Tell me, have you had any dreams lately?"

Daniel was prepared for this question. He had read the Robertson Davies novels, although they put him off a bit on the Jungians if the fictional analysis in those books bore any relationship to a real analysis. It all seemed rather wild at times. In those books, the first dream presented seemed to be given a special weight. So Daniel had combed his mind for an impressive dream.

"I dreamed that I was walking down a long, dark hallway. The walls were lined with a long row of framed diplomas, degrees, and certificates."

At this Dr. Marcowitz looked up at him for the first time. The large black iris struck Daniel as incredibly sad even so hidden on the bearded face.

"Tell me more about these diplomas."

"They were indistinct. I don't know anything more about them."

"Have you seen diplomas like this before?"

"I don't know. It makes me think of my grandfather's medical degree. My father's diploma. They were always in my house growing up. My own diplomas too, I suppose. Phillips Andover. Brown. Harvard. But in the dream, I don't remember any specific insignias. Is that important?"

"You tell me."

Daniel suddenly found himself not wanting to say too much, not wanting to say the wrong thing.

"I don't know."

"Perhaps the dream has to do with your wanting to enter the Jung Institute."

"You mean another diploma?"

"Perhaps. Perhaps you believe you need another diploma to hang on your wall of diplomas."

"Maybe."

"In that case, I am sorry to say the prognosis is not very good, Dr. Osgood. I fear the Jung Institute is not the right place to assist you in hiding out from being a doctor." This was provocative, confrontive. Daniel was used to that. Still, he was taken aback.

"You think I am hiding out from being a doctor? How could you possibly know that after fifteen minutes?"

"Well, there is the evidence of your own dream. And then, of course, I know a little about doctors. Perhaps you came to the right analyst after all. I do know that specializing in psychiatry is one of the very few ways to be a doctor without really being a doctor, isn't it?"

"I disagree with your conclusion, doctor. I would need to see more evidence."

"Yes. I can see that. You are only convinced by details and facts. A good suggestion. Perhaps next week we should perform the Word Association test to verify our results. It will take two hours. Next week then?"

So Daniel returned the next week. And the following week. And the following three years.

Sometimes it is possible to trace the origins of your own issues right back up the family tree. Dr. Marcowitz had pointed this out to him. How could it be that Daniel was still suffering today from the fact that his great-grandmother Paula had died of a genetic blood disease called hemochromatosis? (it causes body tissue to absorb and store too much iron). It is rarely fatal nowadays, but back then there was little that could be done. So, in his grief, his sixteen year-old grandfather, the future Doctor Daniel J. Osgood, determined with all his might to become a doctor. That man had truly wanted to be a doctor, to spend the rest of his life trying to save his mother.

And so it began, back in Iowa and the University of Iowa. But twenty years later that wasn't good enough. Dr. Paul C. Osgood, first born son, had to better himself, had to oedipally erect the higher position, starting at the Pritzker School of Medicine at The University of Chicago to become a surgeon, not a mere hematologist, and hence on to Massachusetts General Hospital to become Chief of Surgery.

Except that it was harder than he thought. Daniel believed that's why his father had always been so angry. Not overtly, but in the way that somehow his wife and son could never seem to show enough appreciation for what he put himself through to get there. In the way that Beacon Hill, Martha's Vineyard, expensive food and $400 single-malt Scotch could never seem to be enough of a reward. Dr. Paul Osgood had simply taken the medical profession for granted, as any kid growing up around it would do. So he was astounded, depressingly astounded, by what he was expected to do when he walked carefree into the University of Chicago to earn his medical degree and complete his residency. And he never forgave the profession, or anybody else, for that.

But, by God, his son was going to appreciate what it took to become a doctor even if it killed him. *Off to Harvard Medical School with him. That'll show him.* That'll teach him a little respect. Absorbing the anger, then, without being able to articulate exactly why, Daniel hated medical school. He didn't really want to be a doctor at all. And yet his twenty two year-old ego did not have the strength to confront that kind of anger head on with his father, so Daniel persisted.

And those, Dr. Marcowitz taught him, are the three types of doctor personalities, the three types of medical students he found himself marooned with at Harvard. The ones who desperately wanted to help people, to cure diseases, and crack the code on baffling disorders because in their personal histories there was always a story about someone who had not been helped, not been cured. Someone who had lost the battle to a baffling disease. And occasionally that special someone was themselves. They endured the brutality because it served a noble crusade. And then there were the legacy students, the ones who liked what they saw growing up in a medical family and happily embraced it, at first, only to fall victim to the effrontery of having to work so hard to achieve what they thought they had already been given. They endured the brutality because like any good hazing it was required to join the club. But they gave it all back in spades to the pledges and plebes when it was their turn to induct new members.

And then there was Daniel and his group of smart, beleaguered ne'er-do-wells. They didn't want to join the club. They felt no crusading passion. Every single day in med school only convinced them more and more of how much they dreaded what was yet to come. The stronger ones made their stand against their parents early on and dropped out. The others, like Daniel, smart as they were, had not a clue as to how to outsmart this dilemma. They endured the brutality of their internships and residencies because they were familiar with it from their fathers. They were used to it. It was an advantage, frankly.

Daniel did not stand a chance in that competition. When it came time to apply for a residency position Daniel was paralyzed, having delayed to the last possible minute any commitment.

Surgery was out of the question. His grandfather was far too imposing a figure to follow into hematology. His only safe choices were dermatology, ophthalmology, pathology, and perhaps histology, although it was difficult to find a position. As the pressure of the choice mounted, it was getting so bad he couldn't sleep. All his food began to taste bland, as if something had altered his palate. Somehow no matter what he was doing in the front part of his brain, the back of his brain was always wrapped in thought, pondering the problem. Not consciously, of course, but it was always there. It was like a cloud, a dark mood that settles over Boston for a spring of endless rain.

"You were getting depressed, then." Marcowitz commented.

"I suppose I was. But you wouldn't call it clinical depression."

"What would you call it?"

"Despair."

"And that is different?"

"Yes. Because I was thinking clearly. Because I was grounded in reality. Because in reality my course had reached a dead end."

And then one day—it was in the middle of January in the final year of his internship, he clearly recalled—he was so remarkably tired that he had to leave his shift at the hospital and go home to bed. He napped. A deep half-hour sleep. And when he woke he felt it immediately. The weight was gone. Simply vanished. The cloud had blown away. All of a sudden he was no longer tormented. It was one of the most remarkable experiences in his life.

This interested Dr. Marcowitz immensely.

"Did you dream during that nap?"

"No. Nothing I can recall."

"Hmmm. Interesting. I suppose it goes to show how an un-interpreted dream, even an unremembered dream, can still do its emotional work."

"If you say so."

"Well, what happened next?"

"Nothing. You want to make it so dramatic, Stanley. I'm sorry. It wasn't like that at all. I simply felt better. I had made no decision. Things were exactly as they had been before I slept."

"Yes, well, what happened next?"

"The next day I was in the cafeteria at lunch. Anna was there. Another intern. I didn't know her well, not then. Columbia grad and Johns Hopkins, I think. She was so excited. She had just come back from an interview at McLean and felt she had done well. She had just decided to specialize in psychiatry."

"So you followed her."

"No. I made up my own mind."

"Now, Daniel, tell the truth."

"What? That I made the single most important decision in my life based on meeting a woman? Please."

"You resist this idea?"

"I am embarrassed. What a stupid thing to do. How adrift I must have been. God."

"I am hoping for once in your life you were led, not drifting."

"Oh, please! Not the anima again! Bull shit. A bit of an over interpretation if you ask me."

"And yet you resist all the more."

"I thought the anima was for teenagers. Falling in love. Projection of the perfect woman for me. *La-ti-da. Anima-Shmanima.* I was not a teenager."

"I take it she was painful."

That was just about as much as Daniel wanted to say. He did not go on.

"Fine," Dr. Marcowitz continued, wrapping up the session. "You have just told me how your conscious life came upon an insoluble impasse, resolved only by a dream that you cannot remember. That unremembered dream, we might deduce, was in all probability an anima dream, because the very next thing that happened was that you met an outer woman who showed you a way out of your situation. And that, Dr. Osgood, is not just for teenagers. If a man is not to die from boredom, he needs the anima to get him stirred up about things. Passionate about things. There may be hope for you, after all. If the anima pulled you into psychiatry, then maybe you are more suited to be an analyst than even you suppose yourself. I take it as a good sign."

"Not if she's dead, Stanley. Not if she's dead."

And with that, he left the room.

CAN A MAN DIE OF BOREDOM? And this is not a rhetorical question, because as women surely know, there are so many men who are bored and boring. They do not light up as another man would light up to a toss of the hair or a touch on the shoulder because they do not seem to know the steps of the dance, the ancient dance, the dance of men and women exploring each other, only slightly unconscious of what is actually going on between them.

And if a certain man cannot dance the dance, could he ever be taught and would it be worth the effort? A boring man at a boring party, Daniel knew the time had come to at least give it one last try, even if he were only following the painted feet on the studio floor which somehow represented the foxtrot, as Mrs. Lynch's seventh grade music class had shown him, the only dance instruction he had ever had, how the man leads the lady in the direction he wants her to go by putting his left foot inside of her right foot so that she must pivot. If he was not to die of boredom, he needed to remember how to dance even at a party at the Jung Institute.

"Hello Daniel! It's been too long. I'm afraid I haven't made it to one of these gatherings in several years. It's hard enough to make it to NESJA meetings. How are you doing?"

"I'm well, Donna. How about you?"

"Fine. A bit busy lately. For the last couple of years I have been organizing Jungian study trips. We went to Ireland last year to study Celtic mythology. Fifty people for two weeks. Surely you get the brochures?"

"Oh, yes."

"Well, you must come with us sometime. Next summer we are going to the Greek islands to study the early centers of Goddess worship. It's going to be quite a trip."

This was new—Jungian travel as a profit making venture.

"Is that a specialty of yours?" *One-Two-Three. One-Two-Three.* He was getting better at the foxtrot.

"Yes, recently anyways. I started with ancient Sumer. My God, can you believe what they did to the Baghdad museum after the war? A crime. A true crime…"

He got himself up to date on all the latest about the artifacts at the Baghdad museum.

"Say, I've run out of mineral water and need to go back to the table. Can I get you something?"

By the time he had his water, some silent bell had rung to move the conversation to the next round of soliloquies. The partners had switched without him. So he was left at the table without a partner and would have to sip his water until the next bell.

An attractive middle-aged woman approached. He didn't know her. Although she was as lanky as he was, she slightly stooped. Arthritis? he wondered. Or perhaps an habitual nonchalance?

He couldn't tell. Unlike the other women at the reception, analysts mostly in their sixties and seventies arrayed in their New Age Wild Woman regalia, she was dressed elegantly in black. A New York look, masterfully pulled off. Her long hair fell down around her face, with that stoop, and reaching for a chocolate on the table she did not brush it away. His was beginning to think she was one of the wives occasionally dragged into these receptions by one of the new analysts from another region who hadn't yet figured out that it was cruel to make her fulfill this particular social obligation.

"Dr. Osgood, I presume," she said, looking up, with a slight smile, "do you have a minute?" Seeing her face for the first time—a dark, Eastern European face—he wondered if she were Russian. Polish maybe. She spoke with the faintest trace of a Continental accent. God, he would be embarrassed if she were an analyst coming over from Zurich that he had forgotten already from the last Society meeting. But no, he would not have forgotten her.

"Daniel, please. Yes. I seem to be without a conversation partner currently."

"I know!" she laughed, tossing her hair back off of her face. "Isn't it dreadful! Every year I have to screw up the courage to make myself attend this boring affair."

"I can understand."

"Oh, but I have always come," she recovered, hoping not to cast Daniel in the role of boring analyst, although, he assumed, he surely was just another boring analyst to her.

"Lately I have been trying to meet every analyst in NESJA. It's difficult, you know. You seldom see them out of their…offices."

"Out of their caves, you mean."

"I didn't want to seem flippant."

"Be as flippant as you want. We know we're all kind of kooky. I'm sorry. I don't remember your name."

"Laurel. Laurel Wolff. I don't believe we have meet in person before. I know you only by name, from the paper you wrote on fantasy. We had to read it in class."

"You're in training then?"

"Yes. Stage Two, almost ready for my dissertation."

Looking down, she flipped her dark her away from her face, inviting him to the dance. Daniel was flustered. Mrs. Lynch had not prepared him for this eventuality. The lady was leading. Laurel could see his confusion, but was unsure what to make of it.

"I liked your paper. I'd like to learn more," she tried again. "Dr. Osgood…"

"Daniel."

"I've been meaning to call you, but, here you are." And he could feel it then, or suspected at least that he should be feeling it if he only knew the steps, that the next turn was coming. "Actually I had been hoping to ask if you would serve as one of my control analysts. If you are taking more hours, I mean. If you have time available."

The silent bell chimed. The time was up. The other partners at the party rotated one partner to the right. But Laurel did not change partners.

"I'm afraid I have a problem," he began, breaking the awkward silence, breaking the well-patterned ritual, breaking his promise to himself. "My medical license has been suspended."

That stopped her in her tracks, feet tangling on the dance floor. She could not hide the doubt that washed over her face; the doubt that came from a thought, the thought that came from her unconscious too fast to stop, so that her whole body reacted as if the thought were true and the fantasy of what had happened to suspend his license were absolutely real.

It was as he feared. Naturally people would respond to the first thought that crossed their minds.

"And I didn't sleep with one of my analysands, by the way."

"I...I wouldn't have thought that."

"Liar."

"Well, it happens. I do understand."

"I should hope you would have learned that by now. At any rate, I have withdrawn from NESJA temporarily until this matter is sorted out. I'm afraid I couldn't be your control analyst. The hours wouldn't count toward your graduation anyway, since technically, I am not an analyst at present."

"I am truly sorry to hear that."

And there, on the ballroom floor, at the height of the competition, in that awful moment when the leading man losses his grip and the lady falls ungraciously to the floor is there any greater embarrassment? Is there any recovery? Only this: if the lady is a professional. If the lady is experienced enough to know how to flip her hair and smile as if nothing has happened because the competition is not over until the music stops.

"Daniel," she began carefully, "perhaps given the circumstances you could serve as my thesis advisor. It would mean a great deal to me if an analyst of your standing would advise me."

He looked into her dark, Eastern European eyes. She did not turn away. She challenged him. She knew how to dance.

"Please. A proper end to my training process. You do not need a license, I believe, to simply read something. It wouldn't be a clinical relationship."

His left foot and his right foot were going in different directions. Out of his rhythm, he could not remember whether the next move was in toward his partner, or a spin to the outside, hand over hand, away. She smiled fully for the first time, taking the lead.

"I already have a topic. I want to write my dissertation on *The Secret Garden*."

"Is that so?" he stuttered, suddenly a little dizzy. "I've always loved that story."

"I love it too!" she exclaimed, dancing around him now in a Pasa Doble with her hands on her hips and a swirl of her dress. "I've already written fifty pages! The material is pouring out of me."

"To what end?" he said abruptly, completely out of context.

"To what end? Isn't it obvious?" Suddenly she stopped herself.

"Not so obvious."

"I…I was going to say because I want to graduate. I suppose that's not much a reason, is it?"

"Well, it is a reason. A very pragmatic reason. Are you in such a hurry, then? Tired of it all and just want to get it over with?"

"I don't know."

"Take a minute. Either you are tired of training or you're not. Easy enough to know that."

This has got to be the most exasperating man I have ever met, Laurel thought to herself. *I can't seem to find the right thing to say to him. Does he want to dance or not? What does he want?*

"Laurel?"

"Yes, I guess I'm tired of it. It's been eight years, Daniel. That's a lot of living. I just want to get on with my life."

"Laurel, let's back up. It's just that when I said I love *The Secret Garden*, I meant it. I am simply saying that if you are going to write about *The Secret Garden* then you damn well better be willing to let it get to you. Let it get under your skin. Things would go a lot better if you would learn to find the Secret Garden in yourself."

"Ah yes, ever the Jungian."

"You laugh. I am the one who should be laughing at the idea that a man could ever teach a woman anything about *The Secret Garden*."

"You mean about sex? About a woman's sexuality?"

"That's your interpretation of *The Secret Garden*?"

"Well, it's kind of obvious, isn't it? Mary Lennox is a girl thrown into an old Victorian mansion with two available males, her sick cousin Colin, and the ever cool and romantic Dickon. What does she find?

A secret garden that was dead, closed down by Victorian morality, that blooms into a living growing thing. Mary Lennox discovers her puberty."

"The garden as vaginal mound? Yes, I've read it before. but not everything can be reduced to sex and sexuality."

"A lot of things can." Laurel let her hair fall down around her face again. She had realized she found herself wondering about his sex life; that she didn't even know if he was married, or partnered, or gay. She'd have to ask around the Institute about that. "Well," she continued, "when you stop and think of all those Victorian stovepipe hats and the women's millinery, gardens of flowers growing out of the top of their heads, it's hard to miss the analogy."

"Millinery?"

"A maker of women's hats. From Milaner, from Milan."

"You seem to know a lot about hats."

"I know a lot about Freud. The two most basic things."

"That old sawhorse, Freud wanting us all to achieve mastery in love and work. I don't know, Laurel."

"Mastery of love. Sex, in other words. Basic competence in sex means the ability to achieve orgasm regularly." Sometimes Freud was very practical, she found herself thinking.

"Yes, yes. But I am asking you what does sex symbolize?" he countered.

"Sex?…sex is about sex."

"Ah, the young Freudian hits upon the only thing in the world that is not symbolic. Sex. I have always found that strange. And so did Jung."

"What else? You're going to have to tell me. I don't have a clue." And she didn't. She didn't know anything that could be more basic.

"Before you go running off after sex, it seems reasonable to me that you talk about the real experience of real human beings. The things that people go through in life and what really happens to them emotionally. Find out everything you can about Frances Hodgson Burnett. Don't you think it might help to know a little about the things that happened in her life? Interesting story there."

"And what real human experience is *The Secret Garden* about, then?"

"It's about grief, Laurel. It's about grief."

CHAPTER THREE

AGIC

HAT DO YOU SEE WHEN YOU LOOK INTO PEOPLE'S LIVES? First, you would need a very long lens because you need to see past the common idiosyncrasies in which people appear to be so different from one another. Fast-talkers and shy ones. Deep thinkers and couch potatoes. Beauties and balding mid-life men. You have to look up and beyond the street level and focus on the larger epidemiological groupings.

Because at that level they look very much alike in their heartaches and their joys. Their complaints about their husbands are always within a range, you see. Or the things that happen at work. Or health emergencies and diseases. And, of course, what is going on with the kids. There are differences, naturally, when you look across the spectrum of the generations and of class. But in one way or another they are all making their way around the great circle of the life cycle. The life of the species in the round.

And yet, zooming in, the picture changes. Instead of rows of houses side by side, every one alike, you would see framed a more personal history. History like geology with layers from each succeeding age stacked one upon the other, hard and soft, and cragged fault lines knifing through that show the record of earthquakes, mudslides, volcanoes, and great floods. A landscape of inexorable emotional pressures bending and shaping peaks and valleys. In that way people are as unique as ecosystems, temperate or intemperate, and always in motion.

However, for all of that, if you were to look closer still, zooming in like a microscope to the cellular level the picture changes again. It is a perspective from which the smallest changes have the largest effects. This is the life of the organism itself pushing outward to express its own nature, in spite of everything; whether frost or sun, torrent or soft rain, hard rock or fertile soil. It fights to hold the smallest foothold, exposing itself to life or death, and takes its chances in the wild winds. What else can it do? This you see in people too.

TO A KID A TELEVISION IS A MARVELOUS THING. The people on television are a whole lot funnier than the people in your family, at a time in your life when laughing and playing are the predominate pastimes. Except in Daniel's case, the people on television were the people in his family; his mother, to be precise. And she was very funny on television. Much less so in her life off-screen.

Children's programming in those golden years of television consisted of three main blocks, Saturday mornings being the most important. By that time the networks were also running the yearly specials of *Peter Pan* and *The Wizard of Oz. A Charley Brown Christmas* didn't come along until 1965. Of course Sunday nights with *The Wonderful World of Disney* were a regular. But Daniel's favorite time slot was weekday afternoons, typically at four o'clock. He did watch *The Captain Kangaroo Show* every morning, but the thing that stole his heart was *Howdy Dowdy* and *The Shari Lewis Show.*

Daniel was a sucker for puppets.

When his seven year-old heart was broken by the loss of his best friend, Howdy Dowdy, in 1960 Daniel was looking for a new hero. Now, as an artifact of analysis, not as its primary focus, one of the things that happens is a new appreciation of the impact of events in your life. An awareness of the reality of the hit we take when something, like a meteor, makes an impact.

"*Geschlagen, verstehst du, Daniel? Es ist ein Slage.* A hit. It hits you in the gut," Frau Delarosa was trying to get him to understand. But he didn't understand, not at first. It took him several years to see the telltale signs of craters left in people's lives by something most often hardly even noticed that happened long ago.

Howdy Dowdy was gone, but in Chicago, of all places, someone new rose to take his place. A guy named Bob Bell, who had played a variety of roles in *The Wally Phillips Show*, debuted a new character in that fateful year of 1960—Bozo the Clown. The character was so successful *Bozo's Circus* was born in 1961 and every single child in Chicago watched *Bozo's Circus* every single day after school.

Bob Bell was like a meteor crashing into Daniel's life. But that is not the crater. It is not what happens, *per se*. It is on whom the impact is made. Daniel saw the meteor, but it was his mother who was crushed by its impact.

In the way that events often seem to transpire whimsically just for the sake of making things more interesting, Margaret Osgood was walking down the hallway at WGN Channel 9 in Chicago that very day in 1961 to deliver a news story to Studio One where the evening news would unfold at six o'clock. The young mother of the seven year-old, former journalism major at the University of Iowa, had never gotten her diploma and yet had managed at least to get a job as assistant news editor, mostly on account of the fact that she didn't look like the young mother of a seven-year old. She looked like a co-ed, at a time when being a co-ed was a very new thing. Proud of her new part-time job, she had no idea who Bob Bell might be until that day in the hallway when she bumped into him, literally.

"You!" he exclaimed loudly.

"I'm sorry. I wasn't paying attention."

"You!" he repeated. "Come with me!"

She followed him to a room she had never seen before. WGN-TV had recently moved to its new facilities on Bradley Place and the rooms were new to everyone. Bob Bell dragged her by the hand over to a rolling clothes hanger, pushed her arms down straight, and proceeded to lift three or four mouse costumes up next to her shoulders.

"Put this on," he said.

"But I work in the news department."

"Not today. You have sixty seconds." With that he left the room.

Precisely sixty seconds later Margaret Osgood stood in Studio Two in a mouse costume, still holding tightly to her as yet undelivered news story.

"Well, what'd ya think now?" said Bob Bell to his compatriots—Ned Locke, Ray Rayner, Don Sandburg, and Bob Trendler.

"She's not mousy enough, if you ask me!" Sandburg piped.

"Honestly, you guys are blind," Bob Bell retorted.

"Makeup!"

Another sixty seconds later, Margaret's face had a black nose and drawn up whiskers.

"Now, ya see?"

"Possible," they all agreed.

"Here, read this." Bob Bell tore the news story out of her hands and pointed to one line of script.

"But I work in the news department."

"Just read it."

"Oh no, Oliver," Margaret began, "you spilled the bananas on the floor."

"No. No. No. Read it like a mouse."

"Oh no, Oliver, you spilled…"

"Higher!"

"Oh no, Oliver …"

"Higher! Higher!"

"*Oh no, Oliver, you spilled the bananas on the floor*."

"Say that again."

"*Oh no, Oliver, you spilled the bananas on the floor*," said Margaret Osgood in her new mouse voice.

"What'd I tell ya, boys! Now Oliver's got a straight man, see?"

And all within those three minutes the character of the Church Mouse was born, and Daniel's mother's life in front of the camera began. She lost her part-time job as assistant news editor. She took a cut in pay. She couldn't afford to pay another mother from the Loyola Resident Student Housing to watch after Daniel in the afternoons any more.

No, she had something more wonderful in store for Daniel, although she could never have imagined the impact. Her solution was to shuffle over to his elementary school every day at 2 o'clock, between her rehearsals, pick him up, books in hand, and deposit him back stage at *Bozo's Circus*, where he kept himself out of the way until taking his seat at 3:30 in the bleachers of the peanut gallery to watch the grand hilarity unfold before his enchanted eyes at 4 o'clock on live television.

Margaret Osgood experienced her own enchantment with *Bozo's Circus*. Since she had moved to Chicago, following Paul to medical school, her life had not worked out according to plan. She had planned to finish her degree at the University of Chicago or Loyola, but with no escape from Paul's long hours she found herself marooned with Daniel. During the medical school years she had contented herself with preparing an unending stream of sandwiches and coffee that she delivered to Paul in the library, the locus of their family life at the time.

But by the time of his internship and residency with the ruthless Dr. Cobb, she had given up on being a partner in medicine with him. Dr. Cobb was the kind of professor who insisted that his house staff must be available twenty-four hours a day, and most definitely did not allow time for his students to pursue their medical careers and fulfill the duties of marriage and family at the same time. Residents and interns tried to hide the fact they were married, embarrassed to admit they had any other demands on their lives. If he did find out, Dr. Cobb was quick to assign that student to the night desk simply to enforce the idea that a man could have only one wife, and that wife was medicine.

It was not a lifestyle for the faint of heart. Margaret and Paul took to sneaking time together in the Memorial Gardens where the patients strolled at Loyola. It was the only place she could see him fully awake. Sixteen and twenty hour days during the week left him useless to her and on the two weekends a month he had off he slept straight through until Sunday morning. Twice a month, then, on a Sunday, Dr. Paul Osgood was awake and engaged. In the summers he liked to take his family out to the beaches on the Michigan shore, typically with other medical families. During the cold Chicago winters he preferred to listen to the Bears on the radio, preferably with his band of brothers, while the wives served up kielbasa and beer.

The wives were artificial sisters, women more married to each other, in truth, than to their preoccupied husbands. They exchanged recipes, baby-sitting chores, and Green Stamps. They started scout troops of every kind—Brownies, Cub Scouts, Girl and Boy Scouts. They did it all in the service of their futures in the simple belief that all the months, soon gathering into all the years, they spent away from their husbands would at some magical moment reappear in plenty and in leisure. *How could they have ever known, especially the surgeon's wives, that they were waiting in vain?*

The trouble was that Margaret Osgood was not a woman's kind of a woman. She was always more of a man's kind of woman. Sisters she had in plenitude. Gentlemen admirers were hard to come by.

But the times were changing, even for young doctor's wives. Although she would never have told her strictly Republican husband, Margaret voted for Jack Kennedy in 1960 mostly on account of his looks. Mostly on account of Jackie's looks too. That was how Daniel always liked to remember his mother, the way she looked in that glorious Camelot spring of 1961 in her pale blue dress and jacket with the pillbox hat and white gloves. To him Margaret was the spitting image of Jackie Kennedy, and the prettiest woman he had ever known.

For Mrs. Margaret Osgood getting her small break into even smaller show business was not the most important thing that had happened that day at WGN Channel 9 Chicago. Nor was her freedom from the doctor's wives. The thing that changed her life was the attention and admiration of a group of men who took her into their confidence in a way that a group of doctors could never, never do. In her painted nose and whiskers, surprisingly, she felt like a woman again.

"You know this?" Frau Delarosa queried Daniel.

"Yes, I knew that much even then. I could see the change in her instantly."

"What change?"

"She was happy."

"And what about you?"

"I was happy too. Deliriously happy."

"I am glad for that, Herr Doctor Osgood. Good for you."

In the first place, Daniel never attended another Boy Scout meeting in his entire life. Even better, every day after school his life was, literally, a circus. Ringmaster Ned led the festivities—circus trapezes and magic acts, running gags and a thirteen-piece band, games and contests, and most importantly prizes. There was the daily "fair and square" contest to see who would lead the grand march at the end of the show. There was the Grand Prize Game that matched a boy and a girl throwing ping pong balls into 6 buckets. Well, they didn't always stay in the buckets, of course. They bounced. It was a lot harder than it looked, Daniel quickly learned from the inside. Even a kid could understand that you won better and better toys with each bucket, up to the celebrated Bucket Number Six. "One silver dollar in bucket number six until someone wins them all!" Ringmaster Ned reminded the kids. "And a new Schwinn bike!"

It was only many years later that Daniel realized it must have been a bit of a problem the day he won the bike, his very own Schwinn bike. He was really almost one of the cast, but the men loved him so. They wanted him to have it.

Bozo's Circus was a surprise hit. At a time when the waiting list for tickets extended to ten years and newlyweds were fighting to get tickets for their unborn children, Daniel had a front row seat each and every day to watch his mother and her friends entertain him. It was Vaudeville in a clown's costume, with a little Burlesque thrown in for good measure. Daniel never noticed and never would have known other than Margaret's slip at a dinner party years later that her soft and fuzzy mouse suit was cut to fit her tighter and tighter until—she laughed, sipping her drink—there was nothing underneath.

The men were large, goofy uncles to him. They paraded him around on their backs, swung him in the air, taught him magic tricks and card games. There was Bob Bell asking him to hold a microphone during commercial breaks and paying him with $50.00 bills in Monopoly money. His eighth birthday party was attended by no less than Bozo the Clown himself, Ringmaster Ned, Oliver O. Oliver, and Mr. Bob the bandleader, which would have been the envy of all his second grade friends if he had told them.

But he didn't tell them. Five days a week Daniel and Margaret shared a world of fun and fantasy, their private pleasure. Paul Osgood knew, of course. He knew she had a job. He knew it had something to do with clowns and children. And yet doctors on rounds did not have the time to watch even the most popular children's show in Chicago. They had more important things to do. So Dr. Paul Osgood had never seen his wife on the small screen. Not once.

It was an unspoken collusion, a quiet little arrangement that left both mother and son silent on the weekends while Paul slept and ate his meals with them, then on the weekdays found them boisterous and exuberant.

She was two different women; compliant, unassuming, eager to please, and soothing on the weekends when she cooked his meals and washed his clothes and tended to his ego when he complained of how mercilessly his superiors worked him; witty, lively, brassy, and engaging on the weekdays under the spotlights. Daniel remembered her at a WGN barbecue on a hot, summer afternoon in a hostess top, capri pants, and sun glasses laughing like Sophia Loren. How confident she was. How full of herself and playful. Moving from man to man, whispering secrets. Easy, comfortable, and familiar. Arms entwined. Shoes off. Hands talking.

People can never calculate the impact of the things that happen because they are not trained to reckon the reality of themselves; how things are set in motion by the gravity of even the smallest things and outer facts cannot describe the movement of the inner planets that causes them to flinch or stutter at the oddest moments. It is the law of unintended consequences that wreaks havoc upon their fate in ways that physics can never predict, the stray meteor with its core of iron ore buried deep below the ground that pulls everything to itself.

Television taught him, even then, that things are not as they appear. Perspective is distorted. His schoolyard friends would never have believed that *Bozo's Circus* was in fact such a little place. The studio was so much smaller in person. And the people were shorter. A simple camera angle could make Daniel fill up the screen, same as Bozo, or make the Church Mouse seem like a little vermin in a little hole telling jokes. The walls were not really walls at all, but stapled paper. Every day he watched the men with suits and ties and scratchy faces turn into clowns and circus creatures, and back again after the children had left.

He saw real people behind the painted faces. They had real grown-up voices and grown-up talk and sometimes shouted at each other and said bad things. They could get sick and barely stand. Sometimes when Daniel watched the show behind the glass in the director's booth, he heard their chatter. He watched the cameramen frame their shots and the director barking orders. He saw the camera zooming in as his mother crouched, bending over, and heard the men laughing. He learned quickly what is shown and what is not shown, what is public and what is private, what is acknowledged and what must go unacknowledged.

DR. PAUL OSGOOD COMPLETED HIS SURGICAL RESIDENCY at Loyola Medical Center in the early summer of 1962, having learned the latest techniques in valve replacement and bypass surgery. Those skills were in high demand. People came to Chicago from all over the Midwest to get the lifesaving treatment.

As the time ran out on her quiet little arrangement, Mrs. Paul Osgood had mastered a few techniques of her own. She knew just when to throw the cream pie and how to slip and fall on cue. Her comedic timing was impeccable. It was another kind of timing that worried her.

She started early.

"Paul, don't you think Chicago is the perfect place for you?"

"And play second fiddle to Dr. Cobb forever? I damn well need to get myself out from under him and now's my chance. The world's my oyster."

"But we have so many friends."

"Think of it, Margaret! The Mayo Clinic!"

"Where is that?"

"Rochester, Minnesota."

"Oh, that's much too cold."

"The UCLA Medical Center, only seven years old and already to top-ranked hospital on the West Coast. Heart surgeon to the stars. That warm enough for you?"

"Too far from home."

"Well, I don't see what that has to do with it. Mount Sinai Hospital, New York City. The Cleveland Clinic. Massachusetts General Hospital."

"But I have a job!"

Daniel starred at his mashed potatoes. At nine years-old he was not old enough to understand what residency meant. His father was a doctor. His grandfather was a doctor. Somehow his father was talking about being another kind of doctor and he couldn't understand why that meant they might have to leave Chicago. In the long silence he did look up enough to see the bewilderment on his father's face.

"You have a job?"

"You know I work at the television station."

"Yes, I know that. I am just trying to comprehend why you are telling me this when I am trying to make the most important decision of my life."

When Daniel worked his way through this particular bit of the amanuensis with Dr. Marcowitz in his first analysis, it came as a revelation.

"Put yourself in his shoes, Daniel."

"I wouldn't want to."

"Don't you want to understand your father?"

"No. And I already understand him perfectly besides."

"Interesting answer. No, you don't want to understand him. You just want to go on hating him. Go on blaming him."

"What is there to understand? He's a narcissistic bastard. Aren't you sympathetic to the pain I suffered from being dragged around with him in my childhood?"

"Again, this split we've come across before. From him you want nothing. From me you want sympathy. Good fathers and bad fathers. Mean fathers and fun fathers. Maybe your pain would be more convincing to me if it were real to you yourself. I don't know if your father was narcissistic or not. You throw it around too easily. Too easy, Daniel. You want to get to the real story or not?"

"Yes. Fine."

"Then put yourself in his shoes. A resident finishing in 1962. His wife is complaining she has a part-time job."

"He didn't understand."

"No, he didn't. And you tell me another man alive in 1962 who would have understood. Hell, tell me a young resident today who would have understood?"

Dr. Marcowitz forced Daniel to look into his father's bewildered eyes and to see there the incredulity of a man who worked sixteen hours a day for more than four years to earn the right to practice on his own. The eyes of a heart surgeon, schooled to take every life and death decision on his own shoulders, who was being gainsaid by, to put it frankly, someone who was not a doctor. *His wife*. It was the astonishment of a man who had up to that very moment thought that everything he had suffered he had endured on her behalf and now saw, if only for an instant, that something else might be more important to her.

"But it wasn't for her. It wasn't for us. It was for himself."

"Yes, Daniel. It was for himself and what he entitled himself to take. But it is the same fantasy that many hardworking men tell themselves. They do it all for her. And every time you hear it you need to remember that. They believe that. They believe it deeply."

"It is a lie."

"It is partly a lie, and it is also partly true, if you care to take the trouble to differentiate a little bit. It's true because a man needs to believe in his own worth. He needs to believe that whatever he endures, he does not suffer in vain. So he offers it to her. It's the only way of enduring, like a soldier in the trenches with a picture of his girl in his wallet."

"You make it sound like he loved her."

"Oh really?" Marcowitz laughed out loud. "Loved your mother or loved his anima? Either way, yes. Why not? Why is it so hard for you to think he loved her?"

"Because he didn't act like it, did he?"

"Well, how does love act? Anyway, you take your mother's side every time, don't you?"

"No. I blame her too."

"Perhaps. But she was a doctor's wife in 1962. She followed him. That was part of the deal. Still is."

"She didn't know that."

"I wouldn't be so sure."

BUT IT WASN'T THE MAYO CLINIC. It wasn't UCLA. Dr. Paul Osgood did not get his privileges in Minnesota or California or New York, or even Cleveland.

"Methodist Hospital. Indianapolis. I will be their first heart surgeon."

Now it was Margaret Osgood's turn to be bewildered. At least, she thought, *if I have to move maybe we can move to a larger market station. Los Angeles or New York*. It was a dream that she was dreaming, almost against her will. She had a resume now. She had Bob Bell in her back pocket and the station manager at WGN. *It was possible.*

"Don't be disappointed."

She couldn't speak to him and ran off to the bedroom. If Daniel had the strength of character to endure it, he would have realized that very moment may have been the first moment that it ever crossed his father's mind that he was losing her. But he couldn't do it, not with Marcowitz. That picture would have to remain undeveloped until he was stronger, until Frau Delarosa forced him.

The Osgood family licked their wounds in Indianapolis. Margaret busied herself with the details of the move while Paul finished up, taking Daniel along to shop for houses, row upon row of new three-bedroom brick Ranches spreading out over the cornfields west of town like summer stalks, every one alike. She picked one close to school so Daniel could walk and paid the deposit. Her doctor's life began, with more Cub Scout troops and PTA dinners than she could count.

But in the back of her mind she was trying to find a way. She watched a lot of television that summer, but not the way most people watch television. Margaret Osgood was taking notes. By the time Daniel started back to school in late August of 1962 she had her plan.

WISH-TV Channel 8 Indianapolis, a CBS affiliate back then, filled their primary children's after-school slot with Captain Paulo, a one hour extravaganza of Warner Brothers cartoons introduced by a sad and dour-looking Captain Paulo dressed in his white ship Captain's suit and sailor's pipe. Johnson Taylor, Channel 8's regular evening weatherman had been pulled into the role.

"*Aye, laddies and lasses,*" he would croon, "*thar she blows. Let's see what that land lubber rabbit is up to today.*"

Margaret could see they needed a little help. References in hand from Bob Bell and WGN Chicago, she sprung her plan on Johnson Taylor.

"Look, you're number three in a three station market. Contests, games, and prizes with a live audience are a proven success. I can put this together for you."

"We don't have room for a live audience in the studio."

"This show could pull in all the school-aged children in Indianapolis. And their mothers."

"I'm sorry, Mrs. Osgood. We just don't have the budget. But look, you seem to know what you're doing. I need a weekend weather girl."

"I don't know anything about meteorology."

"Not required. You just need presence. And I can tell right now you've got that, in spades. Why don't we give it a try?"

"Fine. I'll take it."

WISH-TV had granted Margaret Osgood's wish in a most unusual way. True, she could not read the AVN/NGM to plot the cyclogenesis of an orographic lift, but she could deliver tomorrow's high temperature like it was a punch line. She was back in business. Back under the lights. Now all she needed was a few good men.

"But you don't need to work anymore," insisted Daniel's flabbergasted father.

"It's just weekends, Paul."

"That's the point. It's the weekends when I need you."

"Need me for what?"

"Need you to watch Daniel so that I can relax. It's my only time off."

"And what about my time? My time for me?"

"You're off every single day, for cryin' out loud."

"No. I'm not. Don't get me started."

"I want you to tell them it was a mistake. I want to tell them you can't take the job. Tell them your husband won't let you. I don't care. You're a mother. You're a doctor's wife. You have more important things to do."

"Is that what you think?"

"All I want is a little piece and quiet when I'm home. Is that so much to ask? Huh? Just a little respect in my own house. Who pays the bills around here? I do. Who puts the food on the table?"

"I do, as a matter of fact. But I tell you what. You can take your god-damned money, fry it up in a frying pan with some brown onions, serve it with some fresh car keys and stewed golf balls and choke on your own bullshit till your face turns blue. I need this job. I'm taking it."

That was how they fought in the old days, Daniel reflected later with Marcowitz. *Role conflict.* When their roles define them couples need not get so personal. They do not need to carry on their shoulders the burden of relating to a unique individual. The most useful thing about that kind of marriage is that a woman's primary relationship is with the other women, the women of her community. And a man's primary relationship is with the other men, the men of his community. People would think you were nuts if you insisted on getting your relationship needs met by your spouse. Why would you even want to? That's not what a marriage is for.

This is what the Old Man couldn't see, Daniel reckoned. This is what the Old Man could never figure out. Mrs. Margaret Osgood didn't have a community of women. Not in Indianapolis. Not in the suburbs. Not in moving, moving, moving to chase the job. And even if she did, she was becoming something else that she could not explain even to herself. She was becoming a modern woman who was working on her WISH.

Only one thing could stop her. It is the only thing that can contradict a wish, said Freud. It's old and ancient enemy. *Fear.*

To reach out, to stretch, to grasp. To pull back, to tighten, to let go. The impulse and its inhibition.

"You should write a paper," said Marcowitz happily.

"On my mother?"

"Yes, I suppose. On the archetypes of the marriage relationship."

"You think I've got it now?"

"Only if you understand your father for what he was."

"A son of a bitch."

"A man of his times. A man in a role that he could not let go of."

"On account of fear?"

"If you want to understand a man, Daniel, it always helps to know what he fears. Even a man like yourself."

"Or a man like you, Stanley?"

"Yes. Of course. A man like me."

Fear was made real in 1962 in a way that it has not been real before or after that October.

Monday, October 22, 1962, 6:45 P.M. Dr. Paul Osgood, the new heart surgeon at Methodist Hospital in Indianapolis, Indiana is on his way home, driving westward on 16th Street. He is contemplating recent events with his wife, Margaret, that have put the deepest Cold War chill into their marriage he can remember. They are not speaking. Dr. Osgood is confused. He has recently completed his residency at Loyola Medical Center in Chicago with Dr. Cobb, one of the five leading heart specialists in the United States, and had expected to be greeted with open arms and generous offers by leading medical institutions around the country. No offers were forthcoming, however, due to the less than enthusiastic recommendation Dr. Cobb has circulated concerning Dr. Osgood's work. When he learned of this, Dr. Osgood, in an uncharacteristic flash of fury, confronted Dr. Cobb with such venom and vitriol that their relationship was permanently severed. They never spoke again and their animosity was legend at medical conferences for decades to come. Due to this rupture of relationship and good taste, Dr. Osgood was forced to accept a position in Indiana.

He shares none of this information with his wife, however. He is not in the habit of mixing his professional and his personal life, being of the opinion, fostered by his father, Dr. Daniel J. Osgood, that doctors are best advised to keep their professional disagreements to themselves.

Coming into Speedway Township he drives past the southern turn of the Indianapolis Motor Speedway and considers his dilemma with his wife, although he would admit to a vexing irritation in having to take his mind away from his work and his patients for something as trivial as a marital difficulty. They have not spoken other than to make dinner plans and childcare arrangements since an incident in late August when she had mentioned she was considering taking a part-time job on weekends at a local television station. Two weeks following the incident, she insisted he sleep in a separate bed, and there he has remained.

In spite of his reasonable arguments against the need for her to seek employment, she had taken the job and for seven weeks Dr. Osgood has often found himself alone on Saturdays and Sundays with his nine year-old son, Daniel. He is not quite sure what to do with the boy. Being the autumn season, Dr. Osgood tried to interest his son in learning how to throw a football. When this activity was not successful, he tried to teach the lad some chess. Apparently the child did not have the attention span for it. The only successful event was listening to the third game of the World Series together, young Daniel seeming inspired by the home run of a previously hitless Roger Maris in the ninth inning to win the game. Unfortunately, the Yankees crushed the Cincinnati Reds in five games and the Series was over by Tuesday.

Dr. Paul Osgood is at an utter loss as to how to approach his estranged wife. The only solution he can see is for her to quit her job as, incredibly, a weather girl and return the situation to the sane and happy home life he had enjoyed previously. He misses her, he misses that old life desperately, for it was his only refuge from the brutality of the hated Dr. Cobb. In his mind he goes through the things that might have upset her. Perhaps she is not happy with the house. Although at the time he thought a new house would be the most suitable, he has seen older neighborhoods in the four months since his arrival and knows of several other doctors who live in the area near Butler University. Then again, perhaps she misses her friends in Chicago. The resident's families there had been very close. He is feeling a little forlorn in this strange new city, he admits to himself. Or perhaps, she does not like Indiana, or the school system, or the grocery stores.

Options? His first option is to buy her a new car. That always made him feel better when he was a little blue. A Lincoln. God, he loves Lincolns. They way they handle, the way they float right under you. Maybe she needs a trip to visit her friends in Chicago, or her mother back in Iowa. But no, that wouldn't really do if the issue were really the house. It must be the house. There is no other logical explanation. Yes, he must promise her to buy her another house as soon as possible. They had been too hurried. He would take a loss, certainly, selling so soon, but he understands that being a good family man requires making sacrifices for the family. It is a sacrifice he is willing to make. *Good.* He would bring that up with her as soon as possible and everything could get back to normal.

Monday, October 22, 1962, 7:00 P.M. Mrs. Margaret Osgood is completing dinner for the evening. A meatloaf is in the oven, potatoes, soon to be mashed, are on the stove. The corn is boiling. An apple pie sits on the counter.

She watches her son Daniel sitting by the television. A fourth grader at Ben Davis Elementary School, she worries he is not adjusting well. The only life he had ever known had been in Chicago. Although the streets up and down the subdivision are filled with children his age, she has yet to see him ask to go over to another boy's house or invite a friend over. She thinks of him as a delicate, deep-thinking child, prone to ask her questions that make her marvel at his understanding of grown-up things. She has read what Dr. Spock has said about only children (*he doesn't like them*), and fears Daniel has, predictably, learned to identify with adults rather than the children his own age. She couldn't even get him to listen to the World Series on the radio like all the other boys. He said baseball bored him.

Still, he seems happy enough. She has other problems to worry about. Just the other day the station manager had complimented her on her success at the station. The fact that the man always watched two TV's at the same time, one always tuned to his own station, concerned her. But the station manager had said that her lack of experience broadcasting weather reports didn't show. She was a natural. He had even suggested he'd find a way to schedule time for her during the weekdays. Johnson Taylor had a vacation coming up and she could do the whole week while he was gone.

It makes her happy. All things told, maybe it is better to wait to bring up the idea about the children's show again. Wait until she is more settled, until she has all the station folks behind her. They are nice. The weekend crew is fun. Some of the younger cameramen like to flirt. No, it's fine. It is innocent enough. They don't even seem to realize she is older. The attention is nice.

Damn it, why can't she get the attention from her husband? Didn't he understand? *No. Of course not.* He had changed since medical school. Why couldn't they go back to the way things used to be? Margaret could still remember when she had met him in the library or the Memorial Gardens and snuck kisses while Daniel toddled. Paul had seemed interested in her then. They had a partnership. They were building something together.

How could they have lost that? That damn Dr. Cobb. Paul's residency had killed him, she could see that. He was clearly unhappy. *Let's move*, she urged him. *If it's so bad then let's just move and find another residency.* No, that was suicide, Paul insisted. Everyone would ask him what went wrong with Dr. Cobb. Just stick it out. Just stick it out and things will get better, Paul had promised.

And *this* is better? Oh, it enrages her just to think about it. Indianapolis is tolerable. Disappointing, no doubt, but tolerable. And the house is nice. She has always preferred brick homes. So much bigger than the apartment in Chicago. And finally she has gotten herself away from those women and those ridiculous teas with Mrs. Cobb.

It's not Indianapolis. Margaret finds herself enraged because, she realizes, there had always been the unspoken promise that after residency Paul would be his old self again. A promise of return from a temporary hardship. But it wasn't true. *God damn it, that man broke his promise.* She could see it already in Chicago. Paul was just like Dr. Cobb. That awful man had somehow made all his students copy him right down to his blue suits and his god-damned Lincoln.

The old Paul wasn't coming back, she realized. That's when she knew she had to stop waiting. She had to get on with her life. If he wasn't going to be around anyway, she couldn't just sit and wait for the rest of her life. WGN saved her.

Can't he understand this? *The job is the only thing keeping me alive. The job is the only thing making it possible for me to be with him. That job is his best friend.* Doesn't he know that?

Working weekends is tough on the family, Margaret acknowledges. Not the optimal situation. If only there were another way. But no. She has to pay her dues. She had gotten that lucky break with Bob Bell, but now she needed to earn it. Give it year. Then she could move to days. Afternoons. Mother's hours. It's perfect.

Still, *what to do about Paul?* She had made her point, she thinks to herself. That would be the last time he would tell her what she could and couldn't do. A few nights on the couch will fix that right up. *But it isn't just a few nights anymore, is it?* She didn't want to count. She has been meaning to make a gesture, reduce tensions, find some face-saving way for both of them to back down from the brink of something neither of them really want.

"It's the President, Mommy. I don't want to watch this channel," young Daniel interrupts.

"Change the channel, Dear. It's alright with me."

"But he's on every channel, Mommy."

She wanders over to the television from the stove. President Kennedy's face is serious. His voice is trying to be reassuring in that movie star kind of way he has. But even John Fitzgerald Kennedy cannot hide the concern in his voice when he announces 'within the past week, unmistakable evidence has established the fact that a series of offensive missile sites is now in preparation on that imprisoned island. The purpose of these bases can be none other than to provide a nuclear strike capability against the Western Hemisphere.'

"What does that mean, Mommy?"

Monday, October 22, 1962, 7:10 P.M. Dr. Paul Osgood pulls his Lincoln into the attached garage of his home on 16th Street, Ben Davis Township, Indiana. He is quite confused and worried when his estranged wife greets him at the door in tears. At first he blames himself for not having talked to her about the house problem sooner.

"I'm sorry," he begins, but she takes him by the hand, the first time she has touched him in more than seven weeks, and leads him to the television.

"Hello, Danny," he begins again, but Margaret and Daniel are so involved in the television they do not hear him.

President Kennedy is in the middle of 'his seventeen-minute address. He tells the nation that "further action is required—and it is under way; and these actions may only be the beginning. We will not prematurely or unnecessarily risk the costs of worldwide nuclear war in which even the fruits of victory would be ashes in our mouth—but neither will we shrink from that risk at any time it must be faced."

"This can't be happening," Paul says out loud, not realizing he is talking.

Margaret is crying quiet tears, forcing herself to hold back so that she can still hear the President. Daniel, at nine years old, is struggling to interpret his parents' reaction. While he can understand President Kennedy's words, the only context he has for this experience is to take his emotional cues from his parents. And Daniel has never seen his parents in this state before. It is, on the one hand, as if a great wind has sucked the air right out of their lungs and the living room has become a vast stretch of empty ocean. And yet, on the other hand, he senses a great wave of desperation and panic looming in the distance.

President Kennedy is describing seven initial steps he is taking to confront the crisis, including a strict quarantine on all offensive military equipment under shipment to Cuba. The words fall as a hammer blow upon this frightened family. "It shall be the policy of this Nation to regard any nuclear missile launched from Cuba against any nation in the Western Hemisphere as an attack by the Soviet Union on the United States, requiring a full retaliatory response upon the Soviet Union."

"Those Communist bastards," Paul Osgood mutters in disbelief. His unconscious is playing crazy tricks, shooting thoughts into his mind like missiles. *Well, at least I won't have to deal with Dr. Cobb again. Bastard. Is a brick home better protected in a situation like this? Maybe this house was a good thing after all. No basement though.*

Margaret's unconscious is awash in conflicting instincts. Fear collides with her will to live. Self-preservation battles a mother's fierce protectiveness. She looks at Daniel to find him starring at her in wide-eyed fear.

"It's going to be alright, Honey," she says instinctively.

President Kennedy concludes. "My fellow citizens: let no one doubt that this is a difficult and dangerous effort on which we have set out. No one can see precisely what course it will take or what costs or casualties will be incurred. Many months of sacrifice and self-discipline lie ahead—months in which our patience and our will will be tested—months in which many threats and denunciations will keep us aware of our dangers. But the greatest danger of all would be to do nothing...Thank you and good night."

Chet Huntley and David Brinkley appear on screen to repeat, in grave voices, what the President has just said. Margaret, mindful now of Daniel, fights all the harder to keep from dissolving. As Huntley and Brinkley become a droning background presence in a room that seems suddenly empty, Dr. Paul Osgood walks three steps toward his wife, who is on her knees near Daniel, kneels with her, and takes her in his arms. She pushes hard against him, reaching with her free hand to pull in Daniel. The meatloaf in the oven burns.

Monday, October 22, 1962, 7:30 P.M. Margaret announces that she should call her mother. Paul agrees and adds she should ring up his parents afterward. Both attempts are unsuccessful for hours to come. Phone lines all across the country are overwhelmed with people desperate to contact family. Margaret paces the kitchen, throws the burned dinner away. No one is hungry, except Daniel. She bakes him cookies and tells him to get ready for bed.

By 9 P.M., after cookies and milk for all, suddenly hungry, both parents share in putting Daniel to bed. As they kneel bedside the bed, petting his hair, Margaret suggests they pray together. Daniel finds this interesting, as he has only attended church services with his grandparents back in Iowa. Margaret and Paul have not attended church services since arriving in Chicago. In trying to pray, Margaret is hesitant. The words are hard to find.

"Dear God, in this moment of danger, please keep Danny safe."

Paul squeezes her hand reassuringly.

"Keep us all safe."

"Grandmas and Grandpas too," Daniel adds reflectively.

"Yes, Grandmas and Grandpas too. And please help President Kennedy. Give him wisdom and strength. Give us all wisdom and strength."

Daniel likes this. His parents are close, his grandparents have been accounted for, and, for the moment, he believes his parents know what to do. They kiss him goodnight and turn out the light.

Monday, October 22, 1962, 9:30 P.M. Paul Osgood returns to the kitchen and cleans up the dishes. He has never done this before, except on holidays in his mother's home. Since he is a bit rusty in his technique, Margaret helps him.

"Like this," she says.

"I think we should get some money out of the bank," Paul comments without looking up from the dishes.

"I can do it in the morning after Danny goes to school. No, wait. Maybe he won't go to school. I'll just take him with me. How much?"

Paul looks up at her, not really sure how to say what is on his mind.

"All of it."

"Yes."

"I will fill up the car on my way to work. If I don't go, the staff will lose heart. They will look to me."

"I will go to the grocery store."

"Don't forget water."

"Yes."

"We should fill up the bathtub tonight."

"I need to cry now."

"O.K."

"Try the phone again when you finish the dishes."

"Right."

"Then come to bed."

"Right."

Tuesday, October 23, 1962, 3:00 A.M. Paul and Margaret Osgood are cocooned, one against the other, in the darkened bedroom. Neither one has slept, but each of them has been very still, trying not to disturb the other. Margaret speaks first.

"Paul, I need to go to Iowa. I need to be with my family." He does not move or speak, but her words shoot straight through his heart. "Paul?"

"I know, Maggie. I know."

"I am taking Danny. You should come with us."

Paul smiles in the dark. She cannot see.

"If I leave, patients will die, with or without the bombs. You understand? I should stay. I must stay."

"You are a good doctor."

"I love you, Maggie."

"Make love to me, Paul. It will help me sleep."

"It will help me too."

They make love and they both are much comforted from it.

Tuesday, October 23, 1962, 9:00 A.M. From the very beginning, events of this day are very odd. School is not canceled and Margaret walks Daniel all the way to school. At first he is embarrassed. She has not walked with him since the first grade. But he is also rather comforted by it and feels even better when they are on the sidewalk and see all the parents of all of the children walking them to school.

When Margaret returns, she gets in her car and drives to the bank only to find a line of people all the way around the block waiting for the doors to open. Worried now about the groceries, she instead moves on to the Kroger's on 10th Street and finds it also a mad house. The shelves empty. Bread, milk, and water have already run out. People are cleaning out everything—batteries, canned goods, boxes of sugar and cake mix. Taking anything she can find Margaret fills her cart and waits in the checkout line. Strangely, the women there do not talk of the bombs. They talk only of their families, from every state in the union.

Word passes back through the line. The cashiers are taking only cash today, not checks. Margaret pays cash for her cache of emergency rations and goes straight to the bank. She waits in line until past twelve noon.

Presenting her passbook savings, the teller shakes his head.

"One thousand dollar limit."

"But I want to withdraw ten thousand."

"One thousand dollar limit. No exceptions. And you'll have to take fives and ones. No tens or twenties left."

Dr. Paul Osgood has fared little better. Leaving the house at 8 A.M. he found all the gas stations already lined with cars bumper to bumper. He fears to wait any longer. Thirty minutes later he fills the Lincoln and drives downtown to Methodist Hospital. By 2 P.M. there would be no gas left in the city.

Late for his first scrub-in, Paul finds that three members of his team have not reported to work. He is short two nurses and an anesthesiologist. For the first time in a long time he is not angry with them. In fact, he is pleased. Eighty percent of the hospital staff is on duty, better than he expected. All of the elective surgeries have been canceled, but it does him little good. His patients for the day all arrive, complaining of the gas shortage. At twelve he tries to call Margaret, but the phone lines are still busy. He tries again at two and gets through.

"Anything happening? I won't let them play the radio in the operating room. They need to focus."

"No. Nothing new."

"Did you get the money?"

"Only a thousand. There was a run on the bank."

"It'll have to do, then. When are you leaving?"

"Paul, my place is with you. I'll stay till you can go, if you can. I was just scared last night. Better now."

"O.K."

"Come home for dinner."

"Yes. That would be nice."

During his operations there is none of the usual chatter. His staff is all business. In spite of his training he finds himself making absurd calculations. *1,000 nautical miles works out to 1,150 statute miles, or roughly the distance between Havana and Washington, D.C.. But the Commies obviously knew that. Bastards. Indianapolis, Columbus, Dayton, Springfield, Cincinnati, Nashville, all in range. Damn. But Saint Louis, Detroit, Chicago, just out of range. Range of the Lincoln on a full tank is about 300 miles. But they wouldn't hit the cities, not first. Military first. Wright-Patterson in Dayton, mighty close. But the prevailing wind is easterly. Fall out in Dayton would spill over to Columbus, not Indianapolis. The big Russian ICBM's would come later. Out west. Hit our missile bases out in Colorado and Wyoming. Easterly winds. Fallout in Iowa. Damn.*

So that's the story. Dr. Paul Osgood determines his family would be safer where they are right in Indianapolis.

He has a quick break at 3 P.M.. Other doctors are talking about the medical facts. Burns and radiation. They didn't have enough beds and medicine to treat one hundred thousand causualities. They didn't have enough to treat ten thousand all in one day. They casually decide the quick death in the big blast would be preferable. Medical treatment for the radiation victims would deteriorate to nothing in three days all across the country. They joke darkly about having the essential disaster survival kit: *a bottle of brandy and a pistol with one bullet.*

Young Daniel Osgood has an interesting day of his own. At first Mrs. Tolbert instructs the children on how to listen for three rings of the bell and then squeeze low under their desks. They should never, never look at the big light. The children are wild, rambunctious. In nervous fits of laughter they squeal and howl down on the floor together. It seems great fun.

Later the principal calls over the loudspeakers. They have done it all wrong, having forgotten about the windows. Now when they hear the three bells they are supposed to file out into the hallway, away from the windows. Little ones closest to the walls, leaning against the bricks, hands over their heads. They practice five times.

The big siren at high school goes off at twelve o'clock (sirens all over the country go off at twelve o'clock). It's more practice. If they hear the big siren at the high school after school they should do what they've learned at school. Find a wall, hands over head. Never, never look at the big light. Daniel is glad, for the first time, he has a brick house.

In the afternoon the teacher decides it would be useful for them to understand about bomb shelters. Mrs. Tolbert draws detailed plans on the chalkboard. Daniel likes this idea a lot. What fun it would be to dig up the back yard. He determines to ask his mother about it as soon as he gets home.

Tuesday, October 23, 1962, 7:00 P.M. Huntley and Brinkley have been talking about the military buildup. Castro has just placed Cuba on full military alert. American forces are at Def-Con 3. At 7:06 President Kennedy holds a ceremony at the White House, signing Proclamation 3505, formally declaring the Cuban quarantine, now set to commence at 10:00 A.M. the next morning. TV news reports show Russian ships on their way to Cuba. Gallop reports that 84% of Americans support the quarantine/blockade, and 20% of Americans believe it will lead to World War III.

The unintended consequence emerges. People get the idea that something very bad will happen the next morning at 10 A.M. precisely.

The Osgood family—Paul, Margaret, and Daniel—sit down to a perfect dinner of meatloaf, mashed potatoes, and corn. This is the first family dinner they have shared in a long time. Joking and laughing, they are all happy to be with each other. Still trying to comprehend what is happening, Daniel is joyous to see his parents engaged with each other. This fact is far more real to him than everyone's imagined impending death.

Wednesday, October 24, 1962, 5:15 P.M. It has been a strange day. By the time Paul leaves for work at 8:30 A.M., he hears the sounds of backhoes in his neighbor's back yards, digging bomb shelters. Others dig with shovels. Paul has given Daniel permission to dig, but only after school. On his way to work, it's like the Fourth of July. The streets are lined with American flags.

10 A.M. passes with no news. Huntley and Brinkley go on and on about possibilities, with maps showing the reach of the Russian Intermediate range missiles in a big red circle. No one outside of the military has any way of knowing what is happening at sea.

Margaret has finally gotten through to her parents. Their Iowa "Fraidy" shack is stocked and locked. They'll be fine no matter what, they insist. Paul's folks also get through. All is well. Dr. Daniel J. Osgood is busy with blood drives. The whole country is busy with blood drives.

Finally, at 5:15 a Defense Department spokesman announces some Soviet ships appear to have altered course. Already primed from the tension of the day, great cheers go up from every household. Most people assume this means the crisis will pass. But the very next day military forces are put on Def-Con 2, for the first time in U.S. history.

The Osgood family shares another dinner.

Thursday, October 25, 1962, 2:00 P.M. High drama. Even Dr. Paul Osgood takes time from his schedule to watch U.S. Ambassador Adlai Stevenson confront the Soviets in the United Nations.

"Take that, you Commie bastards!" He shouts approvingly.

As the crisis extends, people settle into a grim awareness that the situation could drag on. Grocery shelves are restocked, gas supplies grow, people return to daily life. Methodist Hospital returns to full staffing.

Friday, October 26, 1962, 7:00 P.M. The crisis in the Osgood family is reaching its peak. Margaret is scheduled to report for work at WISH-TV at 3 P.M. the following day. Over a dinner of baked ham, scalloped potatoes, and cream corn, negotiations are tense.

"I am concerned," Paul states at dinner, "that if you go to work tomorrow we'll be separated as a family. I have a bad feeling about this weekend."

"Paul, you have gone to work every single day."

"I am a doctor. It is my responsibility."

"You can help me build the shelter, Mommy," Daniel suggests. Margaret pauses reflectively over a piece of ham.

"Maggie, we have to decide what's most important in times like these."

She waits. She looks her husband in the eyes. She looks at her son.

"Let's see what happens tomorrow," she concludes. "If it's another day of no news, like today, I will go. If it's a bad day, then we'll see."

Saturday, October 27, 1962, 12:00 P.M. A bad day. The worst day, from the public perception. Major Rudolf Anderson's U-2 flight is shot down by a Soviet SAM battery over Cuba. He is killed. Across the nation everyone assumes this can only mean a retaliatory strike on missile batteries in Cuba and their Soviet soldiers. So this is how it begins.

Margaret receives a phone call that the WISH-TV local news broadcast for Saturday evening is canceled. They will stay with the network feed until the issue is decided. She stays home with her family.

At 8:05 P.M. President Kennedy releases a response to Premier Khrushchev to the press detailing a settlement in which the Soviets remove the missiles and agree to U.N. inspection and promising the Americans will withdraw the blockade and give assurances against the invasion of Cuba. Every one assumes this is the final offer. The nation waits.

Sunday, October 28, 1962, 9:00 A.M. Broadcasting on Radio Moscow Premier Khrushchev announces he has ordered the dismantling of the missiles and their return to the Soviet Union. A jubilant nation rushes into the streets. The crisis is effectively over, although several weeks of U.N. visits, surveillance, and blockade remain.

Mrs. Margaret Osgood, reflecting on all that has just happened, decides that in the face of nuclear annihilation her family is the most important thing in her life. She calls WISH-TV and quits her job.

CHAPTER FOUR

THERE IS NO ONE LEFT

HEN SAD THINGS HAPPEN IN PEOPLE'S LIVES, GRAVELY sad events as heavy as the weight of steel beams bending in the hull of a great ship going down, they are often in shock. There is a certain mental unreality to catastrophe. Initially people find it hard to believe that something has happened and will even forget, briefly upon waking, that it has come to pass.

That is because it is so little understood that the reality which we live is a mentally constructed reality. It isn't raw and truly in the present moment. Not at all. It is merely habitual, a habitat of the brain itself, so dependent upon neural memory that everything that happens is always first known in the flash of the synapses calling up what has already happened in the past; and not only the details of what has happened, but the emotional valence of things remembered, whether something was agreeable or disagreeable, pleasurable or painful, benign or threatening.

And no less so the future also. In one great evolutionary leap the human brain could contemplate that what had happened before may happen again and for the first time free us from the endless round of instinct, from pattern and reaction, pattern and reaction, only pattern and reaction. And yet, how crudely we project ourselves forward. The future becomes as real as the past, because it is indeed the past imagined to continue. Only one small area in the front of our most recent brains can play the trick of abstraction and comment that life may change, that circumstances yet to come may be entirely different than one would have expected, that new situations impose themselves. But every abstraction is unconvincing to things more basic.

The shock of unimagined reality is the hole it tears in the past and in the future because it is the anomaly, the thing that has not happened before and is outside of the equation: *The Unaccounted*.

And that is the challenge, retreat or advance; whether the personality will expand to include the anomaly in the mental picture of the way life truly is and adjust the framework of reality to include these larger things; or, pulling back, confine itself to the smaller things that seem more tame and restrict known territory to the beaches, never to risk again to sail where there be monsters.

THE MUSIC CHANGES EVERYTHING. When Lilly Summers heard this for herself she was astonished. Snuggled in a blanket with her feet up on the big green ottoman she balanced the popcorn on the arm of the sofa and drank her Sam Adams beer straight from the bottle. Finishing the dishes, cleaning the counters, changing into her pajamas, she'd been waiting all evening just for this moment when she could sit down with her brand new DVD and watch her life roll by like a movie, set to the rhythms and moods of her own voice.

When she picked it up that morning she hadn't wanted to tell Daniel how eager she had been to watch it. It seemed somehow selfish, she supposed. To watch yourself for two hours. Her entire family was on the films, of course. Her brothers arriving one by one by one after her. Little babies crawling, pulling themselves up on chairs. Portrait shots of them lined up together like ducklings—her in a frilly dress, Tom tucked under her chin in a little suit and tie, Robert still a baby propped between his knees. Billy yet to come. All there. Her Dad seemed to favor long angles of the Christmas trees, assuming for some unknown reason that sitting there thirty years later perhaps she would enjoy seeing the difference between the Douglas Fir from Christmas 1974 and the Scotch Pine from Christmas 1975. The outside shots were better. Her confirmation procession down High Street past the rows of double and triple decker houses to St. Jo's, with all the little girls in their white dresses and gloves. The Memorial Day picnics at the union hall. Dances at the Knights of Columbus. The City of Medford 4th of July parade, most years featuring authentic civil war cannon. All there.

That was not what Lilly saw. *She was looking for herself.* And even if it was a little selfish, she needed the comfort of it. The comfort of continuity. That was why she spent the four hundred dollars to get the films transferred to video and now saved on a DVD that would never fade. She was hoping that in the same way you could lose yourself in a movie for a couple of hours, feeling, in the end, that you knew the characters so well that you could understand their lives and hopes and dreams, that she could lose herself in herself for a couple of hours and also understand her own character.

Lilly was the kind of person who had a set of meticulous picture albums, consecutively numbered, that she actually took out of the shelves and looked through once a year, often on her birthday or sometimes on her mother's birthday. Hundreds of photographs, but they were all old friends as familiar to her as her high school graduating class. Since the house seemed so empty now she had filled the hallways with them, amazed at the difference it made to have them enlarged and set in the dark wood frames she bought at Walmart by the dozens, on sale. Tim hadn't let her decorate the way she really wanted to, but now she had recently found it in herself to change things around and throw up walls of pictures like she had seen in magazines, and those nice little shelves that you could paint to match the wallpaper, a light blue, and use the plastic photo stands. More flowers. More light. Better curtains with sheers. The house was coming along.

She was coming along. So when she had seen the coupon for the film-to-DVD special she knew just who to call with those old films from her mother's things. And here she was, sitting in front of the television, her beer still cold, and watching a movie of herself. *Play.* The black screen opened with a good strumming rhythm from Lilly's title CD, a lilting 6/8 waltz she had picked up from an *Indigo Girls* song, and then just when her vocal began she saw the title appear, fading in with a slow zoom—*Lilly Summers: Old and New.*

Too perfect. Too perfect. He had put her CD cover photo in the background, Lilly and her guitar silhouetted in deep shadow in black and white. She was going to have to unwind herself from the comforter and find the Kleenex already. It was everything she wanted. A good beer and a good cry. The music changed everything. Over the silence of the old films the music track was like an emotional map that showed the way through it; reflective at first, like the quiet pause when entering a great art museum, giving way to a happy childhood song down a long hallway, then turning a corner into a room of wistful sadness with the images of people now long gone, but soon opening to a marble rotunda of light spring sounds and flowers, or exploring a fast-moving exhibit of teenage summers, and ending with a contemplative, open chord meditation on weddings and good-byes.

The wedding was the first images of Tim she had seen in a long time, she realized. It was nearly too much to see. She wasn't ready yet. Her plan with these films, it now occurred to her, had been to find herself in her life before Tim.

How had Daniel done it? Somehow he had taken her lyrics and used them to narrate her story. He had mined the different moods in her music to underscore the different moods in her life. It was like the life review that passes before your eyes when you are dying, as people said, when you can stand outside of yourself and watch the things that happened from some higher perspective. She needed a way to pull back from the day to day details, to get on top of it somehow and look down and see her life as an intuitive whole; the same person, the same spark of being that was her in essence from that first little girl in the flower dress to this woman she was now, in spite of everything that changed, everything that happened, they still must be one and the same. She could feel it enough at least to search for it.

It made her cry, but the tears tasted differently than before. Like the tears you cry returning home from a long and difficult trip, tears of release, tears of letting go. When screen faded to black with the music she stood, gathered her second empty beer bottle and the Kleenex off the floor, and put the DVD back in the case her had made for her.

Lilly Summers could feel a song coming on. One of the great things about having the house to herself was that she could do as she pleased. If she wanted to stay up late and write a song, there was no one else to worry about. Tim would have hated it, would have hated the *Indigo Girls* that she played over and over trying to teach herself to play the guitar again after so long.

Still in her pajamas, she pulled the guitar up close to her chin. If you let the edge of the body touch your jawbone somehow it made the chords resonate in your head, almost as if you were inside the instrument. She liked the sound of her guitar that way, deep and resonate. Draped over it in that position she could reach the legal pad on the coffee table and jot down her lyrics without ever leaving the embrace of her guitar. Lilly started with a G chord, certainly her favorite and on that account changed her mind. All of her songs seemed to be in G, although she could capo the tune up several steps if she liked, but it always still sounded like G. No, this time for variety she experimented with something different. D was more of a soprano range that didn't suit her. The A chord was closer to her alto voice, but that often left you with an F# minor somewhere in the song and her hands still weren't strong enough to play it right. All of which led her inevitably back to the G chord.

"*I've been looking for myself,*" she began. "*I've been looking for my soul…in flowered dresses and ponytails* (drifting up in A minor)…*cut off jeans and fairy tales, polished nails…that tell me who I was…and who I shall be whole…*"

There was a second stanza in there somewhere. She could sense it. "*Far away…*(needs seven syllables apparently)…"

```
…Far away I've always walked
…down the road far from myself (difficult to rhyme)
…down the road far from the path (better)
…to destinations so far from home
…empty nights and hotel rooms/roams/known
…hotel rooms and towns unknown
…and now I've lost my way
…I need to take a bath? (Arrg, fix it later)
```

Time for the chorus. Lilly could feel herself shifting into the 6/8 dance rhythm.

```
…There's a girl (walking up to the C chord)
…There's a woman (back to G)
…There's a person I've known all along (down to the D)
…(now repeat) There's a girl
…There's a woman
…There's a person/lady who lives in a song.
```

Lady who lives, she liked the alliteration of it. Did Emily Saliers in the *Indigo Girls* compose her songs this way? She wondered. Lilly leaned more towards Emily's songs than Amy's, although she had to admit most of the time she could only play along with Amy's good guitar rhythms. She couldn't finger pick like Emily. Not that she wanted to be a professional musician. Her music, such as it was, was for herself. Playing in the Coffee House with the applause from her friends was reward enough. She was happy to buy the new *Indigo Girls* album or catch Lilith Fair when it used to come to the Tweeter Center. Still, someone had told her once: *what's the difference between an amateur musician and a professional musician? A professional musician is an amateur who didn't give up.*

Her music was her therapy, the only therapy she had ever tried or wanted. At one time everybody had been trying to push therapy on her and the Red Cross had even sent people around to her house.

She let them in and made coffee, but she wasn't ready to talk then. Maybe she wasn't ready to talk now. But since she had taken up her guitar again maybe she didn't need to talk about it as much as everybody thought because the main thing was not the talking anyway. The main thing was getting out there again. That was the hard part. And her guitar and her songs were the vehicle, if still a little amateur and corny.

By that time midnight had passed and she put her guitar back in the case. She slept soundly and fully. The DVD with a good beer and a good cry had done its job.

In the morning she called Daniel. Often he wouldn't answer the phone early, until he had completed his walk around the Public Garden and his Starbucks from around the corner and checked his email. But that morning, he answered.

"You still have my CD."

"Excuse me?"

"You still have my CD. When I picked up my order yesterday, my DVD, you gave me back all my films but not my music CD. Remember?"

Her talking voice was still unfamiliar to him, if not her singing voice. He had heard her recorded voice over and over again during his editing and in many ways felt he knew all about Lilly Summers, in truth, probably better than she knew herself. Because Daniel knew the world she had grown up in from the films—the rough and tumble working class neighborhood in Medford, the Catholic schools, her brothers trailing out behind her—he knew the general outlines of her worldview, her opinions, her expectations. With the added guide of her homegrown lyrics he also knew something about her ego development, her self esteem, her education, her attitudes. He assumed she was divorced. He assumed he knew a lot, but because he didn't know the details, *he was wrong*. He didn't know Lilly Summers at all.

"Lilly?…Oh yes. Your burned CD. I remember. Wait a minute…yes, it's still in the computer. Sorry."

"It was good. The DVD, I mean."

"You watched it already?"

"I couldn't wait. I am impressed. You showed a lot of sensitivity. For the music. For the film. All of it. People should know about you. They'd all bring their stuff if they knew how good you were."

"Thank you. I always like to hear what the customer thinks."

"I think it's great. Do you need an assistant?"

"What?"

"Someone to help you. I can't think of anything more fun and more creative than what you do. I could spend all day putting people's stuff together with music. I do some things with pictures. Not like you.

I mean around the house. But it would be fun. I know my way around a computer."

"Sorry, I don't have enough work to need an assistant. When do you want to pick up your CD?"

"I could come in this afternoon before work. Unless you want to keep it."

"Oh, no, I couldn't keep it, Lilly."

"I thought you said you liked folk music?"

"...I guess so," Daniel couldn't remember ever having said something that solicitous to her about folk music. "I mean, I would have to buy it. I wouldn't just keep it."

"You want to buy my CD?"

Daniel paused, confused. "Yes...if it isn't your only copy."

"Oh, I have lots of copies. How much?"

"How much what?"

"How much do you want to pay?"

"I don't know. What do you usually charge?"

"Don't know. Never sold one of my CD's before."

"Twenty dollars?"

"Too much."

"You haven't sold a CD before and already you are having a sale?"

"I'm new to the music business. OK, twenty bucks. But for that much you have to get a concert ticket."

"How much is *that*? I'm losing money fast here."

"It's free."

"Well, that's a bargain then."

"But you have to come. You really have to come if you like folk music so much."

"Come where?"

"To the concert."

"But I thought I was buying an imaginary ticket."

"Oh, the ticket is imaginary. Don't need a ticket. But the concert isn't imaginary, well, except it isn't a concert either...exactly. Just the Coffee House at the Church of the Covenant. Saturday night, 7:30. I'll introduce you to my friends. They all need videos and stuff. Plus they never stop talking so before long everybody in Boston will know what you do. Trust me. You'll make money. Just come. You know where it is, right?"

"I've never been to a Coffee House."

"It's across the street from your office. How could you not come?"

"And I don't even know if I like folk music." Daniel stopped. He hadn't meant to say that.

"Then why are you buying my CD?"

"Because…," *because the customer is always right,* he thought to himself. "Because maybe I'll use it as background music for some other videos."

"You would do that?"

"Yes. With your permission, of course." He needed to find a more graceful way out of this dilemma. "Lilly, I don't know about the concert. I'm reluctant. I don't get out much."

"Then you need to get out more." She wasn't cooperating. "Look, you owe me twenty bucks. Right? Bring it over on Saturday night across the street. If you don't show up, maybe me and my friends will come looking for you. And you don't want that. We're loud and obnoxious. Bye…"

DANIEL'S FIRST PROBLEM WAS WHAT TO WEAR. His wardrobe was hopeless, having lived so long without a woman in his life. In his life as a psychiatrist, he had been fine in a white shirt and slacks with his medical White Coat thrown over an incredible assortment of ties. Moving on to psychoanalysis, he had opted for cardigans and pullovers. He really didn't know how to dress down. Any normal man, finding himself on Newbury Street, would have visited Brooks Brothers or Armani, even the Riccardi Boutique. He would have found no shortage of fashion. Daniel's shortage was in his mind, however, and several more Newbury Streets would not have helped him.

One wouldn't wear a tie to a folk music Coffee House, he decided, so he settled on the blue wool pullover and khaki's, a preppie look he was comfortable wearing since his days at Phillips Andover.

They were all in jeans and tee shirts, of course, lounging in metal folding chairs in the darkened fellowship hall downstairs. A small stage was in the front of the room, set only with a baby grand piano and homemade footlights, just enough room for a jazz quartet. Arriving fashionably late, Daniel found the first act had already started and struggled to see in the dark.

Open Mike Night at the Coffee House was the typical amateur affair—guitars, piano, keyboards, and the occasional saxophone in varying degrees of proficiency ranging from old John Denver tunes and Joni Mitchell to the accomplished composers and poets for whom the Coffee House had been a lifelong avocation. On other nights regional performers from the circuit were invited—Fred Small, the Blue Corn Band, and Lui Collins—with their professional sound boards. But at the open mike there was a simple microphone arrangement, clearly a gathering of a community of people who knew each other well and who were there to provide a safe, welcoming environment for their own self-expression.

Amid the quiet applause after a heartfelt rendition of *Annie's Song*, Daniel noticed Lilly's strawberry blond head looking back to find him. She waved enthusiastically for him to come to the front where she sat with three women and an unusual-looking man. As he walked up the aisle he noticed, somewhat self-consciously, that they were virtually all women. Virtually all couples.

"You're late!" She quipped, clearing a chair for him beside her.

"I was trying to find a cup of coffee. I thought this was a coffee house?"

"Not in a church."

"No coffee?" He was truly disappointed. "Really? You gotta be kidding me."

"No. Just singing." She looked at him quizzically. "You're a trip, Daniel. I would never have pegged you for a caffeine cruncher...Girls, meet Daniel. He's the video guy I was telling you about."

"Hello, Daniel!" they smiled, in chorus. As they looked him over, Daniel could not escape the impression that he had stumbled into a little amateur night contest himself.

"He's a little old, Lilly," Maureen commented to his chagrin. Maureen, in her fifties and matronly sexual, looked somehow out of place with the younger women.

"Don't start," Lilly retorted, somewhat embarrassed. "Pay no attention to Maureen, Daniel. She's just nervous because all of her videos are of the private variety."

"Wouldn't you like to know. "

"And this is Donna, our super-mom. She only has videos of the kids."

"Can you do slow motion? Like when my son is scoring a goal in soccer?"

"Sure...I guess. We'll have to see," said Daniel in growing amazement. He had never been introduced in this way before. Without his doctor's persona, it felt like he was wearing new clothes in spite of himself.

"And Paula. She's like you. She doesn't get out much. This is her first time."

"Nice to meet you, Daniel. I don't have any videos. Never had a camera."

"And Carl. He's just one of the girls."

"They let me tag along."

Daniel's analytic instinct could not resist pestering him with the scent of something secret among these women. It was something more than their easy familiarity. On the one hand he could perceive, to his chagrin, that Lilly was presenting him as a date. Inwardly wincing, he kicked himself for giving in to her rowdy insistence to hear her sing.

On the other hand, even Lilly's prodding and humor with him was distancing, like she was shaking his hand at arm's length. *No, more than that.* Like she had forgotten how to shake hands. Sitting there in the dim light, this circle of women seemed very much in their own private space as comfortable as their own bedroom, oblivious to anything else going on in the room. And they had allowed him as far as the door.

And then there was Carl. The odd man out, literally. He was odd, too tall somehow and uncomfortable in his own skin. His large, nervous eyes looked toward the women longingly, puppy-dog fashion, and in their turn they petted him kindly from time to time, happy to have him at their feet. But there was no embrace. There was no sexual energy left over for Carl.

Is that it, Daniel wondered? The sexual energy was skewed. The women were fierce with each other, but cold to him. They seemed closed in the presence of a man, he and Carl both. They were allowed only so far, and never on the furniture.

"You seem kind of out of place. Have I made you miserable already?" Lilly offered privately.

"Oh, well I'm still disappointed about the coffee."

"Maybe we can fix that."

"I guess I don't understand why I'm here. I notice there aren't a lot of men around tonight."

"I really hadn't noticed," Lilly said, sweeping her eyes over the room. "I suppose this has evolved into more and more of a women's night out. When the folk music starts up maybe you'll feel more comfortable."

"Maybe," he offered weakly. "I guess I just don't want to seem to be intruding."

"Oh." Lilly looked surprised. "Oh, the girls. No. Forget about them. I think they've forgotten how to relate to men. Don't take it personally.

You are not intruding. I think we need to spice things up a bit in our closed little club."

"Club?"

Lilly winced. *How to tell him? You need to figure this out*, she told herself. *You are going to be doing this for the rest of your life.*

"Maybe that's not the right word. It sounds too exclusive. I just mean that we've all been pretty tight for the last three years and I could go for a little fresh air myself."

"And Carl?"

"Oh…Carl. Sweet Carl. He was so lonely. We had a lot in common so we kind of took him under our wing. If it wasn't for us, I'm not sure he'd ever talk to anybody. We couldn't have that. If we didn't get him out with us he might end up more paranoid than he already is."

"Paranoid?"

"You'll see. Trust me."

"I notice that a lot of the women here are couples."

"Oh!" She smiled, leaning closer. "I guess I take it for granted. The Church of the Covenant is an open and affirming congregation, one of the first in the country they tell me…Open and affirming means…"

"I know what it means…"

"They welcome gays and lesbians. I kind of like it. Very different than the church I grew up in."

"You grew up Catholic."

"Yes. Wouldn't my Dad be rolling over in his grave to see me now? But here I am."

"Well Lilly, things change. Even in a culture like ours. When did you come out?"

Daniel hesitated. It wasn't as if he really knew her well enough to ask her through the proper context of a relationship. It was only that the films had made him feel he knew her. Perhaps this knowledge of her would make her uncomfortable.

"No." Lilly shook her head, looking a little surprised. "No. No. No. That's not what I mean. You thought…? Oh, that's kind of funny actually. Wow. I don't think anybody's ever asked me that before."

"I apologize, Lilly. I seem to be getting more confused all of the time."

"No. It's fine. It's fine. Who knows? Maybe I would enjoy being a lesbian?" she said somewhat flirtatiously. "I've never tried it."

At this Daniel was only more confused. He looked away.

"I'm a widow, Daniel" Lilly replied, sounding like an actress speaking a line. Even as she heard herself say it she thought it sounded like somebody else, some other woman, someone she didn't recognize.

He turned toward her, genuinely pained.

"I'm so sorry to hear that," offered Daniel. *Sincere*, she thought. *Appropriate. He still doesn't have a clue, does he?* That was what she liked about him. That he didn't know. Not yet. That for him she must appear as just the average woman. And just at that moment in her life average was attractive. She wanted it more than she wanted anything else.

She didn't want to tell him, not because she found it difficult to tell the story these days, but because, she discovered, she enjoyed relating to someone in the regular way. People treat you differently after sudden violent death. That's what the Red Cross worker has called it. The people who knew Tim didn't see her. They always saw her and Tim, always saw her now with a hole in her life standing beside her. Even when they weren't saying anything they were protecting her, trying not to bruise her. Kindness and cruelness, all in a package.

With Daniel she was free of it. But she was going to have to tell him. If she didn't tell him soon perhaps he would feel a bit cheated later.

"And how about you, Daniel? A woman in your life?"

"No. Not recently."

"That's right, you don't get out much. I remember."

"Hence, I repeat my initial confusion. Why am I here tonight?"

"Because you owe me twenty bucks! Pay up!" He laughed, fumbling with the money from his wallet. "And because you are into folk music...So, how do you like the lesbian Coffee House, without any coffee, now?"

"Not so much."

"Maybe you'll enjoy yourself more when I get up and sing."

"Well, that depends..."

"Depends on what?"

"On whether you are going to sing about coffee or not."

"By some strange coincidence, I got twenty dollars now. If you can manage to sit through the whole thing without squirming too much, I'll buy you a coffee."

"Two coffees."

But she wasn't listening. She had already pulled her guitar case out from under her chair and was making her way toward the makeshift stage. A hush loomed over the animated hall as she came into the lights, and then murmurs and whispers, building to applause.

"She's our little star," Maureen cooed, clapping enthusiastically. "You should have seen her a year ago. She's come so far."

"Do you all perform?" Daniel wondered aloud.

"No. No. We're just here for Lilly. It's good to see her happy."

The crowd of women was already calling out tunes, *Indigo Girls* mostly. It was obvious that Lilly was a regular and they knew her repertoire.

"Galileo!"

"Bright Star!"

"Love Will Come to You!"

"But you always want that one!" She complained to the audience, laughing. "Fine, just for a warm up."

"Wait'll you hear this!" said Donna, tapping Daniel's shoulder and pointing to the stage.

"Makes me cry every time," Carl inserted.

Tuning up the guitar, Lilly waved them off and let the crowd settle. The first lick was complicated, winding up the guitar neck, and even Daniel, knowing very little about the guitar, thought it sounded fairly difficult. To his surprise, when she began she did not begin alone. Every woman in every seat knew every word and it was clear to Daniel that Lilly's role in this gathering had been as the sing-along song leader. The women's voices were strong and clear, breaking into parts even with the complicated harmonies. They loved it. They loved her.

When Lilly sang there was something in her voice. Her waif-ish looks, struggling to pull the guitar strap over her head in the lights, had struck Daniel with the impression of her as a bit of a lost girl. But when she sang he was taken aback by the strength of her voice. One wouldn't have expected such a full voice from such a slight woman. The combination of frailty and strength lent her singing a quality of sadness that broke his heart.

Lilly's friends sang devotedly, Carl dissolving into tears as predicted.

"She's really good!" Daniel suggested, pleased that he liked the music after all.

"That's our Lilly," Maureen smiled wistfully.

When she finished they clapped as much for themselves as for her, calling out other tunes hopefully.

"OK! Okay, maybe later. But I have a new song I want to sing tonight. A new song for the new me."

A quiver of fear trickled up Lilly's spine. Although she was more sure of herself than before, she knew her limits. They liked her because they liked the *Indigo Girls* and their songs were a shared community asset that she had learned to play. But by offering herself in her own songs she was crossing a line, but it was a line to herself only. Unknown to Lilly, word had spread of her, even though she had rarely attended the Church of the Covenant, choosing to make her music her only act of worship. The other women knew, because it is the place of women to know these things and to hold these things respectfully, never even telling her that they knew because they also knew she would have wanted them to keep silent until she herself was ready.

"I am going to teach you the words to the chorus. You all have to help me."

She put the capo up three frets, stretching her range. It was a good tune to learn, a theme song for all the hopes they silently wished her.

There's a girl
There's a woman
There's a person I've known all along

There's a girl
There's a woman
There's a lady who lives in a song.

When it was over, they cried, clapping through their tears. Because they knew without saying what it meant to her. They knew what they had just witnessed in her life and were joyous for her. There was no call to go back to *Indigo Girls* tunes, only kisses and hugs and woman-to-woman solidarity as she walked down from the stage.

"Now do you understand?" Lilly said to Daniel as she sat, her eyes wet.

"Understand what, Lilly? I am trying."

"Why I need these women in my life."

YOU NEED TO TELL HIM, LILLY. YOU NEED TO TELL HIM SOON, she thought again as the cadre walked down Newbury Street to the Green Tea Café. But this was just the thing, you see. Virtually all of the people in her life were from her old life. They knew. They didn't need to be told. So everything about meeting Daniel was new. For all the others the manner of her widowhood was the main thing, but to Daniel perhaps it would only be one fact about her life in the midst of all the other facts he didn't know about her.

Strange. Maybe she shouldn't have invited him out with the girls, plus Carl, in the first place. *The girls will just blurt it out, throw it in his face just to watch him,* she feared suddenly. She had seen them do it before as kind of a safety mechanism, a way to take the higher ground before someone else could climb their pity to rise above them.

Maureen was baiting him already, as they waited for their lattes.

"You mean to tell me you haven't been on a plane since 9/11?"

"Well, I never go anywhere."

"So you've never had to take your shoes off at the airport?"

"No. Why do people take their shoes off?"

"God, Lilly was right. You really have been out of circulation."

"Maureen?!" Lilly spouted. *Honest to God, they were like cats toying with a mouse.*

"So, Donna, what do you do?" Daniel continued.

"I'm independently wealthy." The other women burst into hysterical gales of laughter. "At least I will be soon."

"Not really," Lilly scolded.

"It's what people say, Lil," Maureen countered.

"Yeah, well, people are mighty small, you know," Paula cut in, a little hurt. "Don't even joke about it."

Daniel's eyes rolled in a bewildered gaze from woman to woman, then to Carl who had a strange grin on his face, straining from the center of the group. Even as an analyst, there was something here he could not place, some sheen of human emotion he had rarely encountered.

Hard to explain. When people are caught up in something larger than themselves, elevated unnaturally above their normal psychological constitution, they have an air of breathlessness. It is felt as a kind of intensity of personhood. You can only watch them as you would watch a slender rocket—unearthly fire burning at the bottom, quick away toward the arc of gravity's reach, weightless at the apogee so they say. Sometimes people are both propelled and suspended at the very same time. If you are drawn to their spirit the tightrope walking will weigh you down with its quirky gravity. So casual, and yet so perilous. So dazzling in its way, and yet, so quick and brief, the hot flashing moment of a flash bulb.

"Who do you think we are? Guess!"

"We are kind of like a club."

"I don't get it." Daniel shook his head.

Something about this group of women struck Daniel as odd. That lack of sexual energy again. They shared a secret. No doubt. But they were not close like high school friends, sisters wound round the central pole of personal history. No. They were more like male friends, a platoon of veterans fused together through the heat of life and death.

It's time to tell him, Lil, her inner voice interrupted. *Don't waste his time. This is the point of the evening and you know it. Just put it on the table. Just get it said and move on.*

Lilly caught Maureen's eye, assenting. She pulled her chair close in by the table and the others stopped. They looked at him in a circle of faces.

"We are 9/11 widows," whispered Maureen, turning away from the other tables.

Leaning in around the table towards him, their heads in a circle, one by one they slowly fished a golden chain from around each of their necks and offered him the token of their secret guild. Each woman fingered the soft gold of her husband's wedding ring.

"But it's our little secret."

Daniel looked at Lilly.

"You too?"

"Yes, me too."

"Me too!" Carl piped in.

Daniel paused to take in the enormity of it. They paused to watch him. He looked at them, faces smiling towards him in amusement, but then, eyes lowered, also in grief. And they looked to him expectantly.

"But I don't understand," Daniel said finally.

"What don't you understand?"

"I mean, why you are all together? As a group? Why are you here?"

"For Lilly. To watch her perform. To clap. To be supportive."

They all started talking at once.

"It's just that no one else understands," Maureen began.

"No, they don't know what to say."

"So they say too much."

"And they say too little."

"Then we found each other at the Memorial service."

"And the Red Cross support group. The grief counselors put us together."

"And the Victim's Fund meetings."

"And then our protest march."

"Bastards!"

"God, wasn't that a trip!"

"Wait! Wait…you're going too fast for me," Daniel interrupted.

And so they explained over three more rounds of coffee how they had found each other. In the weeks following 9/11 the shock and terror gave way to the darker realities of unprocessed grief—the day-to-day losses. Husbands who weren't there to take out the trash or drive the kids to soccer practice, or walk the dog. Waking up every morning alone.

At their first meeting the grief counselor had made them talk about the little things, the small things. She called these secondary losses the most painful. Three months after sudden violent death the symptoms are not something anybody else would notice. You simply seem preoccupied. You forget people's names, or lock your keys in the car, or lose track of time and miss appointments. It doesn't mean you're getting better, she told them. It only means you are getting started.

They had introduced themselves in that first support group, as instructed, by the things they had in common.

"American Flight 11," Maureen began, in tears.

"My wife was a stewardess on Flight 11," Carl had said, reaching to embrace her. Gripping her like a mother, his large arms trembled.

"United 175. Do we really have to do this in this way?" Donna protested, a woman in her thirties with young children at home.

"Yes," said the grief counselor. "It has to start to be real."

"United 175," Paula said slowly, looking across the circle to Donna.

"Tim died on United 175," Lilly said through her tears. "You don't have to tell me it's real."

But there were no tears now. Three years out from the tragedy their tears no longer came in telling their stories. They came in the odd moments of memory, the small reminders, the little things that had mattered most.

As Daniel took it all in he pondered. Nothing in his analytic training had prepared him for this. The difference was that their grief was so public they could not escape it. So public and so endless. Neighbors came to their door. Then the F.B.I.. Then the insurance adjusters. And then the endless flood of relief agencies promising help. Catholic Charities. The Red Cross. N.O.V.A. (National Organization for Victims Assistance). All of them promising help. And yet, for all of that, very little help was forthcoming in the early days.

These were women who had to stand in line with volunteer guides through a bizarre supermarket of disaster-relief trailers presenting receipts for their husbands memorial services, for mortgage payments, phone bills, and heating costs as they drifted from trailer to trailer, agency to agency, death certificate and marriage license in hand.

"$1,800. Do you believe it?" Donna insisted. "Three kids and that's all I ever received from the Red Cross."

They endured the clinging grasp of a traumatized nation, boarding buses at South Station for the long trip to New York and the service of national mourning. It was the first time, the only time, they were ever to venture to Ground Zero. Issued respiratory masks, protective glasses, and white hard hats they were led past the Memorial Wall, still aching with its candles and teddy bears, its flowers and fading pictures; across an unsteady catwalk under the outer buildings draped in black netting, and finally a steel ramp ascending toward the incomprehensible reality of what happened there.

"It was nothing like I thought it would be on TV. On TV you were always looking down at Ground Zero, but when you are there you are always looking up at Ground Zero," Maureen reflected. "I had to see it for myself."

"I don't think I could have gone there," Daniel mused.

"Many didn't go. Not that day," said Lilly.

"You have to understand, for myself at least," Paula began, "I had to make it real. That was the worst part, how everything was so unreal. The mind plays tricks. I mean, I saw the plane on television, but I somehow didn't believe it was really Ned's plane. It wasn't until I was there and saw that awful place that I could feel it and start to move on."

Daniel knew that grief was like a quilt, patterns stitched from fragments of memory, and so the work is always in putting things together that have been torn apart. As they talked he sensed he was hearing a story told over and over in their time together, a stitch repeated again and again until the seam was strong. This repetition they allowed one another as the necessary work around their quilting circle for the last three years. It was understood.

To anyone else perhaps their recitation would have seemed flat. But Daniel could feel the weight of each story, stuffed full with warm emotion, held firmly in place along the edges by only the thread of sheer will. The quilter's will. The will to finish and move on, finish and move on, piece by piece by piece.

"Was that day the hardest then?" he asked.

"Oh no!"

Each woman had her own version of bottoming out. For Donna and Paula it was what they grimly called the Second Death. Families and grief therapists counseled closure and in the two to three month range out from the tragedy hundreds of memorial services were held. But, in the relentless cadence of consequences one by one over the months, the widows heard a knock at the door from the local police departments with news from New York that positive identification of remains had been made. Whatever patchwork seams had been woven were now undone, unraveled by cruel choices about what to ask and what to leave unspoken. Every recovered wedding band came at a cost.

For Maureen it was the free vacation. Six months into the grief process a spring basket arrived from one of the various relief agencies offering free vacations to Florida or the Caribbean. At first

Maureen had been eager to put some distance between her memories and her present.

"I wasn't thinking," she shook her head. "I had to fly to St. Thomas. My first flight. I nearly got off the plane. And then I was on the beach. Alone. You understand? All I could think of was this is my first vacation without Donald…and how every vacation would be without Donald. It was too soon. I shouldn't have gone."

She mentioned dating. What fun was going to the Caribbean alone? And yet they were always watching her—her family, her friends, her co-workers. If she were even seen with another man in public the whispers would have ended it then and there. It was too early.

"And you, Carl?"

"One word. Bush. Another word. Cheney. Bad news."

"Don't mind Carl. He's a little paranoid nowadays," Maureen interjected. Lilly caught Daniel's eye.

"Don't humor me, Maureen. You laugh now. Well, it ain't over till it's over, is it?"

"We support you, Carl," Lilly offered. "That's why we went to Washington."

After three months, just at the stage where the shock and denial were giving way to anger, a group of widows from New Jersey started pestering Congress for tax relief. The paperwork was just too much. Lilly explained how every waking minute had been filled with forms, piles of forms taking over her living room floor—insurance forms, agency forms, state forms, federal forms, the September 11th Victim Compensation Fund.

So all five of them went down on the train to Washington as a group, meeting up with the New Jersey widows and chasing down Dennis Hastert, Speaker of the House. It was the first time any one of them had been out of town. They were challenged by the sight of a memorial display of melted steel beams at Union Station, challenged by a high security Capital Building still closed to the public, challenged by congressmen avoiding them in the halls. But they got it done.

"We had the high ground then," Carl insisted.

But as the nation's newspapers detailed the minute by minute events of 9/11, publishing chronologies and timelines, their anger grew. Pressure was building in Washington against an independent investigation into 9/11. Inspired by the New Jersey widows, they were at it again, descending on Washington in June *en masse* to demand a full investigation. They got it done.

"And that's as far as they are ever going to let us go," Carl insisted. "Trust me. They have too much to hide."

"Here we go!" Maureen huffed.

"You know about the assassination team, right?" He held Daniel's eyes.

"What assassination team?"

"Don't encourage him, Daniel." Maureen threw up her hands.

"When Bush got up for his morning jog on the morning on 9/11, a van full of Middle Eastern men pulled up at the security gate of the Colony Beach resort in Sarasota and asked for a particular Secret Service agent by name. They said they were a television crew who had come for a pool-side interview. The Secret Service didn't let them in."

"And the significance of that is?"

"Two days earlier the leader of the Northern Alliance in Afghanistan, Ahmed Shah Massoud, was killed by suicide bombers with a bomb in their news camera."

"I'm surprised. You know this?"

"*LongBoat Observer*, Sarasota, Florida."

"I don't know, Carl."

"Fine. Then there's the seven versions of what Bush knew and when he knew it. The news of the first crash broke while Bush was in the motorcade. Reporters in the motorcade got the news on route. Two accounts claim Bush got the news on route. People at the school got the news before Bush arrived. But in the official White House versions, either Andrew Card or possibly Carl Rove told him about it, and told him it was an accident. Bush's own version, by the way, on *Sixty Minutes*, was that he was waiting in a classroom with a TV on and saw the first plane hit the tower. But nobody saw that. That footage didn't surface until the next day. And he couldn't have seen the second plane hit because there is camera footage of him reading to the class when Flight 175 hit. What's the deal with that? Why would he lie? Even in the White House version Bush stayed reading the goat story and talking for 35 minutes after he was told."

"I have to admit, that really bothers me," Lilly commented.

"You have a point, Carl," Daniel added.

"You bet I do. And what about the three missing minutes on the Flight 93 cockpit voice recording?"

"I never heard of that."

"The Government version, re-recorded on a thirty minute tape reel, by the way, says Flight 93 crashed at 10:03. Seismologists could pick up the crash and say it was 10:06. And witnesses on the ground in Pennsylvania saw the plane in the air around 10:03. And the last sound heard on the tape is loud wind noises, any way, like the plane had a hole in it."

"Is this real, Carl?"

"*CNN. London Times Mirror.* Sure. You bet. We never got the real story on what happened that day. And we're not gonna get the real deal until somebody leaks it later. But I know what went down. And I know what they're hiding."

"Enough already," Maureen insisted.

"I just want to know what happened to my wife."

"I know, Carl. I know." Lilly leaned over to pat his hand.

"We've been trying to help, you know. Trying to do what we can to get a real investigation."

"That Kristen Breitweiser, she's my hero," offered Donna.

"Fighting with the Victim's Fund. Fighting for the 9/11 investigation panel for us."

"You understand that they are calling anybody who asks questions un-American or a conspiracy kook, right?" Carl added.

"But not Kristen Breitweiser," said Paula.

"Not any of us either," confirmed Lilly. "It's something we can do. We'll keep at it, Carl."

"Still pisses me off though. I gotta go." Carl stood abruptly

"You okay?" Maureen queried. "Call you later?"

"No. I mean I gotta go home. Work tomorrow. I'm fine."

"Walk me to the T-stop then," said Maureen, standing as well. She looked to Paula and Donna.

"Me too," Donna chimed in on cue.

"Let me get my bag," followed Paula.

Daniel and Lilly rose to say good-bye.

"I don't know what to say," Daniel offered. "You've got quite a group here. I'm honored. It's been quite an evening."

"You guys get your videos together for Daniel. Tell your friends," said Lilly, pulling on her coat. "Pats game next Sunday?"

"Right, see you there." They trotted off a little too quickly with knowing smiles.

A tingle of panic caught in Lilly's throat. *You're not as strong as you feel*, it occurred to her. *The crowd and the clapping has gone to your head.*

"Patriots?" Daniel mused, clearing a dozen coffee cups off the table.

"Season tickets. Group vote. Gives us a chance to yell our heads off." She swept the sugars and open creamers into a napkin. "So, what'd ya think? I bet they bring their videos in for you. If they don't, I'll make them."

"I think I didn't hear you say anything about what's been hard for you."

"That's because everything is hard for me, Daniel."

"I'm sorry. I'm sure you loved your husband very much."

Why do people always say that, always think that? Lilly wondered. *Respect*, she knew. *Respect for the dead*. Somehow in people's minds the dead have no relationship problems. They simply loved and were loved. Their exit is their free pass out of commitments and accountabilities; their promises and their reckonings can no longer be enforced.

Grief is a spiral, never a straight line. A circle of remembering and forgetting around the central pool of pain that is never far away. People sometimes think that pool can be drained, but what happens in reality is simply that you move closer to it or further away. It is always there. Lilly understood what it was to walk that labyrinth. Even three years later she could one day be walking a distant hill thinking only of her journey onward, and the very next be turned back to feel its presence once more, wounded by the roadside, unable to go further.

"Unfinished business, Daniel. Tim's timing was always wrong."

The table cleared, Daniel turned toward the door.

"I'm sorry. It's really not for me to ask. Ready to go? It's late." He escorted her to the door. She hesitated, then followed him out to Newbury Street.

"I had a decision to make," she said suddenly, looking away from him. "When all of this happened, you have to understand, all these people…they were trying to help me. They were giving me things—food, money, vacations. It was hard for me. I've always been a giver, not a taker. That's not me. And I was getting down. I was becoming that depressed woman you read about. That's not me either. So that was the hardest part for me. Turning into somebody else. Somebody I don't recognize. I had to make a decision. I had to decide what kind of person I was going to be. A small person or a big person."

"So what was your decision?"

"The music. New people in my life." She looked up to his eyes. "You."

Daniel stopped in mid-step.

"Then this was a date, I guess? I don't know, Lilly."

"No, this most definitely was not a date."

"Well, that's good because I haven't been on a date in a long time."

"Neither have I. I don't think I am ready for dating. Even if the girls say that I have to try."

"Is that why they were treating me like a date?"

"They just wanted to see if you were the right material. See if you could take it. None of them have dated either, you know."

"I don't think I want to be a guinea pig."

"So, can you take it or not? It's an unusual situation, I know."

"Lilly, it's just that I still don't understand what is being asked of me."

"I know. The thing is, I don't want your sympathy. I am so tired of sympathy. I just want to be me. Maybe it's enough just for me to know if you liked my singing."

"I liked it, Lilly."

"Then maybe it's enough if I ask you if you want to go to the Patriots game with me next Sunday."

"Is that a date?"

"I guess it is. But only a little date."

"But why, Lilly? Why me?"

"Because you are safe, Daniel." She looked down and away. "Because you are safe and so reluctant."

"Reluctant is the word."

"That's what I need. Will you come?"

When a man is closed, there is always a reason. His heart, even the most timid heart, does not turn away from the world for reasons of its own. He is not by nature uninterested, but unnaturally wounded. And if you think that merely attention and desire will draw him out again, then you do not understand the injury that a woman can inflict upon a man's soul. It is not a little thing. Some harms can never be undone.

For a woman holds the singular power to break a man's trust. Trust in the world. In a way that no other man could ever do, because competitors are distrustful by nature, a woman, acting cruelly, can destroy the basic sense that life is giving and yielding. First from his mother, he must know he can trust to comfort; to withdraw from pain and toil and there be held. And then to his lover, his inspiring and alluring other, he must find the will to fight, the prize worth fighting for, the promise of fulfillment and release.

And should these be broken in him by misfortune or outright callousness then he will withdraw into a deep cave and wrap himself up in himself like a lost boy in abject despair. To be alone is his only solace, and that solace, though familiar, will be a prison and an exile. From that dark cave few ever emerge again, save by the grace of larger things still larger than the comfort and release of a good woman.

"I like football just about as much as I like folk music," Daniel sighed. "But, yes. I'll be there."

CHAPTER FIVE

A TANTRUM

HAT A PSYCHOANALYST KNOWS: *THE RELATIONSHIP between people and things as they are.* Things as they are—*breath, and then death.* No need to fear the truth. Oh, come now, please. Don't rush to disguise it. This is simply how it is for us.

People's relationship to things as they are—instinct and genes. Not to think, but to act. To grunt, to pleasure, and to sigh. Without delay. Without hesitation. You must understand. A human gene, alive and well, does not hesitate, does not interfere with instinct. And if he should interfere this is a sickness. The psychoanalyst knows this, heals this, dispenses with this hesitation. Be fruitful and multiply. Do not wait. Do not hesitate.

And then, what? Let us be honest, for once. Why avoid it? All this is perhaps a little surprising, but not so hidden or difficult to understand. *People's relationship to things as they are when the instinct is not aroused*—to merely pass the time. All these pursuits—do you see now?—they are just to pass the time when we are not otherwise engaged and have no more importance than a game played in the sand under a tree on a bright afternoon too hot to work. And so we pass the time as best we can. The psychoanalyst knows this and does not laugh out loud at foolishness because we are entitled to lighten our burden just a bit. In that way we save our strength.

And then, after and between the start/stop cycle of instinct going round yet another time, there remains only one essential thing—*the curious. Of what nature is this?* The psychoanalyst must ask. Curiosity is of the nature of instinct, surely, a vigilance of certain senses tuned to the world. Sniffing the wind. Scanning the horizon. Bending the ear so faintly that the head rises, and pauses to consider what manner of thing might be there. We await death and return and sleep—but, in waiting, in that space smaller still than a runner's stride, time enough to raise the eyes and to look far and ponder the mist of a dark wood beyond a green meadow. And perhaps remark to others "once I saw a faraway thing of beauty. Have you not seen it too?" And the possibility of friendship, of another person's knowing eyes. "Aye, I have seen it. We must go there one day."

And the only question, you see, is whether this passing curiosity happened to become curious about itself by some unforeseen accident of evolution, whether nature in some wise desires to peruse and evaluate itself. This is possible.

So these three things the psychoanalyst will allow as healthy and in no need of interference on his part: instinct going about its business without hesitation; boredom playing games in the sand to pass the time for idle hands and minds; and also, finally, curiosity casting a thin light in dark places simply for the sake of interest in what might be there. Beyond this there is nothing the psychoanalyst knows, or needs to know.

A DRAFT OF THE NEW FIRST CHAPTER OF HER DISSERTATION IN HAND, Laurel Wolff sat nervously in the big overstuffed chair in Daniel's waiting room. She could just make out the mutter of a conversation within, but not the words. She didn't want to pry, and yet she was curious.

What goes on inside an analyst's office is a curiosity for many people. She could remember her first time walking through Carla Greer's door after her divorce, feeling the anticipation, wondering if anybody could really tell her anything she didn't already know. What made therapists so special anyway? *The books they'd read?* Laurel could read the books just as well herself.

She had decided to see a Jungian because she had run across Jung in graduate school at Columbia. Professor Tawney had given her quite a push-back, being a Deconstructionist. He had no room for the idea of archetypes. Professor Grainger, on the other hand, encouraged her to use the big Jungian symbols. In fact he was glad to read a dissertation that had something original in it. Other than hers, all of the dissertations in Literature were Post-postmodern that year.

Still, it was strange to apply Jung's ideas to herself rather than to Emily Dickinson and Louisa May Alcott. Nineteenth Century American women writers were her specialty. The marriage relationship was apparently not. She knew it was her fault, in a way. Brian had been caring enough, if a little immature. He was teachable, malleable, open to instruction in a woman's ways. And needs. A decent chap, really. So quiet. They were living together, they married, they graduated.

At first she had wanted to open him like a novel and delve into him. Carla Greer had made a lot of that her first year in analysis. Her eagerness to read him thoroughly. *The animus!* Her splendid dark lover waiting to be revealed.

Except he was none of that. Underneath it all Brian was plain and plodding. A details person. Happy enough to spend his hours tracking down the references to Boswell in the literature of the period. 12,414, it could be proved. In those first days of grad school she thought he shared her love of books and talking endlessly about books. And he could talk. He could talk for hours. It was just that she blew right by him. She was the star.

And it made him happy. He was happy to watch her win the academic honors and get herself on a tenure track at Fordham. Brian adjusted, working part-time at City College. He was ready for children and would stay home.

Damn it. Everything would have been so much easier if he didn't love her. It made her feel so cruel to be dissatisfied with him. And she was cruel. It was wrong. It was nasty. It was a student in Creative Writing with his short stories that made her think he was the real deal. Soon to be published. The talk of New York. She wasn't the only one who slept with him, but it made the Jesuits at Fordham nervous.

"You always like the quiet ones, don't you?" Carla Greer suggested.

"Yes. My fatal attraction."

"And I would think the Man of Words as well. You don't seem much impressed with the Man of Action."

Translation: *at one phase in a woman's development the thing that is attractive is the way a man acts, his strength and straight-jawed courage, presaging strong semen no doubt; but at another phase she is attracted to the way a man talks, the way a man thinks when he talks, the way a man writes* (which to her was even better than hearing him talk), *presaging genetically good minds, all in the way of proving that both brawn and brains are essential to evolution through mate selection preferences.* Emma Jung and Toni Wolff had worked this out long ago, cranking out a woman's theory from Jung's views on the human/all too male psyche.

Sub-translation: *some women get off on muscles and facial lines—oh my God will you just look at him; other women get off on words and voice—oh my God will you just listen to him. And all of the women all of the time would prefer a good strong man with a nice face who talks like the Devil.*

Laurel found it always helped her understand psychology to boil it down to the way people behaved in relationships. In that way you could learn a lot about a person.

Painful as it was Carla Greer had made her face what had gone on in her relationship with Brian when she quietly slipped away to Brandeis and found herself in Boston. In the long run she had been hoping that as she tore into him she would discover a truly great man in there, a man to inspire her and challenge her. That's what she projected on to the quietness. To her such a stillness was a deep ocean.

"That's quite a fantasy," said Carla.

"I was only twenty when we met. I wanted to be a writer then, you know. I loved all of those stories about Virginia Wolff. I was just a kid."

"Interesting that you share her name. And you don't want that life any more?"

"No, I am more realistic."

"You gave up so easily?"

Tears came to her eyes with such unexpected force that she couldn't control them. Carla Greer was kind and motherly, touching her woman to woman.

"I don't want to give it up."

"I didn't think so."

"But I must. And so I have."

"Have you?"

"Yes. That's all behind me now. My Ph.D. will have to do."

"And yet you wrote your dissertation on Emily Dickinson. Tell me, what is your favorite Dickinson poem?" The analyst pulled a 1924 *Complete Poems* edition from her shelves. "Read it for me."

EXULTATION is the going
Of an inland soul to sea, —
Past the houses, past the headlands,
Into deep eternity!
Bred as we, among the mountains,
Can the sailor understand
The divine intoxication
Of the first league out from land?

"Oh my! Now that is sexy. You are a Poseidon's Daughter, my dear. A mermaid, through and through. No wonder a man can't get you to plant your feet on the ground."

"What does that mean?"

"You swim in your father's depths."

And with that Laurel was hooked, hooked on psychoanalysis. Damn it all. Her father was such a quiet man. Like so many refugees from those times he would not talk about it. The reality of Hungary became a memory and the memory became an obstacle to moving on and so it was put away with the old clothes and the three-stringed gardon and the rugs. He only said that they were lucky to be in Amerika when Amerika took so few Hungarians that year and that she should be thankful and always do her best to make her way in Amerika.

When Laurel was a rebellious thirteen years-old her mother scolded her to respect her father. Didn't she know who he was? Didn't she know of his fiery, passionate speeches during the Hungarian Revolution, how he fought bravely when the Russians marched on Budapest, of those terrible days in November 1956 when they walked one hundred miles to the Austrian border with baby Laurel in their arms and had to survive in the refugee camps? They would all be dead were it not for him. *Respect, little lanya. Respect.* But Laurel did not know this. He would never tell her.

It was like a story, a lived novel. It enthralled her, but eluded her. All she knew was that in Hungary he had been an intellectual, a university student, but in New Jersey he has a mechanic. A very good and trusted mechanic who liked to read political books and did not like to be disturbed when he sat by himself and thought that *Amerika is not what I expected. Amerika is cruel and too much to do with money. Amerika will never listen to me and will never think of noble revolution and honor. In Hungary there was honor. In Amerika there is only disdain for the way people talk.* And so he did not talk. He was embarrassed to talk. And he was sad, immensely sad and disappointed.

"What are you thinking about, Papa?"

"I am thinking you are not studying. I am thinking you are not reading a book. If you do not read a book, how will you make a university, *lanya*? You want to be a *munkas* like me all your life?!"

Reality. Fantasy. Loss. They are the stuff of every life, of every analysis.

DANIEL WAS A MYSTERY TO HER. She could not fathom how he could be so immune to her wiles. How in one moment he could be so stern and cold, convinced of what he knew like a lonely king on a high frosty mountain, and then in the next moment so wounded, so hurt and vulnerable.

In the waiting room she had passed another woman, laughing as she left his office. *Was this a patient?* she could not help but wonder. So, he is seeing patients after all. *She's there to talk about her sexual problems, no doubt.*

It was one of those things about psychoanalysis. Sex. Sex talk. When given the right space—a relaxed, non-judgmental, absolutely confidential space to talk—people often utilize the opportunity to satisfy their curiosity about what other people are doing. Sharing their fantasies, eyes down, they glance up to see the reaction. Like so many things, they need the reality check. They need to see the understanding analyst does not flinch or squirm uncomfortably.

Laurel had had a dream about her breasts. Not her breasts, exactly, but the breasts of a college friend who was not shy about tight sweaters and tee-shirts. The other girls had been a little envious, actually, of her endowment and her exhibition. In the dream there was a bright shining star on her cream-colored blouse marking just the spot, Laurel supposed, where she liked to be touched.

"And how do you feel about your breasts?" Carla Greer had asked her. "Different women are all over the map on how they relate to their breasts."

Laurel had to reach down for a minute to consult her attitude. The truth surprised her.

"I feel good," she said a little shyly. Carla waited, making her say more. "I've always been…adequate."

"More than adequate. More than a handful is a waste, as some men say."

At that Laurel had to laugh out loud.

"I have been pleased…I mean, other women have sagged. I'm still firm. So, I'm alright in that department. One of my best features."

"Like a mermaid on the prow of a ship."

"Yes. I've always felt good about that."

"And when it comes to sex?"

"I like sex too."

"I mean your breasts. Your breasts are important when you are having sex, or not so important?"

"Important."

"And?"

"And what?"

"And satisfying?" Carla interrogated her with a glance of the eye. "It's one thing to be important. It's another thing to be satisfied. Brian, for instance. He satisfied you?"

"Yes," she said quickly, then thought better of it. "No. He did not pay sufficient attention. I could do for more attention to my breasts."

"And you told him this?"

"No. Well, once maybe. But then he did it all wrong. I didn't ask again."

"And why not?"

"Because I would not wish to appear to be too demanding," Laurel said slowly.

Carla was relentless. "Too demanding for what?"

"For the man."

"For the man…," Carla repeated. "And what is your fantasy of what would happen if you were too demanding? Tell me."

"That…That he would be unsatisfied. I suppose. That he would be unhappy."

"And if he were unsatisfied? If he were unhappy, what then?" Carla in these moments pushed every thought of hers down and down the chain of associations to the very bottom.

"Then, I guess…I guess he would leave. He wouldn't want me anymore."

"So, you remain unsatisfied as a way of keeping a man?" Carla offered bluntly.

"I wouldn't put it that way."

"What way would you put it?"

"If he is happy, then I am happy."

"Satisfied."

"If he is satisfied then I am satisfied."

"Mermaid logic, Laurel. Mermaid logic."

"I don't understand."

"Mermaids are fish below the waist. And fish don't copulate." Carla looked her square in the eyes. "When you do it, Laurel, it's not for you. It's for him. Isn't that what you're saying?"

"Yes." Laurel fought not to give into her sudden tears.

"Well then, your dream is an invitation. An invitation to your femininity. We could go on a bit with your associations to your college friend, but my guess would be she was a more feminine woman. A different type than you."

"Yes."

"And in your dream her breasts are blessed and glorified. She's the kind of woman who puts it out there, so to speak. Other women ask for what they need, what they want. And, believe it or not, their men do not run away from them. In fact, some of the men kind of like it. But you hesitate."

"I know."

"Don't hesitate, Laurel. What are you waiting for? If you want to be satisfied you are going to have to put yourself out there, in more ways than one. Your feminine self. Your feminine ego, technically. You can learn to ask for what you want. Throw a tantrum if you have to, but communicate. This is a big dream for you because you have always been such a father's daughter, as we have discussed. Glorify your breasts, if that is what you need."

Laurel laughed. "It does sound kind of fun."

But that was just the thing. It was one thing to talk with Carla Greer in the confidence of woman-to-woman intimacy. Something like sharing fashion tips or makeup ideas. How different it would be to have the very same conversation with a male analyst. With Daniel. If Daniel were her analyst, would that conversation have been the same? Obviously not. No. It would have been more like exposing her breasts. Like the college girl in the dream. It would have been bolder. A way of saying *look at me.*

And would he have looked then? Would she have wanted him to? Yes. That was the fantasy. To expose herself to him. To get under his skin and break him out of his sternness. To penetrate his impenetrability and make him show himself for once. A little strip poker.

"Sorry to keep you waiting so long," he interrupted.

'Oh," she said, coming to herself. "That's quite alright. You had another patient."

"Interesting," said Daniel.

"She's an interesting case?"

"No," Daniel replied, laying out the new chapter from her thesis on his desk. "Interesting you assumed she was a patient when you know that officially I am no longer seeing patients until this ethical issue is resolved."

"I didn't mean to assume," Laurel stuttered.

"I've always found this phenomenon of the fantasies about people engendered by encounters in the waiting room most interesting. The fantasies tell you a lot about the person."

"It was a mistake. I'm sorry."

"You said you were controlling with Martha Fleming, as I remember. Didn't Martha pound into your head you have to pay attention to things like this?"

"She mentioned it, yes. I don't know that I've ever really understood what I am supposed to do with that material."

"Analyze the hell out it. Get to the bottom of it."

"I'll try to remember that. So, who *was* she, if not a patient?" *Do not hesitate,* Laurel remembered. *Make bold and ask for what you want. Throw a tantrum if you have to.*

Daniel paused to consider this quagmire she offered him. To engage, or not to engage. He still did not have straight in his mind what sort of relationship with Laurel he actually wanted. Being free to decide was an unusual situation for him, most of his other relationships being defined so clearly by his various roles. It surprised him to be thinking of choices at all. And yet that was the only small gain he had made in these last few years after his analysis with Frau Delarosa. Because previously there had been no room for decision. It was out of his hands. At one time he had been so closed and so hurt the functioning was automatic. He simply could not do what he was not emotionally prepared to do. It was hopeless.

Sometimes in the course of a long analysis together the analyst and analysand come across the central issue. There are many things in a person's life, of course. Never just the one thing. And yet, sometimes there is a central core of gravity around which all the other complexes orbit, that one essential thing so large it cannot be moved. Not by force of will. Not by clever technique. Not by any countervailing force available to consciousness.

And so they must wait. The great dead weight of mournful Saturn does not countenance any little thing and will answer only to its archetypal foe and nemesis, jovial Jupiter. It is not for the analyst or the analysand to decide. They must wait for nature to take its course.

When Daniel had first seen *The Secret Garden* he had been without hope, knowing as he did from Frau Delarosa, at last, what ailed him.

"Do you enjoy the theater?" she asked him back then, out of the blue.

"I haven't been in many years."

"I should think it would appeal to you, being such an observer of other people." She laughed to herself as if he wasn't in the room. "Two kinds of people, *nicht wahr*? Those who watch and those who perform."

"I suppose so."

"There is a play in town. A musical. I saw it last night. Very psychological."

"Music and dancing? Not for me."

"Very little dancing. Too sad a thing for dancing. At any rate I thought of you. *Natürlich. The Secret Garden.* You might profit from it."

"I have patients in the evening."

"Herr Doctor Osgood, listen to me. Perhaps the play's the thing wherein I'll catch the conscience of the king. Do you know what that means?"

"Of course."

"*Doch!* I mean, psychologically. Symbolically. It means sometimes we need to see ourselves performed. When you dream of a play, for instance, what might this mean?"

"That we are seeing an inner drama."

"That we are seeing an inner unconscious drama. A drama of the unconscious played out without the interference of the ego. And when we see our own little lives played out at a higher level, perhaps it pricks us."

"I am surprised you know this word in English."

"Fine, *geschlagen* then. It hits us. I fear that given your situation we will make no progress against it through the conscious level. You have to gain a larger perspective on your own suffering. You cannot hope to solve the conflict, but only to grow out of it. An irrational problem requires an irrational solution."

He hadn't wanted to go. Not at first. There was the matter of going alone, which, truth be told, had always bothered him more than he let on. And then there was the issue of the energy required to steel himself against the venture over to Bolyston Street and the crowds of strangers.

And yet, there he was, dressed for the theater and snaking his way through the foyer of the Colonial and the mobs of Boston socialites in heels and little black dresses, Armani suits and Zegna silk ties, to his first row seat in the Mezzanine level. His father could still get good tickets, after all.

Alone in the aisle seat, hands in his lap, not a single person around him that night would have had any idea at all just how hard it hit him. Even if they saw his eyes moisten, and that is all anyone would have ever seen from Daniel on any night, they could not have guessed how *The Secret Garden* struck him full force. He did not know, he did not understand himself. He had done it for her, for Frau Delarosa, because although he didn't want to admit it to her face-to-face he was stuck in the transference with her—her big motherly Swiss presence—and was loath to disappoint her. So he went.

She never knew. She died before he could tell her, as he wanted to tell her. As with so many things about analysis each and every situation is unique. The best one can say is that it is not uncommon for the big revelation to come quite consciously in a moment you can identify and perhaps say *this is the day that I understood and was moved*. Except that no sooner is it spoken one finds oneself, for the sake of the truth, saying just the other thing: it is not uncommon to be moved—and to be moved so profoundly, in fact, that it may be a healing, as far as healing goes—without realizing at the time that this was the one essential thing. For Daniel it meant that one day he was walking down Newbury Street and realized that he had been living a new life at least for the last three years. And it was because of *The Secret Garden*. Because of the play. Because of something Frau Delarosa had asked him once.

It wasn't fair to Laurel to keep this from her, he realized. She was writing a thesis, just an exercise, something she might very well leave dusty on the shelf once she got it accepted. He could not blame her for that. And yet for him she was dealing with life and death. She was holding his life in her hands. She was dealing with the one essential thing. No. It would not do. He would have to tell her soon.

The synchronicity of it all had been seductive. He could never have refused her that night after he learned about her interest in *The Secret Garden*. But it was also she who was seductive. She was pretty, in her dark way. Direct. Sometimes confrontive, if a little academically entitled. He found himself noticing her prettiness, and that was new. Unwanted, even. Sometimes the smallest changes have the greatest consequences.

Still, Daniel hesitated. He could not choose yet what he wanted from her. He had first to decide if he wanted anything at all.

"Daniel?" she said at last.

"I'm sorry. I was thinking of my old analyst and what she would do in this situation."

"In what situation?"

"In a situation where the analysand keeps probing into the analyst's personal life."

"You are not my analyst. I am not your patient."

"No. Not at all. But I find myself thinking the comparison is apropos."

"I'm just asking because I would like to get to know you a little bit. You're not so easy for a person to get to know."

"No. I guess not."

"You're impenetrable sometimes, actually."

"Impenetrable? As bad as that?"

"Just a little small talk, Daniel. It wouldn't hurt from time to time."

"And since we are getting to know each other," he said, turning towards her, "may I ask who was so emotionally impenetrable to you?"

She stopped to consider if she were making progress with him or not. "Father."

"I see. And what was your reaction to that part of him?"

"Like any daughter, I was always trying to unlock him."

"And succeeded from time to time, I would think."

"Why do you say that?"

"Because you keep treating me like I am emotionally impenetrable and then unlocking me."

"Maybe that's because it's something I'm good at. Maybe it's something you need." She countered.

"Maybe you should stop treating me like your father."

"How would you prefer that I treat you?"

He stopped, clearly unable to answer the question. This satisfied her because she could see she had broken his analytic persona. "Shall I treat you like an analyst? Or perhaps a respected teacher and mentor? Then again, perhaps you would prefer I treat you like a friend. Or like a man? You are all of those things, Daniel."

It felt good to her to be out there. Maybe her analysis was having an effect after all.

Daniel sighed. "I think I want you to treat me like an advisor. A thesis advisor. For today."

"In other words, you're going to give me a hard time?"

"That's my role." Daniel withdrew a large red pen from his desk. "You don't like it?"

"Didn't I tell you to use real life examples?"

"Yes."

"Are you afraid to use them?"

"In a way."

"Look, it's really very simple. Gather the associations. Just like a dream you've had. '*When Mary Lennox was sent to Misselthwaite Manor to live with her uncle, everybody said she was the most disagreeable-looking child ever seen.*' Does that remind you of anything you've ever experienced?"

"Well, Frances Hodgson Burnett was carted off to live with her uncle in Tennessee when she was a girl of fifteen. But it was not a mansion. She lived in sort of a log cabin in abject poverty."

"And was she disagreeable-looking?"

"Her biographer remarks that she was a plain woman, in fact."

"Fine. So, you want to identify Mary Lennox with Frances Hodgson Burnett?"

"Yes. And no. It's dangerous, you know, to read the writers into their characters. Poor form."

"Poor analysis."

"So what is the point of this exercise?" Laurel protested. Perhaps it was an academic prejudice, but she resisted his method of entering the story through the biography and personality of the author. If that was his agenda.

"Just stay with the image, Laurel. Go on."

"I am thinking that Frances Hodgson Burnett was famous for her rags to riches stories. *Little Lord Fauntleroy. A Little Princess.*"

"Riches to rags to riches," he corrected.

"And Frances Hodgson Burnett herself started life fairly well off. Her father was a manufacturer. It seems he sold chandeliers, silver, and other furnishings to all the other manufacturers making their fortunes and building their big houses in Manchester."

"England."

"Yes. I did not realize this before I started my research, but the American Civil War was devastating to Manchester."

"Yes. They needed the cotton."

"Her father had died in 1853, when Frances Hodgson Burnett was only three years-old. So her mother tried to run the business. The war did her in. So she sold the business and moved to Tennessee, near Knoxville, where her brother promised better times. But it was 1865 in Tennessee."

"Riches to rags."

"Well, and then her mother died just five years later, leaving twenty year-old Frances in charge of the family, by now in a dilapidated old house in Knoxville. Her only income was her stories sold to magazines."

"And the rest, as they say, is history."

"Frances Hodgson Burnett was to be quite wealthy from her stories, if a little imprudent with her money. But, quite a story, nevertheless."

"Slow down, Laurel. These things are useful to know. But you're rushing over the painful part."

"The deaths?" she offered reluctantly.

"Yes, but let's stay with the money, for now. Do you know what it feels like to lose everything?"

"No."

"Really? You are sure?"

"Daniel, honestly. If you want me to be frank, I haven't ever had enough money to lose a great deal of money. Have you?" She tossed it back to him angrily.

"I have not lost a great deal of money, exactly. Recently there is a strain. But, I know the experience. It's not just the money. Haven't you known anybody in this story before? You emigrated to this country, correct?"

"My parents came from Hungary, yes."

"And?"

"They lost everything. Yes. Yes, I see."

"Do you?" He paused. "What was the impact on your parents?"

"They were happy to be in America. Happy to have escaped."

"I don't think so."

"What do you know? I heard this every day growing up," Laurel protested.

"Oh, I don't doubt that. I just doubt that happiness is the whole story. I doubt it entirely."

"They worried about the family left behind. Brothers and sisters. If that's what you mean."

"I only want you to slow down long enough to experience the emotional impact of the things that happen to people. Haven't you covered this in your own analysis?"

"Yes, I have. But I fail to see what that has to do with my thesis, Daniel."

"Well, for one thing, it seems only fair to Frances Hodgson Burnett that if we're going to analyze her we also consider the things in your own life that come into your writing. What's good for the goose is good for the gander. Unless you are afraid to tell your own story."

"Am I afraid to put it on paper? To show it to my committee? Yes. Sure."

"Then maybe you can have a little appreciation for what a writer goes through. The other point is that you want to be a psychoanalyst. Without including yourself it's all just a clever intellectualization, isn't it? Boring and sterile in the end. The thing is, Laurel, all we have to work with is ourselves. That is the only real technique. Just ourselves and the bit of emotional clarity that is analyzed out of us."

Laurel felt her stomach drop. She felt it sometimes with Carla Greer too. As if she were on the verge of something. Something she couldn't understand. Something that eluded her. Intellectually, she protested. These were often just clever Jungianizations, it seemed to her. They were so intent upon subjectifying every little comment, every little story, every little idea. Wasn't it possible just to consider what was being said on its own merits without always having to question who was saying it?

"And you wrote things like that in your own thesis?" She said at last, finding a different spin.

"With a lot of help. I admit it wasn't easy at all to attempt it."

"And what was your topic then? What's good for the goose is good for the gander."

"It's in the library at the Institute, if you really want to know. My topic was the death of the anima in a man's life. Is that honest enough for you now?"

Now that is interesting, she thought. *A bit obscure, but interesting nevertheless if it had to do with what he thought about the relationship between men and women.* She would have to check it out of the library first thing.

"Speaking from personal experience, I suppose?"

"Yes. Speaking from personal experience. But, once again you push away from your own experience. Let's get back to what you know."

"What I know is that when something happens, something large, people close down," she said carefully. "They go into survival mode."

"Yes, that's a start."

"And when they close down, it's like a shell. Everything gets reduced to putting one foot in front of another. To surviving one more day. They harden themselves."

"Yes, they do. And then?"

"And then what? I feel like you are trying to make me say something analytically brilliant. I don't know if I can."

"Brilliance is not required. In fact, it may well be a defense. Just tell me what happens to the hard shell after the crisis has passed."

"The shell remains."

"Yes."

"They remain emotionally impenetrable. Somehow they are still lost in the old battles."

"'When Mary Lennox was sent to Misselthwaite Manor to live with her uncle, everybody said she was the most disagreeable-looking child ever seen.' Now we are getting somewhere."

Again, she felt her stomach drop. There was something here just out of reach. His method seemed to be to treat characters as real people. And yet that cannot be so. Characters in books, in children's stories, in fairy tales are, well, just characters. They never lived at all. How can they have real feelings when as characters in stories they can have only points of view?

"Okay. Mary has hardened herself and that's what makes her such a disagreeable child. She was orphaned," Laurel began, not realizing what she was really saying.

"Yes. And neglected even before that, if you read the story. But not only Mary."

"Colin?"

"Colin whines a bit too much. No. I am thinking of Archibald Craven, her uncle. Emotionally impenetrable in his grief."

"So that is the initial situation in the story? What's wrong in the old manor house is that everything is closed down emotionally."

"And that is the dead garden," Daniel said with conviction.

Her stomach dropped a second level. There was such pain in his voice when he said it that it made her want to take him in her arms for the sadness of it. Somehow when he spoke of it the dead garden was real, as if it were just around the corner in the Public Garden behind a stone wall. As if he had been there himself, died there himself.

But she resisted, in spite of wanting to embrace this part of himself he was showing her. She didn't want to accept that somehow stories could be real.

"Yes. Yes. So the Secret Garden is simply the opening of the heart. I don't know, Daniel. Too easy."

"Simply the opening of the heart? You find it so easy to open a dead heart, do you?"

"No, I suppose not."

"No, you would not find it easy at all. Okay. You may be analytical again now. What does this mean, something so simple as opening the heart?"

"To love again."

"And what is that?"

"Attachment theory? Bowlby? Separation anxiety, despair, detachment? What do you want me to say? Honestly." She waved her hands and pouted.

"Include Bowlby in your paper if you want. Mary Lennox would fit with separation anxiety. We are just laying out the field for today. But I simply mean what is involved in learning to love again?"

"Trust."

"I suppose. To me, if you'll forgive me for being so old-fashioned, it has to do with libido. And the attachments of libido."

"Sex, again, in other words."

"No. Energy, to be less Freudian about it. If I were to love again I would need to find the emotional energy for it. But that's the thing. I really have no control over whether I feel love or do not feel love. No one does. It is like a spring of water. Either it is there or it is not there. How will you make it flow again if there is no water?"

"Poetic."

"Jung's image, not mine."

"You make it sound so difficult. So complicated. People are falling in love all of the time, too easily if you ask me. Why make it a psychoanalytic bugaboo?"

At this, Daniel laughed heartily.

"You're laughing?" she continued. "I don't think I have seen you laugh this entire hour. I'm serious. I have read everything I have been required to read. Jung, Freud, Bowlby, Winnicott, Klein, and on and on. Such a fuss. Do you realize what people who are not psychoanalysts think of all of this crap? Oh…," She stopped, suddenly doubting herself. "You're going to be mad at me now."

"No, Laurel. I am glad for a laugh. It never hurts to remind ourselves that we take it all too seriously. Of course! Love is always laughable when it's happening to somebody else. It's only when it's your problem that it seems so serious!"

"Ha-Ha. Very funny."

"Well, have you ever been in love?" he asked her.

"Of course"

"Married?"

"Yes, I was married." *Now we are getting somewhere*, Laurel thought. "And what about you?"

"Never married…Past tense?"

"But you were in love?" She continued.

"Depends on what you mean by love. What happened to your marriage?"

"Don't avoid the question. Keep it simple. Either you were in love or you weren't."

"I was involved in a libido attachment once, yes," said Daniel, smiling.

"What happened?"

"I asked you first."

"It didn't work out with him. So, what happened?"

"It didn't work out. Satisfied with that?"

"No. There's obviously more to it than that."

"Exactly. That's exactly what I am saying. The reason psychoanalysts go on and on about all this libido crap is that there's more to it than that, as you say. What is Mary Lennox's libido problem?"

But Laurel didn't want to talk about Mary Lennox anymore. "She is bored. She is unloved. She is not interested in anything except herself."

"Yes."

"Until she starts to love Dickon."

"Oh no. That is later. Pay attention to the details. Many other things have to happen first. Mary is first interested in the robin, as I remember. In Jungian terms we might say that might have to do with something of the spirit. Of the spirit of nature."

"Are we going archetypal here? You want me to say that Dickon is a spirit of nature?"

"Well, he could be seen as a representation of the Great Pan, most certainly. It is the magic of nature that is the heart of this story, after all."

Intellectually, Laurel understood this comment. But emotionally, it confused her. Again, he wasn't talking like her professors used to talk at all. It was more like a personal experience for him.

"And people just don't fall in love, you know," he added suddenly. "Not starting from where Mary starts. There is a great deal of preparation."

"Explain."

"Libido has to do with the things we get interested in, fascinated by, attached to, passionate about. The question is why we get interested in some things, but not interested at all in others. Or fascinated by something or someone in particular—a book, a movie, a hero, an idea, Jung, Freud, a man or a woman. Why him and not someone else? And then very often for some inexplicable reason suddenly the libido is gone. We're just not interested any more. It bores us now. The tide of libido has turned."

"I get it."

"But what if we're suddenly incapable of being interested in anything? Everything seems dull. No one seems interesting. Nothing excites us, engages us, gives any pleasure."

"Depression."

"Yes, one of the symptoms of depression. Anhedonia. The inability to take pleasure. But that's an extreme case. I'm talking about everyday life. Let's say a client came to you and complained of not being interested in anything anymore. What would you do?"

"Medication?"

"Just treating the symptoms. No. Be an analyst."

"Look at the dreams? You're making me guess again, Daniel." She was exasperated.

"And you shouldn't be guessing by now, should you Laurel? These questions will be more difficult on your diploma examination. Laurel, how do you reengage a person's energy?"

"I don't know."

"You can't. You can't do it. Nobody can. You can't make a person start to take an interest in life again just by sheer force of will. Or persuasion. Or coaxing."

"Prove it."

"Have you ever been in that situation?"

"No."

"I have. Trust me, it's true," he said with a faraway look. "Wait a minute…you mean to tell me that after your husband you had no difficulties in dating again?"

"Well, some difficulties. Yes. It's a grief process. The loss of your marriage."

"Oh, it's that and much more."

"You can't push it. It takes time. You have to wait."

"Wait for what?" he insisted.

"Wait until it's time."

"How long?"

"I don't know. Several months. Several years. I don't know, some women just jump right back into a relationship instantly. It's different for different women."

"And who was saying love isn't complicated? Right. I agree. Men go through it too, you know. There is an inner process. You can't consciously control when you're ready to reengage. But what if it's been ten years and still you cannot reengage?"

"Then you got a problem."

"Like Archibald Craven, you see? After ten years, is he ever going to come back to life? It's a fairy tale, of course. A curse was laid upon the kingdom and everyone went to sleep and nothing had changed in ten years. That is the situation Mary Lennox finds herself in when she arrives there. That is the situation you find yourself in when your client walks in the door. I repeat, what can you do?"

"Pray for rain."

"Oh, I like that. You are closer to being right than I suspect you understand."

"The rain is a libido image."

"Yes. All I really want you to take away from today is that it's a mystery. This grief process, if you want to call it that. This individuation process, if you like. Never forget, Laurel, why things start to grow again after everything has died is a mystery. In fact, one of the most ancient of mysteries. It is not something we can do as analysts. We can only set the proper conditions and hope that nature, human nature, takes its course. Our only hope is that nature wants to grow. That the human psyche wants to develop."

He stopped and looked at her for a long time. His thoughts were far away, on a stage under the bright footlights at the end of Act One where he heard the music swell and saw the little girl pass through a long line of ghosts to stand at the door of a garden with a key she had long sought. It occurred to him, looking up at Laurel, that he could do no more for her. He could only show her the door.

"And, that is the Secret Garden."

Her stomach dropped a third time. He was telling her a story, but the story was his own story. She felt, for the first time, that she was standing closer to him than she might have hoped. Closer to him, perhaps, than any other person had stood in a long, long time.

"I understand," she said respectfully.

"But," he hesitated here. She was drawn to the sudden pain on his face, looking towards him, but as he paused she had to look away. "Sometimes there is no recovery. That is true as well."

He stood, staggering a bit under the weight of it, it seemed to her, and handed her the pages of her thesis again. As much as she wanted to comfort him, to reach and touch him in that moment, when he extended his arms with the papers in his hands, it was a distancing she dare not violate.

He waved her out the door.

"You must include that in your thesis. Sometimes the Secret Garden is never found."

CHAPTER SIX

WHEN THE SUN WENT DOWN

ET US NOW CONSIDER WHETHER THE ARC OF A HUMAN LIFE is predictable or if in some profound way it may be considerably unpredictable. The life cycle is surely predictable, an unbroken chain of human evolution in which a human life has been fully lived countless times over from crying birth to exuberant childhood through lusty adolescence and coupling and uncoupling. And then mid-life, a noonday sun that soon casts its shadow and falls into relentless night, and so we fall also, sometimes gracelessly if we do not mind our place; and others are more graceful if they can see the shadow in themselves and know that even death is just the organism becoming itself, as it was on the day of its birth. No different. Not really. The way through is individual and unique, but the form, the pattern it imposes, does not concern itself with little things.

Of the little things that fall together to compose a life, however, there are one or two that make all the difference. This is unpredictable. When tragedy strikes, or gross misfortune, or the tidal wave of history. Or, better yet, something so small as to pass unnoticed. How can it be that one little thing may be the pebble in the great wheel of life that fouls the gears and slows its progress until everything comes to a standstill and cannot proceed until that grain of sand is removed? That is the power of the small. That is the challenge of the individual.

DANIEL STOOD, SWAYING ON THE HANDRAIL, in the press and crush of the Red Line rush-hour all the way to Harvard Square T-stop. He walked slowly, too slowly for the masses anxious to get home as they bumped past him up the stairs, because he was never in any hurry to visit The Old Man. No. He preferred to take his time and at least enjoy the walk, as he lived for walking, out from the busy square to the river, turning right on Mount Auburn Street, past the hospital and to the nursing home.

In the past he had argued with his father about whether it might be more suitable to live in one of the those new Extended Living Centers in Sudbury or Concord. Places like that had atriums with elegant windows looking out over the Concord river, hardwood floors in the dining area, Mozart and Brahms on the weekends, and full-time activity directors keeping the shuttle buses busy. He could afford it. But no, his father had lived in Boston too long. "I don't want to live out in the sticks!" he insisted, finding it difficult enough to move across the Charles River into Cambridge, where he could at least keep the river in sight and in the spring watch the shells of the rowers—one-man, two-man, four-man—gliding gracefully by his sixth story window. To the proper Bostonian, if you lived beyond the last subway stop you lived in the sticks.

There was no talking to him. He had lived alone for too long. More than thirty years. Dr. Paul Osgood was as obstinate as ever, especially in old age, maintaining with a surgeon's swagger that he knew better than anybody else on a wide range of topics ranging from the stock market to the proper way to wax a Lincoln to retirement living. Like so many things about the shock of reality to people who think they know better, Dr. Osgood had only succeeded in making himself more unhappy than even he was inclined to be; an unhappiness, characteristically, that he was quite unaware of, and hence projected out into the great wide world out around him.

"Why are you so unhappy, son?" Paul Osgood offered, sitting up on the edge of his bed in the little room after the brief handshake that was the only contact between these two untouched and untouchable men. "Has something happened?"

Daniel had given up long ago on psychoanalyzing his father, on any thoughts of helping him leap the gaps in himself to grasp just a few essential insights that might have tempered his bitterness toward the things that had befallen him.

"I lost a patient, Dad. It's kind of getting to me today." Paul Osgood extended a shaky hand. Daniel pulled him upright from the bed, reaching for him as he tottered.

"Don't!" He grumbled. "Leave me be! I can make it myself. I'm just a little slow, that's all."

Daniel found it painful, in a distant way, a surprisingly objective and matter-of-fact observation, to watch the glacial shuffle of his father's small feet, shoes untied, never lifting from the ground, but sliding on the linoleum floor. His arched back bent full over to the floor, extending his large head, frozen in rigor, out over his shoes, which were the only focus of his concentration one small slide at a time.

"What about the Sox?" he said halfway down the hall. "I fell asleep last night."

"They lost."

"God damn Sox."

When they approached the elevator, Daniel took his arm to guide him over the uneven step. Dr. Osgood pulled away. Head down, he willed his right leg over the steel threshold inch by slow inch. Reaching around him, Daniel held the door for a long minute.

Reaching the first floor Daniel's father tottered toward his table in the dining hall, set with white linen napkins, silver cutlery, and fresh flowers. Thirty years ago the Cambridge House had been the picture of elegance, a retreat for so many of the doctors of Paul's generation. By now the peach walls were faded and the plaster cast ceiling medallions cracked. Waiters in white jackets brought the coffee and salad, hailing Paul by name.

Daniel poured a practiced half-cup of coffee, black, into the bone china cup. The cup jumped precariously in Paul's right hand, aching toward his mouth.

"Napkin, Dad," said Daniel reaching.

"Leave me be," Paul insisted again, slurping little enough coffee to make the exercise worthwhile. Hand straining, he aimed the coffee back toward the saucer. "Say," he spoke up, "I missed the paper this morning. What did the Sox do?"

"They lost, Dad."

"Again? God damn Sox."

In Daniel's mind he had seen the Parkinson's coming long before his father, shortly after a severe case of the shingles. It took a doctor's trained eye to see it in his gait, the way his footfall slightly shortened, the way his neck stiffened as he walked. Sitting with Stanley Markowitz, his old analyst, in a Newbury Street café outside in the summer heat one afternoon twelve years ago, he shared his suspicions.

"Do you think I should tell him?" Daniel wondered out loud.

Dr. Markowitz studied his coffee for a long, long time.

"And why would you tell him?" he said, suddenly serious.

"Because his hands are gonna kill somebody," Daniel tossed to him impatiently. "And because nobody else over there is gonna have the guts to tell him, before it's too late."

"Don't gloat."

"Give me a break."

"I mean it. Don't gloat. Don't tempt Captain Karma. He'll slap you upside the head."

"I'm not gloating. And you don't believe in crap like that."

"Don't be so sure."

"Of gloating, or of your crap?"

"Both. It's a little too sweet, don't you think? Standing in oedipal triumph over the ruin of your father?"

"That isn't what I had in mind. I was being practical."

"Sons and fathers. Grace and gracelessness. Don't blow it, Daniel."

"I thought you weren't my analyst anymore?"

"I'm not. If I were I'd be making you figure it out for yourself. But as your friend I'm telling you to be careful what you wish for. You should know that for yourself by now anyways."

"Know what?"

"That at a certain age every man sees his father stumble. Has to take the reins. Has to change shoes, walk in that other man's shoes and take the lead. It's a big moment. Welcome to mid-life."

"Push him aside."

"That's just the thing. You can be graceless about it. Let your complex get the better of you and you make things get ugly. But it will not serve you well."

"And you know this? You have seen this?" Daniel challenged him angrily.

"Yeah. I screwed up. Do as I say, not as I do."

"Why not? Why shouldn't I? He deserves it, after all."

"You see, Captain Karma again. You feel so sure you know what he deserves. I wouldn't be so sure. Don't interfere with a man and his fate."

"Character is destiny."

"In so many ways," Stanley toasted him with his coffee cup. "It's your own destiny you should be concerned with anyways. Your own character. That's the complex, Daniel. I mean, is it *still* all about your getting your father at this point in your life, or is it about living your own life? I thought I made you stand up to your father complex, or maybe you were just faking it?"

"Remains to be seen, I suppose."

"That's right. What I say to you doesn't make a difference. In one ear and out the other. It's only what you do that has an impact."

"As usual." Daniel held his coffee in both hands, looking down. "So how do I handle it gracefully?"

"Let him go his own way."

"Say nothing?"

"If he stumbles, just keep walking. Don't look back until he asks."

"And if he kills a patient?"

"Then that's his responsibility, isn't it? His moral dilemma."

"That's harsh, Stanley. Truly harsh. And if his colleagues are too gutless to confront him?"

"Their moral dilemma."

"My moral dilemma too. That's what I'm saying."

"No. He is a doctor charged with his patient's care. They are doctors, charged with their patients care."

"I am a doctor."

"No. You are a son. He is not a patient. He's your father, living his own life, making his own mistakes, or successes, or compromises. Why would you intervene?" Stanley looked up. "That is, unless you fear to see him fall?"

"To keep him strong, you mean? As an enemy?"

"As a nemesis. Maybe. I don't know. But, I do know this. To see your father fail, it makes him human. Breaks the projection. It opens the possibility of relationship. Man to man."

"That'll be the day."

"You wanted the graceful way. There it is." He paused. "Right in front of you…like me…when I failed you."

"And I said it didn't bother me. You tried your best."

"But we didn't fix you, did we?"

"No."

"No. Because your father is not your problem, in the long run. So I sent you to Frau Delarosa. Now we're friends."

"Same deal?"

"Same deal…Look, finish your coffee. They need the tables."

Daniel noticed Dr. Stanley Markowitz was looking older himself. More frail. A bit slower in his stride.

"Oh, and another thing," Stanley offered as he left. "You need to think about what kind of people doctors turn into when they can't be doctors anymore."

"You've thought a lot about this."

"I've thought a lot about not being a doctor myself. Whether I can break out of this persona, find the other parts of myself. Do something else. Or whether I'm as one dimensional as all those other guys and can't let go."

"How you doing with that?"

"You tell me?" He shrugged his shoulders. "They say in Israel things are wide open. Been thinking about that a lot."

"And you wouldn't be a doctor?"

"No. I hope there's more to me than that."

It was the last time he ever saw Stanley. He'd offered to help him move, when the time came, but Dr. Markowitz refused. They had exchanged a few letters.

"The food is lousy today," former Dr. Paul Osgood commented. "Let's go out next time. Get into town."

"Sounds good, Dad. I'd like that. Maybe go to the *Mistral*? I know you like it there."

"Or the Harvard Club. I need to see some friends over there."

"Fine. I'll set it up."

But Daniel knew he wouldn't be setting up an outing. His Dad hadn't been out to dinner in several years because making their way through the narrow rows of tables would have been too difficult for him to navigate and he refused the use the wheelchair. Earlier on when Daniel had made the arrangements, Paul Osgood had come up at the last minute with half a dozen reasons why he couldn't go that day. Daniel soon discovered it was more important to let him talk about it. About his old life. About his doctor's life going on and on as it had always unfolded. As if nothing had changed.

"What do you hear from your mother?"

"She's dead, Dad."

Paul Osgood ignored this resolutely. "I need you to tell her I want to change the settlement. Don't want the lawyers involved. I'll make it worth her while…I think I want to keep the house in Beacon Hill. It'll make it easier to get to work when I get old. What'd you think about that idea?"

"I don't think she'd go for it, Dad. Lot a history there."

"No? Damn. Brookline's a pain. Damn Green Line." Paul Osgood had not been on a subway in several years.

"I know. Give me the Red Line any day."

"Did you know they don't have a Scully Square Station anymore? Some damn thing called Government Center. I can't even find my way around on the Green Line."

"Dad, that was years ago."

It had all been years ago. Margaret Osgood, in her compromise with herself, had dutifully shouldered the burden of Boston, forsaking the corn-row houses of the growing Midwest for the row houses on Beacon Hill, as her ambitions trickled away like the winding narrow streets from the top to the flat land in the Back Bay—quite literally Boston's sewer, now filled in and covered over—which had become passing elegant, as she had become herself. In long black evening gowns she set a light in the window, if shaded by her graceful valances and stylish lambrequins, a light to capture the ostentatious and the well-heeled like summer moths flocking to her dinner parties. She presided over them queenly, impeccably, and triumphantly. If you had asked Daniel how he liked to remember her best he would have told you that in his mind she lived always as he had known her then, with the glimmer of pearls around a thin lovely neck, and diamonds on her elongated fingers, touching as she talked, bare arms with her muscled skin arching in conversation to laugh, embrace, and toss her long hair. The perfect hostess, wife, and mother.

There are things we remember, without a thought, and things we forget, with a little effort. Not a repressed memory, *per se*, but an overlooking, a hurrying past, a back closet where things go until we are ready and needful. And Daniel might never have been ready if he were not one day needful of the memory, but only because his analysis had hit a wall and progressed no further. It was like that with Stanley Markowitz, so many things that Daniel had thought about but never spoken, pondered but never put together. So Markowitz sent him on for a second analysis. He might not have gone. He might not have ever remembered. But for Daniel it was required, of course, as a condition of his training. Frau Delarosa was so cold and stern she wanted to kick him out of the program.

"You have no sex life, Herr Doctor. This is unnatural."

"With respect, Liebe Frau, there are those for whom sex is not so important."

"*Das stimmt aber nicht!*"

"Nuns. Priests. Celibates of many kinds. Virgins."

"*Doch!* They have sex lives! Have you ever analyzed a priest!"

"Some people are mild in temperament. Mild in libido."

"Some people are blocked, and this is a sickness. Your sickness."

"Frankly, I don't see the use of it at this point in my life." He was serious at the time. He couldn't see how it was of any concern to the Jung Institute to pry into the sex life that he didn't have.

"*Pas auf*, Daniel. I make no jokes. Do you think I could ever in good conscience turn you loose on analysands, female analysands, with a sexual problem of your own? It would eat you alive in a minute. No. Without this, you can go no further."

"You would stop me?" cried Daniel, astonished, and a little frightened.

"I would have an ethical obligation to do so."

"I assure you, it's not a problem."

"*Doch!* I assure you that it is a problem, and a serious problem."

At this Daniel was suddenly angry. He rose from his chair to leave the room, the first time he had ever done so in her presence.

"I'm not a virgin, you know. I slept with a woman…once," he slung at her, walking away.

"Yes? And this was…successful for you?" she said, nonplussed.

It was too much. He left the appointment, hurried down the hallway and out the door to the street, and quickly home. A long and bitter night followed, troubled as he was by the prospect of being forced from his training even at that late stage; troubled also by the painful memory of Anna, his onetime fiancé, and their tryst.

Could it be as bad as all that? He wondered. He had not thought about it in so long that when Frau Delarosa confronted him he was, at first, completely taken aback, and then, when he remembered Anna, totally blocked. *Is this really required, to tell her this? To re-live the unlived? To unlock the box of what two people say to each other when they are quite alone?*

"I lost a patient!" Anna screamed at his door in tears, throwing herself on the couch in abject pain.

He had followed her into the psychiatric residency. Why? It's just that she was so lively. So funny and fresh, quick-witted, a bright bird of endless fascination darting around him, turning his head, leaving him speechless. Anna was the kind of doctor that patients fall in love with because she was such a presence in the room, a healing light. They felt better already just laughing with her. Her attentiveness sprung from her true gift and love of people. Every anxiety, melancholy, trauma, addiction, and delusion she treated with seriousness and respect.

"She's dead, Daniel! They called me tonight."

He never told her, of course, never let her have the slightest indication that in the terror of not knowing what to do with himself he had simply followed her light out of his dark tunnel and on to McLean Hospital where he could simply be near her; share grand rounds, argue over cases, joke about the patients through the endless nights, daft with sleep deprivation. All of the things he loved about her.

If it is love. Is it love to be entertained? To be helped in a dark hour? To be respected as a colleague and a buddy in trying circumstances, sharing learning and growth and adversity together?

Now that is a life for many a couple. Something not to be dismissed out of hand. Because life is lonely. There is much to be said for civility and kindness and steadfast partnership when, all things told, there is so much more to life than fierce attachment and shattering pleasure.

And what then of falling down love? Weak in the knees, staggering, panting, breathless intensity? Shall we name it the body's infatuation, pheromones unleashed like melting mountain snows cascading through the brain like spring swollen streams?

Two bodies can devastate each other, while two personalities collide. The wreck is cruel and painful. Love does not liberate our limitations. Our unworked inadequacies impose themselves on the people closest to us with unremitting certainty. Two bodies can withdraw, and yet, two personalities must mingle, one dancing ever with the other like seedlings planted side by side and rooted in each other, each straining for the sun, and it is simply so that if one should push down upon another to gain advantage in the struggle of life and death one personality will wither and perish if it does not have the strength to tear itself from the ground and leave.

Now that is closer to love by far. To sacrifice the sunny heights for someone else, to lift up instead of pushing down, to hold another life above your own and to be astonished that she unbidden will stand aside for you and bid you onward in the very same way. *After you, my dear. Oh no, please, after you, I must insist. Let us go together then.* Whether two bodies or two personalities, the sacrifice and patient waiting that love demands requires a different sort of person. A completed and whole person, which is, to say the least, never fully achieved in this lifetime. So can it be that what we're looking for is the completing and becoming whole person through the very vehicle of this loving?

Who might that person be? Frau Delarosa knew this, as she told him later. Frau Delarosa knew when she confronted Daniel with his sexual problem that he could never be a psychoanalyst because he was not becoming whole. She knew he had to face it, to know his own deepest wound. To see his own dead spot for what it was—the imprint of life itself branding him forever so that he would never forget the power of larger things to burn us in a moment. And that is a wounding. Wholeness demands it. And a man who cannot be overpowered by himself—body, soul, and mind, one organism—is a man who cannot love, and, failing love, is a man who should not be a psychoanalyst.

But she did not yet know the wound, because Daniel had not yet remembered. He did not wish to remember.

That night, with Anna balled up on the couch, he reached for her for the first time. Putting his arms around her he pulled her close while her tears ran. His arms were clumsy, unpracticed. He did not know how to hold a woman. But she embraced him, taking his hands and laying her head on his shoulder. She cried for two hours because she had never lost a patient to suicide before and had always believed that her charm, her goodwill and genuine devotion to them would save them in the end. She was mistaken.

Looking up after her tears were over she held his eyes.

"I don't think I should be alone tonight. Cah I sleep with you?"

Daniel did not have the heart to tell her that no woman in his life had ever asked that of him before. He said simply,

"Yes," and plunged in.

Strange as it seems to modern eyes, he dressed for bed in his silk pajamas and laid himself down to sleep. Confused, she tarried in the bathroom and pondered the meaning of his strange behavior, then, bright as she was and soon to be a psychiatrist, decided he was the sort of man not to take advantage of a woman, which endeared him to her. Plotting next how best to proceed with this situation she stripped to her underwear and tee-shirt and snuggled in beside him where he turned away.

Time passed. A lot of time. Still he did not move, breathing easily and rhythmically, apparently, without advancing. And yet, she noticed, also not retreating from her.

"I'm hot," she whispered. "I'm going to take my shirt off."

He made no response as she quietly slipped out of her top and nuzzled her breasts along his clothed back.

Time passed. More confused still, she had to stop and think for a long while, analyzing the situation and concluded from her woman's heart, putting her psychiatry on the shelf, that here was a reluctant man, a man shy with women and probably not so much experience. She wondered if he had ever had a sister.

"Aren't you hot too?" she ventured gingerly. Trying to give him the emotional space he needed, she colluded with his hesitance. "Take your shirt off. You might sleep better."

In the dark, he complied, taking of his shirt and tossing it aside, but turned away again and still did not say a word.

She felt his shoulders, strong shoulders. Running her fingers over the back of his head, his hair was short for the Eighties, but fine and smooth. Anna could smell him now, breathing on the back of his neck, the smell of expensive soap. *Funny,* she thought. *These Boston doctors and their Puritan ways.*

Sneaking her leg between the back of his knees, at first she liked the feel of the silk pajamas. She liked the feel of being in control, rare to her with other men. She liked also to be taken, but for tonight it was enough to seduce him step by step and feel her own power. Her timing had a rhythm, whether ten minutes or five she couldn't tell in the dark, so when the time came she decided next to tease him with her legs.

"How can you sleep with your pants on? You must be suffocating."

She tugged gently at the waist and he reached back to help her, without turning over. Her bare legs against his were smoother than the satin, an indescribable gloss of marmalade on peaches, or wax on soft gold somehow still warm and liquid.

Though he could not find a place in himself from which to speak to her in that moment, he enjoyed and adored her. In a truth he could not comprehend he sincerely let himself believe that after her painful tears she needed sleep and comfort. He would never have hoped that she would open herself to him in this way. He was happy enough to be so close to her. Even when she complained of being hot he took her at her word because he knew he didn't know anything about women at all and it was possible that in women the heat disturbed their sleep for all he knew.

Yet in removing her shirt he let himself awaken to the fact that she was wanting something more. He didn't move, he didn't speak, because he feared to do or say the wrong thing, when by his inaction he was progressing further than he had ever progressed before.

There is something to be said for going slowly, she realized, enjoying herself. When she had had enough of legs, she reached around to find him. He was not asleep. She let herself ascend and descend, reveling in her power to make him or unmake him at her choice. It crossed her mind to undo him then and there, but she was feeling hungry for his lips. So she turned him towards her, unresisting, and sat across his chest, first guiding his hands upward to her breasts. She found him eager but unskilled. Entwining her fingers in his she taught him, leading again. She showed him the rhythm of it, the kneading without grasping, the teasing without twisting. Attended, she reached down to his chest with her own hands. Even the in the dark it was a broad, firm, masculine chest. He seemed surprised.

Rising on her knees she took his hand once more and guided him to her.

"Gently," she whispered.

He found it an odd sensation, better even than her bare legs against his own. Hers was the archetypal yielding *Yin*, the smooth lotus petal, and he understood as he had never understood before how a man goes sick with love and will faint from the fever until he feels it again.

"Daniel, are you a virgin?"

He did not answer, but Anna had had enough of his foretaste and reluctance. She was ready to begin in earnest.

"Oh, kiss me now, Daniel," she swore, falling on him.

He took her hair tenderly in his hands and held her eyes where he could look at them.

"Anna, I am afraid."

"I will show you. You don't need to be afraid."

"I am afraid of what this will mean."

She stopped, seeing the sincerity in his eyes and realized how this all had progressed without her quite intending it. Or had she? Anna had certainly noticed him in their time together, noticed his quick wit, matching her stroke for stroke, his easy competition with her, not fearing or defending against her diagnostic skills and bedside manner like the other residents. He was not like any other doctor she had ever met. Not aggressive. Not full of himself. Not condescending toward her own ambitions. A friend.

And maybe more than a friend, if this were her test of him. But a strange test. A strange evening. His body inspired in her body a different part of herself. It was something new and bold in her.

"I don't know what it means," she said at last.

"Then, I think, I shall kiss you, but only kissing."

Considering this, she consulted her body, which was in no doubt, but seeing his eyes discovered that the better part of valor was to leave, to fight another day. That almost satisfied her.

"You are certainly quite a gentleman, Doctor Osgood."

As the word left her mouth, she felt its cold sting. She had said the wrong thing, reminding him of their professional relationship. Her almost satisfied body might have decided to push past his well-mannered self-control in the name of conquest, but she had broken the spell unwittingly, and instantly regretted it.

"Then kiss me, Sir."

She settled for playful. His untrained lips were useless and all too quickly her breathing steadied, her blood flow returned. Her first chance at him was over.

"Like this," she coached, taking his lips into her hand and molding his mouth to hers. "And then softer…you see? No, firm too…Soft and firm, I know it sounds paradoxical."

"Am I doing better?"

"You need more practice."

"Then let us practice."

They practiced. He was an eager student, improving in great strides. But she tired of it.

"I think now that I am very tired, Daniel. Let's go to sleep," she said, meaning it absolutely. Because she was tired, the evening caught up with her as the pain of her loss descended on her once again. She cried herself into a quick sleep while he held her.

At dawn she woke, fully awake, and quietly dressed.

"Thank you, Anna. I am very happy," he said as she turned.

"That was a strange first date, you know. My strangest yet, I would say."

"Maybe I can do better next time."

"Are you asking me out?"

"I guess so."

"Fine. But I drive."

"Sure."

Anna was perplexed for the rest of the week. Her supervisors comforted her, trying to explain the typical psychiatric line that doctors are only doctors. The patients are, in the long run, responsible for themselves. And she should learn from this that a mental disorder is serious business. Lives are a stake. Sometimes, much of time, the illness wins. Get used to it. Suicides are a fact of life. This is what we do.

She did get used to it. And also she did not get used to it. Because she was a woman. Because she was a woman and a doctor and was strong enough in herself not to let the men convince her that people are diseases. She knew that from her mother, because she loved her mother and her mother was very ill and she knew before she ever entered medical school that love and madness exist side by side and that she would not stop loving her mother because she suffered from manic depression and was difficult and dangerous sometimes.

Anna had the right stuff. She had only to learn that she could not fix her mother by loving her. She could not fix her patients by loving them either. And yet this simple fact was not printed in any of the textbooks that she mastered expertly. Nor would any of her supervisors ever take the time to figure it out and help her see it. It was not required to pass her boards and become a good psychiatrist.

No, Anna was not perplexed about how to be a doctor. She was perplexed about Daniel. Her experience with him had turned out to be a vexing combination of a promising, teachable man and an unpromising, reluctant lover. *How can he be so nice and at the same time so irritating? I don't want a gentleman, but I do want a gentleman. Is this guy simply inexperienced or is he immature?*

Instinct took over. Anna realized it wasn't going to be practical to wait for him to just grab her and throw her down. He wasn't ready for that. So when she drove up to Beacon Hill, lost for half an hour on the one way streets that never seemed to connect one to the another, even though she had been to his house before, she hauled him off to a quick dinner then quickly out to her apartment where she threw him down on the couch and showed him without asking just what her hands could do to him. There was nothing gentle about it. And, damn it all, *he* was going to learn to use his fingers and satisfy her. She wanted it. She was ready. She did it.

Fine. Open the wine. Anna hadn't wanted a cigarette in a long time but as she sat across from him on the couch, legs crossed, she could have used to smoke to help her settle down and figure this out. She was acting like a teenager. Hell, *he* was acting like a teenager. What was all this about? She bored psychiatric eyes through him like he was a diagnostic problem the attending physician had sent her just to confuse her and chide her about it in the morning.

She sipped the wine, considering him sideways. *Well, he's got the looks. No question. Not going to be a problem. Maybe a little exercise, a little time with the free weights, fix him right up. He's eager. I know he likes it…teenage sex and all not withstanding. And he's respectful. Attentive. Not intimidated by women. A gentleman, of course, and probably brought up right. Did you see that Brownstone on Beacon Hill?*

So what's your problem?…Hmmmm…Ferocity, meaning the lack of it. Drive. Ambition. Taking the world by the horns. Taking me by the horns. Is he a wimp then? No. Stands up straight enough. It's just…it's just, something about him I can't quite put my finger on.

On the other hand, I got enough ambition for the both of us. I got my own ferocity, at least he's teaching me that. And that's not all bad. Not bad at all, really, when you stop and think about it. I am in control.

"You like that?" she said suddenly, peering at him over the wine glass at her lips.

"I liked it."

"Then make love to me, Daniel."

He put his wine glass down and was suddenly serious. *Something I can't quite put my finger on.*

"Anna," he said with a genuine pain of his face. "I'm not ready for that."

Lifting her head, she threw down the rest of the wine and sat the glass on the table.

"When *will* you be ready for it?"

"When I decide if I am in love with you or not."

Daniel spoke these words with such a careful sincerity that she could not refute the truth of it. She had never heard those words come out of the mouth of a man before. And just in that moment she was pretty sure she might never hear those words come out of a man's mouth ever again.

"I can respect that," she said, astonished. "Let me know what you decide. I'll be right here, waiting."

He slowly finished his wine. The bottle was empty.

"I'll catch the Green Line home. No need to drive."

"That's fine," she stuttered, still in shock as he gathered his things and left.

She had two blinding insights that night, curled up on the couch in the dark under a comforter. Difficult to decide which one was the more important. When he said *when I decide if I am in love with you or not*, when he made the feeling of love a condition of the act of making love, he was talking like a woman. He was saying something a woman would say. Why would he do that? Because there was something about him she just couldn't put her finger on until that moment. *Because he was feminine.* Because he was a feminine kind of man. He thought like a woman would think. That's what it was.

How strange. But stranger still, insight Number Two. In that very moment she loved him. Not a realization of the possibility of loving him as she would have expected, but something that had broken right through to the unforgivable level—she loved him. She already did.

Not possible. She hadn't even slept with him yet. Well, she had, but that was different. She hadn't consummated him. It didn't matter. It was too late. The only thing stranger than Daniel's reaction to her advances, and stranger still than their first two dates, such as they were, was her strange love of him. She loved a feminine man. It was only later, much later, that she realized she had tipped over into this opposite attraction because somehow in being a feminine man he had induced her to discover herself as a masculine woman. And she liked it. She liked it a lot, for reasons that were not clear to her for a long, long time.

And so, once more, the psychoanalytic question: *what is love?* Among all those other things—help, comfort and kindness; pheromones and devastating pleasures; sacrifice and patient waiting—love is surely also the discovery of, soon followed by the exploration of, other parts of ourselves, our whole selves coming into being. Surprising selves. Things so long unlived that we would never whisper them aloud. Yet intimacy is very quiet and quieting. Quiet enough to hear the unspoken whisper and invite its secret, shared, often without the words for it. Shared. Received. Returned unbroken. And safely kept, it speaks again. Only deeper. And that is trust. And that is love.

When Daniel, inviting her for the first time, took her to *Maison Robert* to delight her in French delicacies straight from Paris and there confessed his love Anna was astonished. Astonished at herself. Astonished because he had offered her a ring, on bended knee, and she accepted after only those two weeks. They were engaged. And the whole hospital soon buzzed with the surprising news of it. Nurses shook their heads, for reasons not so psychoanalytic. Doctors shook their heads, for reasons most analytic. But it was nevertheless a fact. Anna and Daniel had gone off and done this one crazy thing. Love never ceases to amaze people, and rightly so.

However, psychoanalysis, knowing love for what it is, must also, by needs, know what love is not. When you ask people why they got married they will quickly tell you—*because we loved each other*. And that truth, being not the whole truth, is a dangerous truth. What is the unacknowledged truth? The shadow side of love.

If Anna had been honest with herself, and being in a state of love she could not have done so that night—no blame—she would have had to admit that the impulse to marry was none other than the overwhelming need to grasp her new found self and never let it go. In that her instinct served her well. In fact throughout her residency it had been growing day by day, her sense of holding herself against the men, her strength to do it. To have the strength of her convictions and enforce them. To decide and to act. To be sure of herself as doctors must be sure of themselves.

There is a price to be paid to think like a doctor. Every woman doctor must confront this. Because the medical profession in theory and practice and training is of the left brain. And men live out of their left brains.

Anna, grounded in her mother's pain, was loathe to pay this price, even if she could not articulate what was bothering her. She was smart as the best of them, as studied and well-schooled. She had the advantages of being highly motivated and through her own life experience being intimately familiar with mental illness at a level only long years can teach. *So why wasn't she sure of herself yet?* In her third year of residency time was running out.

Time was out. That was the impulse to marry. That first night with Daniel she had cried so intensely because the suicide reminded her in no uncertain terms how she must doubt herself, and in doubting she could not see the way forward. And in that state of mind it is not too difficult to understand why unconsciously she would look to a doubting man like Daniel to absorb all her feminine doubt and put it there on the bed and conquer it, once and for all. To take his masculinity and pump it out like steroids to strengthen her muscles.

The experience was so intoxicating that when he asked her to marry him she wanted it signed, sealed, and delivered as soon as possible;

having it in hand, needing never to let it go. For Anna, to be a doctor was the highest good and to marry a doctor the way to seal her place.

Except that Daniel was a doctor in name only. But he had reasons of his own, if unconscious and unspoken. How he hated it when Frau Delarosa laid it brutally before him, after risking in that next session after he had walked away to tell her what had happened with Anna. Down to the last detail. He had never once told another living soul of what passed between them and when it came to the catharsis, his letting go with Frau Delarosa, it broke in him with the very same energy with which it had been bound up all those years. He was in tears.

Pitilessly Frau Delarosa would not let him go. Because pity cannot heal. Mercilessly she beat him over the head with the inescapable logic that the reason he had got down on his knees that night to propose to Anna could only have been that he knew very well he had a sexual problem and that he was grasping at the only woman ever to get so far with him because if he did not bind her up with him before he could no longer make excuses for himself then she would see right through him and get away.

Frau Delarosa would not let him shrink from the shadow side of love. She stripped him naked because, she later told him, she feared from long experience that it might be the only chance she would ever get to make him look at himself as he really was, to see the truth of himself and what ailed him, and maybe the only chance to heal him. A valiant effort. But, sadly, it was not enough, she soon realized.

Celebrating their engagement, Anna and Daniel withdrew to his Beacon Hill home. She was radiant, confident, and glorious, firming up on every side. She stripped him in the living room and led him into the bedroom to make a man out of him then and there. Throwing back the linen sheets, she pumped him full.

"Do you love me?"

"I love you, Anna."

"And I love you."

When she mounted him, he winced, dazed at the fury of her passion. She started. Slowly, at first, restraining herself.

Closing her eyes, she lost track of him, moving faster. Losing her restraint, faster still, she cried out until in one violent leap she suddenly lost him.

When she opened her eyes, reaching with her back hand to readjust, she felt nothing there. Nothing but his shame. Confused, she continued, deluding herself that he was still with her. But he was far away, farther away than she had ever seen a man be from a woman in a moment of desire.

"What's wrong?" she said, more to herself than to Daniel.

"I think there's a problem."

And the problem was Daniel. His lack of drive. His lack of ambition. His lack of ferocity. His suddenly feminine, yielding *Yin* energy.

"I can fix it," she offered, in growing desperation.

"I don't know what to do," Daniel said, looking away from her.

"I do."

She took him in both hands, praying almost; praying for fire in the wet chill of the night falling as she rubbed the stick furiously, blowing on the kindling and waiting for a spark. But he was a fresh green log, too damp, too cold to burn.

"We have to stop," he whispered, turning to the edge of the bed and holding his head in his hands. Anna felt the creeping cloud of doubt that she had worked so hard to avoid. Maybe she had been wrong to push him so fast. Maybe she needed to take his inexperience more seriously, honoring his reluctance. She thought of a dozen ways in which the truth would not appear to be the truth, because she did not like the sight of it, plain as day and lying right in front of her.

"I'm so sorry," he began, unable to look at her.

"It's alright."

"The only thing I can think of is maybe this is not the place."

"These things happen, Daniel."

"I didn't think it was going to bother me so much. But…this was my mother's house, you know. My mother's bed. How stupid! I'm really being just stupid."

"Relax, Daniel. You've got to relax. Have a little patience."

"I don't think I can do this tonight."

"I know. Just hold me, Daniel. Just hold me and tell me that you love me."

They lied down, back to front, but neither of them slept. The next morning, making her rounds at the hospital, Anna flipped. Anna flipped a switch in her brain. She entered her left brain, closing off her right brain because it was too painful. She thought like a doctor, remembering her textbook on sexual disorders and attacked the problem by reviewing Masters & Johnson and the recent literature on treatment for the impotent male. The twist was that typically females were non-orgasmic, not men, and the treatment involved a slow, careful process both psychological and practical—familiarizing the woman with her own body, alone and privately at first, graduating to successful self-stimulation, and only gradually proceeding to manual stimulation by her partner over a period of weeks, and then very carefully introducing penetration, always with her in complete control, until she was relaxed and comfortable enough to achieve orgasm through intercourse successfully.

Anna would later go on to become a brilliant sex therapist, and Daniel was her first case. She regarded him as a problem that could be solved, a disease that could be cured.

The psychology of it was cognitive behavioral. You had to find the thought behind the action, or, in this case, the inaction. *My mother's bed. I am afraid I will get you pregnant. My religion taught me that sex was dirty.* Something like that. *Fine.*

Then you teach the patient thought-blocking. How to counter that disturbing thought. Argue with it. Discuss it to death. Substitute a new thought. Anything. Just don't let that thought run your life.

So she set out to cure him with a little operant conditioning. Back to what worked and to what had made him comfortable. Positive reinforcement. For two weeks there was nothing but hands and fingers. She rewarded him.

Phase Two. The psychological. Long talks ranged through the evening about his fears. *What was he afraid of?* He couldn't tell her. He didn't know. No religious hang-ups. A little concern about pregnancy, to be sure. He was unsure about having children. His mother's bedroom, obviously, but Anna wasn't about to make that mistake again. First a successful treatment and then she could later desensitize him to his own home.

No. There must be something more. When the patient cannot tell you what is wrong there is a great temptation to imply, to deduce from the available clues the original crime, like Sherlock Holmes, spinning the truth from the most unlikely little details.

In her growing desperation she leaped at hunches. It occurred to her that he was a gay man and didn't know it. He was a feminine man, as she had already noticed. Although she inquired of him his feelings for men, he wasn't buying it. *No. Absolutely not.* She wondered. Mildly reassured, she then remembered an obscure theory of vaginal phobia. Something like claustrophobia, but in this case the fear of the enclosed place was localized. Was he concerned about being trapped? Was he concerned about how it would feel in there? *No.* Absolutely not, not as far as he could tell.

Through all this doctoring, Daniel suffered bravely, indignity upon indignity. A proper patient. What had he to say for himself? In college and med school he had told himself he was simply too busy, too focused to be concerned with relationships. Yes, he had seen the *Playboys* and *Hustlers* and all the other things the guys brought for him to see. No big deal. To be honest, he could barely remember having sexual thoughts in high school, and somehow they had passed on to other thoughts. No, he hadn't masturbated since then, she forced him to tell her. Maybe this was the problem.

When Anna suggested they consult a sex therapist, he agreed. It was a strange turn of events for the young doctors to be on the other side of the consulting room. They had read all about it. When the sex therapy couple—they worked as a pair—heard of Anna's treatment plan they were pleased. They congratulated Anna and Daniel for being such an open, modern, loving couple with good communication skills. Good prognosis. It just took a little patience.

But Anna's patience was running thin. It had been four weeks since their engagement and still they had made no progress other than the sex manual. Expressing her need to start to see something different the sex therapists recommended oral stimulation. They wanted to teach her the technique right on the spot. No, she didn't need lessons. Still, Daniel would have liked to have had the technique described.

At home that evening at her place Anna took the job in hand.

"Maybe the doctor was right, Daniel. This is the closest thing to intercourse. You'll see. There is nothing to be afraid of."

"I'm not afraid, Anna."

In her mind she was hoping for a breakthrough, for something so deep and tender to touch him, caress him, kiss him that whatever psychological devil held him back would be blown away. This was her gift. This was the best she could give.

Too much. Too far. Too late. Suddenly a switch flipped again in her brain, swinging wildly to the other side. She was no longer a doctor. She was a woman again. A perilously unsatisfied woman and climbing him she demanded her satisfaction.

But he could not endure it. He went away and hid, hiding himself from her in a cave too deep to reach and though she banged and hollered at the door he would not come out.

"Daniel," she cried in agony, tears in her eyes. "If you loved me you'd fuck me."

He looked at her in shock. He couldn't think of a word to say to her. When she rolled off of him and cried the rest of the night, batting him away when he tried to touch her he was left with only one thought going round and round in his head—*if this is love, then I am unfit for duty. If this is love then I am unfit for duty.*

"ARE YOU SATISFIED YET??" Daniel swore angrily at Frau Delarosa, finishing his story to the bitter end.

She had looked to her notes the entire time, leaving him to himself to tell her what he must tell. In the long silence that fell over them, so quiet that Daniel could hear the spring robins in the cherry tree outside her window in full bloom, she closed her eyes. She needed to consider something that had weighed on her mind during his soliloquy.

The analyst searches for the primal stories. For that day when something happened that wounds the tree. And hearing that she must consider whether or not the consequences flowing from the rupture are commensurate with the nature of the injury, whether the punishment fits the crime because in human affairs, unlike the courts, it is the punishment that is self-evident, for years and years, whereas the crime remains a mystery, if it is ever known at all.

There is such a thing as a screen story, as Freud himself first noticed. Sometimes the analysand will offer you a memory, a story that tells the story. And it may even be that for a long time, without quite knowing it, he has attributed to that tale all the meaning of his suffering. And, more importantly, for the analyst, all the feeling of his suffering. It is an honest rendition. And yet, the unconscious plays you tricks. The defenses have their place, after all. And disguise is the best defense. The feeling of one memory is offered up by another memory which is not its native home. In this way the deeper story is protected.

So Frau Delarosa had to consider the feeling equation. Whether a thing is as ruinous as it sounds, and conversely, whether some things are more devastating than the patient has ever suspected.

"There is hope, Daniel," she said at last.

"No hope, Frau Delarosa. She ruined me."

"She reinforced the problem, no doubt. But she may have helped to cure you, if you will get yourself up off the ground, Herr Doctor."

"But she broke off the engagement then and there. Gave back the ring. Two weeks of dating, four weeks of being engaged to be wed. That is the entire extent of my love life. She said it was a mistake. She was right."

"Did you love her?" Frau Delarosa asked abruptly.

Daniel hesitated. "As we discussed, I thought I did, but I was only grasping. I acted foolishly."

"*Doch!* Did you love her?" She repeated, more firmly this time.

"I don't know." He was suddenly tearful. "Yes. Yes, I tried to love her."

"I think so," she said, nodding her head. "I think so. Hence, I say there is hope for you yet, Daniel. Your feelings got the better of you then, for once. You do have the capacity to love, though one would scarce suspect it. You can be a tender and patient man when you are in love."

"But I failed," he said.

"Yes, but you are not dead at the roots, as I feared. If you loved once, you could love again."

"Fail again. I could never risk it."

"No. You should not risk it until you know what is ailing you."

"But I just told you. Anna ails me. I cannot face myself."

"There is more."

"What more?"

"The business with your mother, Daniel."

"My mother is dead."

"And yet she lives on…in you."

"I'M TIRED. TAKE ME BACK," Dr. Paul Osgood announced after his dinner.

"You want me to stay and watch the Sox game with you? Afternoon game today," Daniel offered, helping him struggle out of the dining chair.

"No. I stayed up too late watching the ball game last night and now my constitution is all out of whack, if you know what I mean."

Taking his arm, and his father did not resist this time, Daniel guided his slide step toward the elevator. Once inside, Paul Osgood felt chatty.

"How's your time at the hospital? They treating you right?"

"I don't work at the hospital any more, Dad. Strictly private practice."

"Sorry to hear that." His father considered this. "That McLean is a good place. World famous, you know."

"So they say."

"I still think you would have made a good surgeon, though."

"Thanks, Dad."

"It's in your blood."

"That's Grandpa's field, as I remember."

"Ha! Ha! He could never have been a surgeon though. Didn't have the hands."

"Really?"

"No. He was a shaker. Like me now. God, look at me." He held his hands in front of him, low under his bent shoulders. "That's why your mother married me. Because I was a surgeon."

"I know."

"That's why she left me, I guess. Because I was a surgeon too. But I loved her anyway."

"I know, Dad."

"Maybe it's not such a bad thing you weren't a surgeon after all. Helps you keep a wife."

"If I had one, Dad."

It had to do with Daniel being in high school. It was a matter of calculating the absolute minimum amount of time it would take Margaret Osgood to convince herself that Daniel was going to be alright. A fine young man, confident in himself.

"The boy's got smarts, just like me," Paul insisted to Margaret. "I'm not gonna stand by and watch a waste of talent. Hell, God knows where he's gonna end up with this god damn school busing. Roxbury, no doubt. Is that what you want?"

"No, Paul. I just want him home. I want him where I can see him."

"It's just Andover, for cryin' out loud. Or Exeter. You can drive up there every day if you want to see him so badly."

"Maybe I will!" she said, just to flaunt him.

"You would, wouldn't you?" he laughed. "Drive the Lincoln all the way up Route 28? Seriously, I've already talked to them. Full fee. They can get him in there."

"I know. I know. I just think we're better off asking Daniel what he wants to do with his life."

"How should he know? He's just a kid. It's our job to do what's best for him. And right now the best thing is to get him out of Boston before he turns into some god damn hippie or Black Panther or worse."

Given the times, and 1968 was already promising to be a troubling year in Boston, and most other places for that matter, Margaret Osgood had to give in to her husband's wishes to get Daniel safely situated in boarding school. At Phillips Andover he would be safely cocooned with other boys of his own station in life, and separating him from girls was not a bad thing either, although they found their ways to meet the girls from Abbott even under lock and key in Phillips dorms, she supposed. Founded in 1778, the school promised the best education Paul's money could buy, and, she hoped, a place where Daniel could discover his talents in music and art, maybe the theater. If he could just find one good professor, one man stronger than Paul, maybe he could love that man enough to escape being a doctor and fight for himself against his father. In spite of Paul, maybe it was a good idea after all.

Daniel was noncommittal, with a typical teenage carelessness. Still, she could see he was worried about high school in Boston. There had been fights in his junior high school that year. Racial tension was growing.

So they drove him up there with all his things to drop him off in Andover in the early fall of 1968 while the nation was still reeling from the Democratic Convention in Chicago.

But that wasn't the time. Not yet. She had to wait. Though she didn't drive to see him every day, as threatened, she saw him often enough. She was looking for a sign. Margaret Osgood was waiting for that moment when she could see her son's personality reach beyond itself and become engaged. That one teachable moment when he would be taken with a passion for something that he truly loved. That would be her sign that he was on his way without her.

"I read a great novel," Daniel announced in early February, 1969. "Dr. Clanner says it's a great novel of our times."

"What's it about?"

"A prep school boy who goes to New York to find out about sex."

"Oh...*Catcher in the Rye*, I suppose?"

"A great novel of our times."

"Does it make you want to run away to New York?"

"Actually he wants to run away to Massachusetts or Vermont. Shows what he knows. But you know what I was thinking?"

"What?"

"I was thinking I could write a novel as good as that. A great novel of our times. Dr. Clanner says I'm a good writer."

"I see. You should show me one of your stories sometime."

"Show you? Jeez. You're my mother. You wouldn't understand it."

"Because I didn't go to Phillips?"

"Because it's about sex and stuff like that. Like J. D. Salinger."

"I thought you were going to be a doctor, Daniel?"

"Hell no."

"Well, I guess you better write that novel then."

"I will. I want to work on it over the summer. Dr. Clanner says he would help me. So I was wondering if it would be alright if I stayed up in Andover this summer? Dr. Clanner says he can get me a job and I could still have time for my writing. What'd you think?"

"I think you better ask your father."

"What'll he think?"

"I'll find a way for him to think it's a good idea."

"Okay. Great. You wouldn't miss me or anything? You know…mother stuff."

Margaret Osgood paused. "I would miss you, Daniel. I will always miss you. But you're your own man now. You have things to do."

So it was settled. Daniel had embraced what Phillips had to offer him and his mother made sure that his father thought he would be ahead of the other boys if he stayed to have the "total experience." Paul Osgood liked the sound of that.

Margaret lingered with Daniel when they brought him back in June after a short break. She met the summer house residence parents and fussed with his room, arranging his towels and straightening his shirts so they wouldn't wrinkle.

"Enough, Mom! I'm ready." His voice had dropped and he sported a dark whiskered face that needed shaving.

"I'll write you." She clutched him to her fiercely.

"I know."

"No matter what, you finish your novel, Daniel. You understand?"

"That's the plan."

"I mean it. NO matter what." He looked surprised. She released him. "A great novel of our times, right?"

He laughed. "That's the plan."

Margaret Osgood had plans of her own. No sooner had Paul dropped her off and gone to park the Lincoln that he found her on the stairs, suitcase in hand.

"Daniel forget his bag?"

"It's my bag, Paul."

"Looks like you are going on a trip," he said, trying to hide his nervousness.

"I have a job."

He saw it in her face, that look he had not seen in more than six years. The spreading devastation made his hands shake.

"I think that would be alright," he offered feebly, knowing he was already too late.

"The U.S. Agency for International Development. I've volunteered. They took me. I'll be a secretary."

"The what?...Isn't that some kind of a Kennedy, Democrat, peace for the world kind of crap?" he said in spite of himself.

"It's in Saigon, Paul. They are sending me to Saigon."

"No, Margaret. No." For the first time in her life she saw tears in his eyes.

"And I'm going. I'm leaving today." She felt strong when she said it. *Strange*, she thought to herself. *When I was thinking about it I was so afraid. When I talked to them on the phone and mailed the application, I thought it would be hard. I thought when I told him I might have to push myself. But this is easy. I'm not afraid at all.*

"We could make it, Margaret. You and I. We made it before."

"Not really, Paul. We didn't really. You only thought we did."

"By why so far? Why Saigon? I'll worry, Margaret. It isn't safe. My God..."

"Time to explore the world, Paul."

"I thought I was your world."

"This...!" She waved her free hand over the Beacon Hill Brownstone. "This is not my world, Paul. Never was."

"But you'll come back...?"

"Well, we'll see. I don't know. It's a big wide world out there, Paul. I just want to see what I can do."

"You can do a lot," he said, his tears finally breaking through fully.

"Good-bye, Paul."

And she was off, off into the great wide world, first New York, then London, then Thailand, and on by military flight to Saigon and the Mondial Hotel USAID Annex in Cholon.

She mailed her letter to Daniel, written a week before, from New York, telling him in her own motherly way that every person has more things inside of them than they ever get to live out. And he should understand that when you love somebody you have to make sacrifices, and that's what you should do. But she wanted him to also understand that even in making sacrifices, even in holding back, there is still something growing inside each person and you have to keep it growing. *You can't let it die. You understand that, don't you Son? You can't let yourself die inside because of holding back from doing something that is growing inside you.* That's what she was doing. That's what he should do too. *Like the novel, Son. Like a great novel of our times. You need to let it keep you alive inside.* Daniel, turning seventeen, did understand her. Because of the novel. Because of J. D. Salinger and running off to New York without telling anybody. But she was running off to Saigon and that was even cooler to his way of thinking. Maybe he could run off too and find his way in the great big world. That was not what ailed him.

She wrote him often, regaling him with stories from the war. Soldiers that she met. Diplomats. War correspondents. A lot of men. *They even have a television station over here, if you can believe it.* And Daniel practiced his writing on her, writing funny scenes from his classes.

And Dr. Paul Osgood worked. He was a good surgeon and he knew no other way. He was trained not to let his personal life interfere with his professional life. Not a single one of his colleagues could have said they noticed any change in him at all.

Her lawyers served the divorce papers in October. He did not resist her, although his lawyer wanted to go after her for desertion. She wanted the Beacon Hill house, which Paul found curious. But after that day on the stairs something inside him never wanted to set foot in that house again. So Paul Osgood moved to Brookline with a circle of friends around him and their wives to look after him at the awkward dinner parties that Christmas season.

She came home that Christmas, excited to see Daniel. Sharing the house alone for the first time they were like two kids on holiday, eating whatever they wanted, staying up all hours, talking incessantly about their new lives. Daniel read to her from his novel, several chapters completed and she debated with him, gently, about the proper qualities for a great novel of our times. There should be a love interest, certainly. And adversity. And triumph. Most of all triumph.

"I have news," she told him. "I've taken a job at the television station, AFVN TV Saigon. As a weather girl. Do you remember, Daniel? Do you remember when we lived in Chicago?"

"I remember, Mom."

"I've made it like *Bozo's Circus*. It's more than weather. It's comedy and pranks. Songs and dancing. The guys love it. You should see it. The guys send me all kinds of greetings to send out over the airwaves. It makes them feel like home, you know?"

"Sounds great."

"I was thinking, when the war is over, this will give me a resume again. This will get me going. Maybe I can come back to Boston and get back into television. What'd you think of that?"

"If that's your dream, Mom, you should do it."

"That's right."

"Are you alright, Mom? I mean, are you safe?"

"To tell you the truth, I love the guys so much on weekends sometimes I go out there."

"Out to the war?"

"I've been to Pleiku, Con Son island, the Nha Trang beaches to work on my tan, the Marines in Quang Tri. Flown in helicopters. Got shot at."

"You got shot at?"

"Yeah. Several times. Isn't that a gas? Don't tell your father. He'll just fret. It's for the morale, Daniel. Keep the guys up over there."

"I don't know, Mom."

"Just live your own life, Daniel. Don't worry about me…Now, let's talk about colleges with good writing programs."

For all of that Daniel was stunned, completely stupefied, to be sitting with his father in the Brookline house on a Sunday evening in late winter 1970 watching *Sixty Minutes*, his father's favorite show, when Dan Rather appeared with a story on Mecong Maggie, the pin-up weather girl. She had been appearing on camera in her bikini with the day's high and lows painted on her body, *Laugh-In*-style. Dan Rather reported she was the "mini-skirted heat wave who raised troops' temperatures." From bases and camps in the South to GI's in hooches in the North her show was the most watched feature of AFVN TV Saigon.

"I'll be damned," said his father incredulously.

"She told me not to tell you. She said you'd worry." Daniel looked reluctantly toward his father, but Paul Osgood slapped him on the back and rolled on the floor in such hysterical laughter that Daniel thought he was going out of his mind.

MARGARET OSGOOD WAS KILLED IN THE WINTER OF 1971 when her helicopter was shot down near the Montagnard villages. Already accepted for his freshman year at Brown, Daniel didn't know until two weeks later when his father called him at Phillips with just a short, brutal recitation of the few facts he was given by the army. Her death was not reported in the media until well after the war because the army wanted to keep up morale. It took six weeks for her body to be flown home to her parents in Iowa for burial. No funeral was ever held for the disconnected family.

Alone now with his father, the young man and the middle aged man were comfortless; Paul, because he did not have the capacity to enter into this pain, and Daniel, because he did not have the capacity to leave it.

Daniel wept when he told the story to Frau Delarosa this time. Although he had told her the facts of his mother's death early on in the analysis, because he had never told the story in this context, in the context of Anna and what had happened, it had never connected deeply. Frau Delarosa let him cry without intervening. It was her job to help him find these disconnected feelings. She let him sit with this for many weeks. An hour would pass without a word. The great inner work is like that. Simply presence. Simply knowing and to be known, without denying or wishing away or hurrying along. It was what she could do for him with her large, severe, Swiss presence. Like a grand-mother. She knew enough to let him work without talking about it.

"So, this is it?" he said, at last, after many weeks.

"This is what it is. No more. No less."

"And there's nothing to be done?"

"And what do you wish to do?"

"I have no idea what I want to do."

"You have had dreams?"

"No. No dreams."

"Then she is not cooked yet, the unconscious."

"But I need something,"

"When there are no dreams, when there is no way, then sometimes we turn to the sandtray."

The Jungian sandtray is a simple wooden box, thirty inches by twenty inches, filled with sand. Something like a larger version of a Japanese stone garden miniature. Typically the analyst has a multitude of play figurines, about the size of the fingers, which are collected over a lifetime and can fill many shelves. Figures of every sort—animals, plants, historical characters, fairy book creatures, and mythological animals. People often assume the setup is for children. And though it is used extensively with children, it is adults who most often have the greatest difficulty in learning to play.

So it was for Daniel. He had no idea what to do.

"I would say," she instructed him, "that you should simply look over the figures and try to feel the ones that seem hot."

"Hot?"

"The ones that appeal to you. For you this may be difficult. To feel what appeals to you."

It was difficult. Daniel had to fight past his skepticism, his left-brained doctor's training, to find what made him smile. Or feel sad. Or other feelings he did not understand. He chose a porcelain robin Frau Delarosa had brought from Switzerland, a plastic Collie, and the figure of a Chinese wise man with the long, thin beard.

"Now, place them in the tray and let your fingers feel the sand. Arrange the figures as you wish."

The sand was cool to his touch. Clean, and smooth. He understood the concept well enough. He had studied projective testing and knew the blank sandtray was an empty slate on to which he would write something. But what was he writing? The Chinese wise man he placed in the center. The dog beside him like a good friend. And the robin out on the edge of the tray, out of the box, looking down on the others.

"Very good, Daniel. And I think, best you stay with these images for a bit. I am going to have a smoke."

He starred into the almost blank sandtray for a long time. After a while the blankness of it no longer pleased him. He built up the sand to put the wise man and his dog on the top of a hill, then fenced them in, then decided it should be more like a Chinese painting he had once seen of a quiet mountain side overlooking a village. There was a plastic white lily on her shelf and something moved him to build a little pond and place the lily there. The time passed quickly. At the end of the hour she called him.

"But what does it mean?" he asked.

"Enough for today, I should think. Next week, Daniel."

Daniel was surprised how the image of the Chinese village stayed with him through the week. He found himself thinking about it. His next session with Frau Delarosa he set right to work on it again, using the same pieces. They didn't speak. He stopped asking for the meaning.

Another set of weeks went by as Daniel spent time in his village. Frau Delarosa smoked and read the newspapers without commenting. Yet he was pleased. He had no words to talk yet, and still, perhaps for the first time in his ten years of analysis he could feel inside himself that something was happening. Something he could not explain and yet also did not wish to explain.

His dreams returned. Dreams of doctors, hospitals, and sick patients. They analyzed them week by week, association by association, and slowly the sandtray faded away back into its corner where he had barely noticed it all those years before.

One day towards the end of his training, he came in and announced to her that he had chosen a thesis topic.

"What's this?" she questioned.

"Eleven years is a long time. I think I am getting ready to graduate, if you will let me."

"A man like you? Are you cured then?"

"Most definitely not."

"Good!" she laughed in her big Swiss laugh. "What is your thesis?"

"The death of the anima in a man's life."

"The death of the anima?"

"*Doch! Liebe Frau*," he chided her.

"Explain yourself."

"When a man cannot be seduced by the anima, cannot engage the world with passion, then we may think of it as the death of the anima. Projected out, this would be something like the death of a lover, or wife. A sense that he has nothing to live for."

"But the anima does not die."

"Yes, theoretically this is not possible. However, is there no such thing as unrecoverable grief? A man whose love she has taken to the grave and will not return?"

"The death anima. She is powerful by seducing a man with death. She is the anima still."

"Argue if you want. My thesis is trying to explain why some men seek death in such a case."

"You must find a fairy tale to support your argument."

"Yes, I know. I have not found it yet. But I will." When he did find the right fairy tale, after Frau Delarosa had died, it was *The Secret Garden*.

"Herr Doctor, why would you write such a thesis?"

"From the sandtray. May I explain?"

Although it had been more than a year Daniel skillfully reconstructed his Chinese village piece by piece. It cheered him to see his old friends again—the dog, the Chinese wise man, the robin, and the white lily.

"Do you see, Frau Delarosa?"

"Yes. I see. I see Vietnam."

"You knew?"

"But it does little good for me to know. It only matters what you know. *Nicht wahr?*"

"*Stimmt, Liebe Frau. Das stimmt.* Yes, my village was Vietnam, and I found myself thinking of my mother and her time over there. How alive she must have felt. Like she always was, when free, alive and vibrant."

"Tell me, where is your mother in this picture?"

"She is the robin."

"As I suspected."

"Yes. She is watching over the peaceful scene. Watching over all things."

"And the death anima? Where is she?"

"She is the robin also. They are one and the same."

"And you, Daniel. Where are you in the picture?"

"That was the missing piece, you see. I was watching from a distance, not putting myself in the picture. In other words, I am in the same position as my mother, watching over all things."

He selected a second bird from the menagerie on her shelves. A blackbird. Reaching across the sandtray to his mother's perch, he placed his own bird beside her. Frau Delarosa cast a long sideways glance at him.

"You wish to join her in death?"

"I do, *Liebe Frau*. Because she is my lover. Because she is my spouse. Because I love her more than any woman in the world."

"And hence, you have never been unfaithful to her."

"No. It was not possible."

"In that way, you were never impotent. You realize this?"

"Yes. It is simply that my heart is given to this woman, and I can serve no other."

"That is it then. That is what ails you."

"There is no cure. Only death, I suppose."

"You will not take another mother? There remains the lily. Perhaps you do not know this, but the Chinese believe the lily has healing properties. An ancient wisdom."

"Oh, you have helped me, no doubt. To let me feel the mother," he thanked her, lowering his head. "And by doing so it is possible you have only bound me closer to her. By separating me from my mother you have freed her to be a stronger anima. Yes, I know the symbolism of the lily and the Chinese also say the lily means *love forever*."

"That may be so. And yet, you see now they are different?"

"I understand the two loves. Yes."

"What will you do now?"

"I will visit Vietnam. I have already made the arrangements."

"A little bit dangerous."

"Yes, a little bit."

"Herr Doctor Osgood, you came to this interpretation of the sandtray by yourself?"

"Yes, *Liebe Frau*."

"Fine. You may finish your thesis and graduate if you can. I will not stop you."

IN THE LONG SLOW WALK BACK to his father's room, Daniel thought about the many things he had never said to his father. Things, perhaps, he should have said. And yet, he realized, looking back, that if he had said all the things he wanted to say so many of them would have turned out to be things he should never have said. Because he did not understand. He did not understand his anger toward his father, as natural as it was in response to his father's many shortcomings, was at the very same time his anger at him for driving her away. Only lately could he understand that this wasn't true. Margaret Osgood was the kind of woman who flew away and would have only flown away sooner in his life if his father had not found a way to keep her, however temporarily. No, better not to force upon people things they cannot understand. You have to meet people where they are.

Coming up to the bed, his father sat.

"You said you lost a patient."

"Yes, Dad. Suicide."

"I lost patients," Dr. Paul Osgood said with clear eyes. "Several dozen."

"Did it bother you?"

"Yes. Every damn one of them. It bothers me even now."

"It bothers me too."

"Don't let them tell you it is not your fault, Son. They were always telling me sometimes the disease wins and there's nothing you could have done about it. Horse crap. You take it personally when you lose one. You fight for life, Son. That's what a doctor does. You fight for life and you never give in."

CHAPTER SEVEN

LET THEM LAUGH

IT IS SAID THAT SIGMUND FREUD FACED A DILEMMA. FOR having committed himself to the idea that the various fixes in which people find themselves could be explained by the sexual drives and the failures of libido, he had painted himself into a corner. He could not account for the self-destructive impulses that were all too obvious in people's lives. How could the pleasure principle in itself become so distorted that pain might become a secret pleasure?

Freud decided he must recognize a force in the human soul as gratifying as pleasure—the death instinct. As surely as we crave the pushing pounding surge of life rushing through our veins, what we desire is also release, to be spent entirely with nothing left to give, and hence to sleep. The great tide of libido turns and in that moment we feel its tug. Surrender. Inevitable entropy. The sweet release from interminable struggle, never to rise again. An end and a withdrawal, a farewell and a dark freedom. This is greatly to be desired.

It is also said that in the great festivals of more ancient days the New Year was often celebrated with a mock battle between competing sides. Old Man Winter dressed in straw or moss appeared in the village and was confronted by young Spring with his ivy cloak. Or horse-mounted troops of young men fought on May Day, the winter troop in furs and the summer troop in leaves and flowers, bashing each other splendidly in ritual combat, to applause and delight. An ancient battle. An eternal conflict. The soul's decision.

IN THE CONFUSION OF THE NARROW WINDING STREETS atop Beacon Hill a strange blue and silver RV wound its way on a quiet Sunday morning. The *Pat T-Wagon* was oversized, 32 feet long, too large for the old streets, only narrowly avoiding the rows of cars parked single file up and down the hill block after block without a break or space. Rumor had it that the whole of the Back Bay had only ten thousand spaces for which the City of Boston had issued more than twenty thousand permits. On a sleepy Sunday morning there was less chance of finding a slot than of finding a public toilet.

Bedraggled and confused, Daniel perused his wardrobe once more, still in his pajamas, when a long blast from the horn of the RV shattered his concentration. And then another. Daniel froze. Looking out from the upstairs window to the street at the Itasca Sunrise RV with its satellite dish folded down on the roof among a maze of other antennas, he thought perhaps some political event was unfolding at the State House and that a television remote truck had been dispatched to cover it. At the third blast he hurried down the stairs, tripping, dashing madly from room to room to find his coat and shoes, and finally hopping out the open door just as the mighty fourth blast echoed through the sleepy Sunday morning streets.

Pulling his coat over his pajama sleeves, he was confronted with the sight of a huge bald man, his head clean-shaven, painted, so it seemed, in deep navy blue on the one side and in glistening silver on the other. He took a step back and inspected Daniel head to toe in a long glance.

"No way in hell I'm lettin' you in the RV dressed like that," he barked.

Nervous neighbors peered out of the surrounding windows to investigate the commotion. Lilly peeked briefly around the open door of the Itasca, smiling at him and waving. Maureen followed, laughing hysterically. Two cars were already on the street behind the van, tooting impatiently.

"You're early. I'm not ready. Drive around again," Daniel offered.

"I don't know if I can find my way back up here. Jesus freakin' Christ, how do you people live up here?"

"Five minutes."

"Yeah, right. It's already nine-thirty, Jack! Well, five more minutes and we're leavin' without ya cause with all the traffic we'd miss the tail-gating."

"Five minutes."

He waved at Lilly as they left and hurried back through the open door, up the stairs again and into his closet, throwing clothes this way and that on the unmade bed. Daniel didn't own any licensed football apparel. If it wasn't in the L. L. Bean catalog it wasn't in his closet. Settling for the only pair of jeans he owned and his Harvard sweatshirt, he threw on his Dockers and was out the door again, without shaving or brushing his teeth, only to find the *Pat T-Wagon* jumped up over the curb on the other side of the street. A large hand, attached to even larger tattooed biceps, reached through the open door and pulled him up into the open couch with no more effort than if he were curling 150 pounds.

"You're the guy, right?"

"Right."

"The video guy."

"Right."

"Daniel, meet my brother Robert," Lilly began, patting him on the shoulder from the bench behind him. "And that's Billy on the other side, and Tommy driving."

They grunted their greetings each in turn, painted faces blue and silver glancing back briefly to look him over. Billy, turning round from the swivel captain's chair, decided to be friendly, Daniel reflected, probably on account of his big sister.

"Heah's ya beah, Jack!" he hollered, extending an open Silver Bullet of Coor's Light. Roughly translated, Daniel presumed, it meant something like—*to make you comfortable as our sister has commanded us, please partake of our beer which we have paid for, not you, and in this way you will be one of the guys.* To drink another man's beer is to be hospitable, especially at nine-thirty in the morning. Daniel drank. Now if only he understood the meaning of Jack. Casting an eye across the aisle of the Itasca, he saw Carl seated along the dining booth with Donna and Paula. Carl saluted him with a Coor's of his own. Daniel drank again.

"Billy calls everybody Jack," Lilly translated, from the couch behind him where she sat with Maureen, who caught Daniel's eye with a knowing look, raising a beer and smiling.

"Drink up, Jack!" Maureen lampooned.

As the RV swayed from turn to turn speedily down the hill and out to Storrow Drive the beer on his stomach, without breakfast, was like a too sweet cotton candy on a carnival Tilt-A-Whirl.

"I notice your face isn't painted, Maureen. Where's your team spirit?" Daniel countered.

"A women's face is always painted, Jack. Unless you think we always look this good." She laughed. "But your green face would make you a Jets fan, and we can't have that around here."

"You a Jets fan?" Robert injected incredulously.

"God no! Not since Namath," Daniel protested from sheer Boston instinct.

It was a fine late September morning, the brilliant sun in the windshield as they climbed up from under the city southeast toward Braintree. The air was already frosty with the taste of winter to come and the last leaves of the trees were tipped with white. Turning towards Foxboro, the crew chatted amiably, Lilly's brothers anxious to interrogate him on his opinions ranging from the Patriots front line—*he didn't know*—to South Shore vs. North Shore preferences and where he had gone to high school. *They were not impressed*. The only useful thing they could get out of him was buying tips about video cameras, which they all owned, and home video systems, which they all wanted to own.

"You really ought to go with component video," Daniel instructed them, finding his stride. "Three separate channels. Red. Green. Blue. And a projection system. You haven't lived until you've seen the Super Bowl on Hi Def projection as big as a room."

"Better than the bar?"

"Hell yes."

Now this guy knows what the hell he's talking about, their blue and silver faces said, nodding in agreement. Lilly sat back to take it all in. She was more nervous than she could say. Nervous, because her brothers were noodges. Nervous, because not so long ago Tim had sat in this very RV with her brothers and was every bit a part of them. The damn thing about the Patriots was that game day had been Tim's favorite thing in all the world. It had been Lilly who had talked the girls into season tickets as a group outing after 9/11, after the Pats had moved to Gillette Stadium. In those first days the familiarity of it had been comforting, a reminder, somehow, that life went on. That she could keep her old life in spite of everything. But now she was beginning to wonder if the Patriots were not more like the wall paper that Tim had liked so she kept it around and then one day she had found it to be an impediment, not an encouragement, to moving on and had changed it.

Still, men liked football, at least the men in her world. A free ticket to the Pats game was something to be appreciated. It surprised her when she asked him. She didn't have it thought out at all. *No.* It was hard enough to invite Daniel to the Coffee House. Just a little experiment, something she could have gone a month without trying again. The football game never crossed her mind. Why had she rushed in? *To show my brothers*, a voice inside answered. *To show them I am not defeated. To tell the truth, to show them I do not need Tim. Did not need Tim. To get them to let go of him. To get them to let go of me. I am alright. I was alright before and I am alright again.*

She didn't know how to tell them that sometimes she thought they loved him more than she did. Married so young, her brothers were still in high school. Tim was their man, their *who-I-want-to-be-when-I-grow-up* man for all men. He knew everything, had done everything, seemed so in control and so ahead of the game. He demystified their women problems. Got them jobs. Fixed their cars. Taught them how to work hard and how to move up in the union. Maybe he really was the best man they had ever known, as they said tearfully at his memorial.

How could she tell them? They didn't know. They didn't have to be married to him.

Lilly knew what only a wife knows. Not simply the little tasteless habits that annoyed her. Or the little blemishes with his body. Or his sexual idiosyncrasies. Rank him a big C, passing but not brilliant. His infertility problems and the lack of a baby. More than that Lilly knew what was missing, the terms of the deal about how things would be between them that two people make without ever mentioning it. When they were dating, still in high school, she had no idea that she, like an untrained lawyer, was writing a contract line by line; what she allowed him, what she denied, what she might ask and even demand, and what she must never say. To date someone is to arrange, to test the limits of things and make them just so. Inbounds. Out of bounds. Fair. Foul. Off sides. Illegal contact. Illegal use of the hands. Unnecessary roughness. The rules of the game defined.

His rules. That Tim was first. That Tim was dominant. That Tim controlled the money and made the big decisions and surprised her with them as a special gift. That he would take care of everything and she would respect that. Honor that. Feed that. And pleasure that.

How could she not love so big and giving and lovable a man as Tim? Because she was not in high school anymore. She was not in high school when she married him but he was so beloved of her father, her brothers, her friends from the good old days that no one, except her mother, who looked at her with knowing eyes that dare not speak, no one else could have ever doubted for a minute that he would make her happy. So she could not doubt it herself, even if she knew, but locked away in the smallest, quietest, most timid part of her heart, that she was strong enough to be herself. Herself alone.

A while ago, just past her thirtieth birthday, she thought she could do it. She thought it was possible to stand him up and make him see that they would be better, better than they had ever been, if they could be two strong people making a life together. Not just the one and his helper. But two. Two together.

When you set out to change the rules you had better be prepared for the gridiron clash of large forces. He did not take it well. She wanted her own money, not a weekly budget. She wanted to get out of town, out from under her own family and his family to see who they might be if they were just themselves. She wanted voice lessons and interesting books and women friends who were not wives of football buddies.

That was not the deal. Why was she making trouble? He thought she was just crazy at first, something to do with women's television programs and Oprah, but when she persisted he yelled. And when she saw him get inconsolably quiet after that she knew that she was breaking his heart, breaking his heart because she was asking him to give up what he loved most. Lilly realized for the very first time that this was the only life he knew and had ever known. He loved his high school. He loved his friends. He loved being what he had once been, a football star and someone to be admired. She realized that he could not live without the people around him propping him up with the image of himself he needed, like a long steel mirror that would never bend. Her husband Tim had no ambition to ever be anything other than who he had been all along because it was so sure and certain and in his mind there was nothing to be risked when there was so little to be gained.

But 9/11 changed all that. The risk caught up with him after all. When Tim branched out into contracting, she thought he was making progress. At least he was expanding his circle outside of the union. He bragged to her brothers about the freedom of working for himself, inspiring their envy. His first trip for the National Contractors Convention had been to Vegas. Tim hoped to bring a little West Coast style to the eastern Ranches and Capes he was building. Although he wanted her to go with him, she had declined. Every hour out of the salon was lost money to her. When the next convention was to be held in Los Angeles, promising tours of Universal Studios, he asked her again. And this time she would have gone with him, except for the little matter of what she needed, her own life separate from his.

She was in the middle of pushing him this way and that, like the Patriots' defensive tackle, to see how strong he really was, to see if she could get him to bend, to give ground without giving her the sack. She was in the middle of finding herself. But when he died like that, so spectacularly and so publicly, he achieved a form of beatification. Who Tim was became unassailable and sacrosanct when he died for his country, as everyone said, and somehow everything he had ever done and everything he had ever said became unimpeachably genuine.

She was in shock, of course, in the beginning. Her family rallied around her—her mother as grief-stricken as she was because Tim had been a son to her for nearly twenty years. Billy wanted to run off and join the army right then and there. Tim's family too, all of them collapsing around her in a hammer vise of help. Their outrage became her dotage and, like Sleeping Beauty, she fell under the spell of all the clinging vines of mourning.

The first thing to break the spell was her anger at Tim. He had left her in the middle of a fight, the good fight, the fight for their marriage and their happiness. And she was not done with him yet. Having no opponent, her opponent was herself. At first she took it out on her family, on her brothers because they were big and strong. They let her flail without flinching.

That was better, in a way. Better than the hard-core reality of fact that Tim wouldn't be coming back from Los Angeles. Feeling a way through the anger she found that subtle trick in her mind of trying to go on believing the story as it had begun—that Tim had gone to Los Angeles to his contractor's convention. That was the story the last time she had seen him and somehow he was still there until the reality of the fact that he had forgotten to take out the garbage set in with her. *No. He hadn't forgotten. He was dead.* The thousand other little things spoke in the same small voice. They would sit there unmoved until she moved them because he wasn't there.

This was the disillusionment stage the grief counselor from Catholic Charities explained to her, the second stage of traumatic grief. *Great. They had a name for it. And how many other freakin' stages do I have to go through?* Five. Maybe seven. A long time.

In off moments, hiding herself from the relentless comfort of others, which was at the very same time a great pain, she found herself thinking about how he died. Not the impact itself. She had seen it. She had watched it, not knowing it was Tim. Thirty minutes later when she heard on the television it was United 175, she knew his death was instantaneous. No. That was not the problem. She found herself thinking about what he did before the impact, the little details. In the Boston Globe she had read there was a phone call from a female flight attendant on United 175 to United's system operations center in Chicago saying the crew had been killed and a flight attendant stabbed so she wondered—*did that piss Tim off? Did he try to do something? Did he see New York from the air and know what was going to happen?*

The grief counselor urged her to pick her story and let it go. *Fine. In my mind he did something. He confronted them. He only stopped because of the danger to the other passengers. He didn't look out the window. He never does.*

When the grief counselor suggested she attend the Red Cross group with the other widows Lilly was ready. Ready for a sanity check. All of these things had rattled around in her brain and she had no one to talk to, especially not her family. And the girls were great. Only they could understand the problem with other people's kindness. That it was self-serving, that doing something for her was about doing something for themselves. They didn't mean to be selfish. And she didn't mean to be ungrateful. The girls understood.

When the Red Cross stopped sponsoring the grief counseling after the anniversary memorial, which Lilly attended at Ground Zero, they all decided to just continue themselves. Even with Carl. They started around dining room tables and quickly decided in addition to their private table talk they needed to get out a bit. They needed safety in numbers. She needed the support of the girls around her to go out at all.

And yet, for all of that, they did not understand Tim. They did not understand what she could not say because she knew from the way they talked they still loved their husbands. Not a single one of them, she feared, would embrace her if she said that Tim was not a saint. Tim was not a hero. Tim was someone standing in her way.

And the guiltiest voice of all: *he was in her way no longer.*

For three years she had hidden herself from herself because it was unspeakable treachery to his memory. Her grief counselor had warned her early on of survivor guilt without the slightest idea of what she was saying. Because it wasn't survival guilt. It was the sure and certain, if untouchable knowledge, that she would have lost her fight with Tim anyway and broken his heart to save her own. And that three years later, even without 9/11, she would probably have been exactly where she was that day. Alone and on her own, without him. When all was said and done she was left with herself.

So strange. Impossible as it seemed to anyone around her, Lilly was surprised to see that the details of her life had changed very little. She still went to work. She still drove the same car. She still had the same family and except for the girls she still saw the same friends. And although family and friends were grieving, were they really any more wounded by the fact that he died on 9/11 than they would have been by the gasping revelation that she had left him to find her own way?

No. She could not say this out loud, even to the girls. They were too enshrined with their husbands. And wife. Especially Carl. She could see that to him her death was like a Mafia hit in the movies and that he had committed himself to getting the bastards, all of them, who had personally arranged to hurt his family. Carl worried her.

Only Maureen had stepped outside the box. Only Maureen had once let slip in group that she and her husband were having problems. And from the look on the other women's faces, their anguished double-take in forcing themselves to listen to another woman's pain as they all obliged themselves to do, while at the very time the involuntary twitch of facial muscles turning away from her, there was no doubt.

"I guess people need to believe that their pasts are manageable." Maureen told her privately in a break.

"You don't?" Lilly questioned.

"Sweetie, I lived with Donald too long to kid myself. It was what it was. Nothing changes that. Not even this."

"But it's so bad."

"Yes. It's terrible. It's tragic and sad. For me, every day is still September 12."

"I know."

"But I tell myself something I heard once. We all start again. Don't know when. Don't know how. But it happens. Somehow that makes me feel better."

"I wasn't ready. Yet."

"You're never ready, girl. I lived for twenty years thinking today might be the last day of my marriage. The last argument. The big blowup. And when the big one came, still I wasn't ready for it. But that's the thing. It was coming. No way around that."

"You sure?"

"I'm sure there's no way around the truth between two people."

The big things, in retrospect, are inevitable, whether we like it or not. They have their time. A big event like 9/11, a big ringing bell that tolled, foretold the cultural end of the Twentieth Century as clearly as the sinking of the Titanic had heralded its fearful beginning. The big turns are like that. Something gives way from underneath and the great large expectations of how life should be lived give way with a shudder and the sound of breaking steel—assumptions, assurances, appearances crushed under the weight of inexorable forces that must have their way when set loose in calamity. These great large things shape us because like it or not we do not live our own lives only; we must also endure the life of our times. We do not seek them. They find us out of their own.

THE PREGAME PARKING LOT AT GILLETTE STADIUM—a thousand RV's, SUV's, trucks, vans, and station wagons—was a carnival of gridiron gluttony and Marti Gras grogginess differentiated only by the fact that the men were bare-chested, not the women. Hawkers waltzed from party to party selling florescent light sticks, caps, T-shirts, trinkets, and programs. The scalpers, always wary, ducked in and out of closed circles, doing a good business. An instant city, block after block in geometric rows, had gathered as a rolling Flea Market, poker game, tourist trap, and pick-up parlor.

Pouring out of the *Pat T-Wagon* with war hoops and chest-thumps, jerseys quickly cast aside, Daniel found himself confronted with three burly brothers painted with scarlet letters on their bellies. A big T. Then an A. And Billy with a large red P.

"T.A.P.?" Daniel wondered aloud.

"No, Jack. Look..." Billy wheeled round the right end, pushing Robert to the left. "P.A.T." They lined themselves up.

"Go Pats! Who-ah!"

"But you need an S," Daniel complained.

"That's right," muttered Tommy, breaking rank and unlatching the back door of the RV. "We're one short."

Lilly looked down to the ground, moving to the side of the RV as the equipment rolled out like a Boston College moving van on freshman arrival day—a six-burner gas grill, three coolers of beer and soda, pallets of hot dog and hamburger buns, rows of Kielbasa stacked by the dozen. With a practiced precision that impressed Daniel a green Astroturf carpet, lined with white ten-yard stripes, rolled out the bottom of the Itasca to form a patio, which was soon covered with an awning that Robert and Billy spooled out from two swing-out poles. Up went the satellite dish, 500 channels, lighting up the 32-inch television by the couch and another out under the awning. Condiments in big steel trays along a fold-out table lined up one after the other, with two beer kegs chilled and tapped. The booming stereo system blazed, and finally a device Daniel had never seen before—a stainless steel contraption strapped to the bottom of an Oster blender jar.

"What the hell is that?" Daniel laughed, amazed. Tommy smiled darkly, reached down and snapped a cord on it like a buzz saw, and proceeded to fill it with ice from the cooler, lemon juice, powered sugar, and a healthy dose of rum.

"That's the Daiquiri Whacker."

"I'll be damned…a gas-powered blender. You don't use a mix?"

"Special recipe." Tommy fired up the blender, poured a picnic cup full, and offered it to Daniel.

"Mighty fine."

"Save some for me!" chirped Maureen, joining them.

"The Daiquiris are my favorite part." Tommy finished off the pitcher in their three glasses and started up a round of margaritas. Pulling Daniel away, Maureen leaned in to him.

"Time for you and me to have a little talk."

"I take it there's a lot of alcohol involved."

"You ain't seen nothin' yet."

"Maybe I should slow down then. Save some for later."

"Little hint." Her eyes brightened. "The game is called last man sober is a son of a bitch."

"Maybe I better get you another drink then."

"Not for me, Bucko. For you. Male bonding ritual."

"Yeah. I noticed."

"So the question is, what are you doing here?"

Daniel took a look at the woman across from him. He found Maureen to be a quick, bird-like spirit, matronly some would have called her on first glance, but her legs were thin as a robin's. She pecked, no doubt, but with a humor that only made her as stout as an English barmaid. In his practice he'd seen women like this before, women in their own world who knew their territory. Matriarchal women from matriarchal mothers and grandmothers. They generally appeared in analysis during mid-life, when the children were leaving the nest, looking for help in getting over the shock that they had mated weak men like their fathers, in spite of their best intentions. The breakthrough for them was always getting them to see they were going to have to take on the world for themselves, most capably, rather than waiting for their husbands to suddenly sprout wings.

"I was kind of asking myself the same thing."

"Answer the question."

"She invited me. I said I'd come."

"Out of sympathy."

"Out of respect. Respect for what she's been through. What you've all been through."

"So? What's the difference?"

"Sympathy would mean I was doing something for her. Respect means I'm aware she could do something for me. It would be an honor."

"Bullshit. Still, I almost believed you anyhow. You're a strange bird, Daniel. Kind of out of your element, aren't you? Not what I expected. Not like Tim."

"You knew Tim?"

"No. But look around you. Not hard to guess."

"No."

"Lots of ghosts here. Just sayin'."

"I'll be careful. She's fragile, I know."

"Wrong again, Bucko. She's the strongest one of us."

"Stronger than you? That would surprise me."

"Not all that glitters is gold, Daniel," she said, raising her glass with a sigh. It was as if she had opened her coat, a great dark coat, just enough to show the weight that hung around her neck like a black pearl.

"But you do glitter, Maureen. You're a gem." They clinked glasses and Maureen folded herself back into herself and waved him off with a brush of her hand.

"Remember the S, Daniel," she said, walking away.

"S…?"

"S stands for Tim."

The others had settled in around the food and Daiquiris. From the grill the rich smell of lost summer filled his nose, Robert's kielbasa simmering, hamburgers and hot dogs on the side. Daniel joined Carl, Donna, and Paula in the folding chairs, backs to the wind, looking a little chilled. As they chatted it occurred to Daniel that the touch of alcohol he felt on the tip of his nose, pleasantly numb, was disinhibiting his typical reserve. And he needed that. Not only did he find himself confronted with a group of new people, lively talkative people with more to discuss than travel tips for introverts, he also had to find a way to engage Lilly's brothers. Maureen was right, he was out of his element.

And yet Maureen could not have known that this was precisely his mission. Though they did not often meet, the Beacon Hill Brownstones and the Southie tenements, except in the ritual combat of Harvard and Boston College hockey, they met in Daniel. These hard-tone intonations, rough hands and rough mouths, love of family, class, and loyalty to the old neighborhood, were the bread and butter of every Boston soul. The heart of the city was a working-class heart, a heart as big and as strong as working-class hands.

If he were ever to come down from the abstracted heights where he had lived for so long, observing without participating, Daniel would need a heart. A big Boston heart. And so he welcomed them. But he drank another Daiquiri just for good measure.

Presently Robert appeared, loudly, with Lilly behind him bearing a tray of fresh cooked kielbasa. In spite of himself Daniel looked doubtfully at the large sausage. The thought of it didn't seem to sit well with the rum in his stomach.

"Now you-ah in foah a treat," Robert proclaimed proudly. "They-ah's nothing' betta than hot kielbasa and a cold be-ah. Fresh kielbasa, not the smoked shit."

"Maybe a burger, Chief." Daniel punted, catching a beer tossed in his belly like a tight end on an in-route.

"Have you evah tried it?"

"No."

Robert chomped half a kielbasa dangling at his mouth on a fork and washed it down with a beer.

"Nothin' like it."

"Great."

Grabbing the plate from Lilly's hands, Robert planted himself in the chair beside Daniel in a chummy way, the way the jocks in high school patted your back in the lunchroom when they wanted your table. Lilly found an empty chair on the other side of Daniel, the first time she had sat next to him all morning. Daniel started on his kielbasa one careful bite at a time.

"You like the digs?" Robert began.

"Damn fine set up. Thanks for the invite. And the booze. You live like kings."

"God damn right. Nothin' betta than the RV life. Me and my brothers, Lilly too, kicked in to buy it couple a yeahs ago. You can get right down on the beach in Chatham with this rig."

"Satellite digital television too. What else does a guy need?"

"Just a woman."

"Damn straight. You married, Robert?"

"Not at the moment. You?"

"Never been married."

"Sounds bad. You'ah not a que-ah are ya?"

"Don't think so. You never know about people, though, do you?" Daniel risked. Robert took in the challenge with a hard eye, drank a beer and laughed.

"Na. I guess ya don't. Can't tell on the outside. Take that Ca-al ova theya. Funny guy. Hey Ca-al!" Carl waved from across the patio. "Ya gonna get painted up with us today and show ya team spirit?"

"I'll pass. Maybe next time." Carl insisted.

"See what I mean," said Robert, leaning in. "That Ca-al's been with us a dozen times and he's still a pussy."

Daniel took refuge in a large gulp of kielbasa.

"You a pussy too?" Robert said with an easy smile, but hard eyes.

"Robert!" Lilly barked, in her loudest big sister voice.

"Just havin' a little fun, Sis."

"No," Daniel interrupted. "That's alright. You got paint?"

"No shit?"

"Paint me up. Why not?"

"Daniel, you don't have to do that. The boys are perfectly fine," said Lilly, more than a little irritated.

"It's alright, Buddy. I was just razin' ya," Robert offered.

"I know. I just think it's time I got the full football experience."

"Damn straight. I got the paint in the RV. Face paint too?"

"The whole deal. Yeah."

Before the astonished eyes of all present, Robert led Daniel to the door of the Itasca. They all stood and followed.

"This oughta be good!" quipped Carl, grabbing his drink.

Arranging himself in the oversized captain's chair, Daniel prepared mentally while Robert dug around in the back bedroom to find the paints. Throwing up her arms, Lilly poured water from the sink into a plastic bowl. When Robert brought the paint, she perused the brushes with an artist's eye. She shook her head and rummaged through her purse to find a makeup brush. The crew leaned their heads through the door, two by two—Carl, Paula, Donna, Timmy, and Billy. Maureen tried to push her way through, anxious not to miss any of the fun.

"Is this stuff, you know, going to be stuck to my face for a week?"

"This is called Krylon Aqua Color, Daniel. Comes off with soap and water," she said, contemplating his face. Lilly turned to her brother. "Out! Out! Shew! Go on."

The onlookers groaned with disappointment as they realized she wasn't going to let them watch and sadly went back to their drinks. She slammed the door shut.

Lilly stood back for a minute evaluating the situation. Even though she realized from the distancing grunts of her brothers when she had told them she wanted to bring a friend to the game, a new friend, a friend outside the widows, that they were going to react with their own measure of protectiveness and working-class pride, she had not factored their hostility into her equation. *It's hard enough to deal with myself,* she lamented silently. *I don't need to deal with their bullshit too. Robert's gonna hear about this when we get home.*

"This isn't what I had in mind," she began, worried about Daniel.

"What did you have in mind?"

"Something safe. Something we could do together with a lot of other people around."

"So far so good, then. Lots of people. I'm not so good with lots of people, you know."

"You're a little shy. I noticed. But I'm not sure this is what you want to do."

"Too much?"

"I should have known Robert was going to be hard on you. You don't have to humor him. It's none of his business."

Daniel looked at her softly. The muscles in her shoulders were like a football player hunched at the line of scrimmage, bracing himself against the struggle of competing weights throwing him from side to side.

"Lilly, paint my face."

"Daniel…"

"It's okay. It's gonna be alright. You remember you asked me if I can take it? The group. The girls. Your situation."

"Yeah, but I forgot about my brothers."

"I can take it, Lilly."

"You have to tell me why."

"Because where I come from people are boring. I am boring. I need to stretch myself. This is definitely not boring."

"So it's not for me? Because I don't want you to do this for me."

"Yes. It's for you, if you'll let me. You're not boring. And besides, I'm a little drunk. What else I am going to do drunk like this at twelve noon on a Sunday morning?"

"You're drunk?"

"You're not?"

"Welcome to my life on a typical Sunday," she sighed, giving in. "Alright. Close your eyes. I need to start with the eyes. You trust me, don't you?"

"I'm not going to look like a freak or anything?"

"Yes, you are going to look like a freak."

"What the hell. Just do it then."

Because the paint came dry in the can, Lilly mixed them with water by hand using her makeup brush. She began with the white first, using that as a base for the design she had in mind. Mime-faced, Daniel reached for the mirror, but she brushed his hand away.

Lilly next started with the silver paint which was much thicker and more difficult to spread.

"Um…my face feels crusty, like it's going to break if I smile or move my lips. Is that normal?" Daniel observed.

"Quit complaining."

Half of his face done in silver, she began with the royal blue on his left side, angling down from the thick eyebrows.

With quick passes along the edges of the white, she finished, a star over his left eye. When she handed him the mirror, Daniel laughed.

"Paul Stanley from KISS? Give me a break."

"Best I could do on short notice."

"If my friends could see me now…Oh well. Okay, now for the cold part."

"You're sure you want to do this? You won't catch cold or something?"

"I'll be fine."

She reached for the bright red paint, cleaning her brush.

"Take off your shirt."

Quite against her will Lilly blushed as red as the paint. Hiding her face, she looked away. Daniel also, surprised by the moment, hesitated. He knew very well that this little experiment in living was somehow out of the range of what he had done before in trying to fix himself. But he had not considered her needs. Not until he saw her lonely struggle, like a mountain climber on a solo ascent up the steep imposing incline, head bent and knees weak from the effort, driven forward only by sheer force of will to conquer the unconquerable. Maureen was right, if analytic instinct pushed him toward helping her, then he must stop. Helping would only get in the way.

"Lilly, let's make a deal," he offered when she turned, embarrassed, to face him. "Just friends, okay? You and I."

"Yes."

"Does that help?"

"Yes."

Taking off the sweatshirt, he closed his eyes so he would not have to watch her. The brush was warm, soft like the touch of the tail of a black angora swishing against his skin. But he hardened against it, his stomach knotted. The air moved. He could sense the pressure of her body bending lower, to one knee, as her breath quickened with quiet tears. Her brush was now unsteady.

"You used to do this for Tim? Like this?"

"Every Sunday," She almost whispered, fighting her tears.

"So this is difficult for you."

"Yes."

"I understand." Daniel hesitated. "I didn't mean to…"

"No. Don't you apologize to me, Daniel."

"Okay." Daniel opened his eyes to find her eye to eye with him as he sat.

"Tim is dead. He's been dead a while now. Time for me to move on."

"Maybe you're not ready yet."

"If I don't move on, I will never be ready."

"It just hurts me to see you in pain."

"I can take it. If you can take it, I can take it. Deal?"

"Deal."

A loud bang on the door startled them both. They jumped, Lilly's hand trailing off in a swirl at the bottom of the S in his solar plexis.

"Hey ya's! Gotta go! Game's gonna sta-at in fifteen minutes," cried Robert.

Lilly reached down, wetting her finger, and brushed away dripping paint. Suddenly a panicked gasp arched her nose.

"Oh Jesus, it's not dry. I forgot."

"I'm coming in!" shouted Robert, barging through the door. "We gotta go!"

"The paint's not dry, Robert…Give me a sec."

"Jesus, Joseph, and Mary!" he said with a laugh, taking in Daniel's new persona. "This is a football game, not a freakin' Trick or Treat. What'd do to him, Sis?"

"Maureen!" screamed Lilly, head and shoulders bobbing out the door. "Maureen! Hair dryer!"

A general panic set in, bodies crashing to and fro in the narrow doorway, heads sneaking around to get their view of the action, legs bumping and jumping in the constricted hallway. Daiquiris tumbled to the ground, with swearing. The steel trays crashed in the sink. It was the endgame of the pregame, the two-minute drill, the no-huddle offense.

"Hair dryer!" Maureen reported, cold steel flashing from her purse.

The blast of hot air struck Daniel like a hurricane, baking the paint on his face at 150 degrees. His hair flew out at odd angles.

"He needs a haircut," Maureen observed, arms folded.

"I wasn't gonna tell him," Lilly admitted.

"And maybe part it on the other side," Paula added thoughtfully, pushing his hair the other way.

"Do you mind?" Daniel protested.

"Don't talk! Paint's still drying," Lilly commanded him.

"Gotta go, Sis!" Robert pleaded from the open door.

"Sixty seconds."

"We can't even finish packin' up."

"I'll stay. I'll fix it. You go on."

"We'll help her!" assented the widows.

"Done!?"

"Done! Daniel, just don't blink your eyes or open your mouth for a few minutes."

Carted out the door by three burly brothers he looked back at her with eyes as wide as the low September moon.

They hurried to the gates, Tom and Billy quickly outpacing them. Carl was nowhere to be seen. He must have stayed with the women.

"Now look, Buddy, let me explain the rules to yaas," commanded Robert, whirling him through the gates. A full size Patriots helmet dangled in his free hand. "In the faast place, you gotta understand that as fan you gotta take it as yaa pasonal responsibility for the outcome of any home game. That means loud. Yaas get it?"

"Ummm, Hmmmm," mumbled Daniel, trying not to move his lips, still wet.

"And another thing. Sittin' down is faa pussies. If ya want to sit on yaa ass, why didn't yaas stay at home? See? Sittin' is faa tea paaties. Standin' is faa football."

In the swirl of the crowd up the wide stairways, excited fans whooped when they saw their faces and bare chests. Total strangers slapped them stinging on their backs.

"And this is anothaa rule. If ya holla like a maniac in the wrong spot, people gonna think Brady threw a touchdown, see? Don't do that shit. Two yaad gain, clap yaa hands two times. Ten yaad gain, clap yaa hands ten times. Big play down the middle, sideline catch, yell yaa head off, but save some. Touchdown I wanna see yaas screamin' like a teenage geh-el at Backstreet Boys con-set. Right?"

"Ummm, hmmmm."

They topped the stairs at the Mezzanine level, pushed along the crowds past the beer stands, pizza, and bathrooms. Approaching a long hallway opening to daylight at the far end, Robert pulled him aside.

"And don't faa-get DE-fense. This is the Patriots. This is freakin' Bill Belichick! Fahst down tackle, 50 percent. Second down tackle, 70 percent. Tha-ad down stop, 100 per cent. Faa-th down crunch time, sackin' the quaata back, howl like a motha fucka. And don't be waitin' faa the freakin' Jets to come out of the freakin' huddle. Raz 'em. Caa-se 'em. Make shu-a they can't he-ah shit. This is yaa personal job. But rememba, when the Pats has a third, it betah be as quiet as Tiger Woods putting for buddie in the end zone. You talk, you die. Got it?"

"Ummm, hmmmm."

"And since yaas been a brothaa today and what not, I'm gonna make you the Helmet Man, see? Special hon-ah."

He snapped the helmet down tight on Daniel's astonished head.

"What's this for?" He protested, makeup cracking on his lips and jaw.

"Faa good luck! Now let's get in th-aah and kick some ass. I'll be right beside yaas."

And with that advice, Robert slapped him on the back of the helmet and threw him in there, like a coach with a reluctant rookie. As Daniel emerged up the sloped walkway a field of emerald green, impossibly green and vital, extended before his eyes. The clamor of the crowd, the sheer physical weight of heavy air and hubbub, broke over him like flood waters cascading down from above. The teams were set for the kickoff, opposing armies in cold blue and virescent green glaring at each other in a din rising louder and louder like the racket of steel swords pounding on burnished shields. As the ball rose high into the air deafening thunder shook his legs, the girders beneath him jumping and thumping. When it came down to the green jersey two steps back from the goal line, the rabble jeered and swore in anger, then cried out again in thirsty revenge and bloodlust. A mighty hit. First down.

As Daniel made his way along the row behind Robert—helmeted, face-painted fiercely with a white star over his left eye, and bare-chested with a scarlet S—other fans adored him. They hugged him. They urged him on with hoots and hollers. Billy waved them ahead and shoved a beer in Daniel's hands. The seats were excellent—first row on the first deck.

"*He's* Helmet Man!?" Billy protested, turning Tommy toward Daniel to see for himself. Robert smiled wickedly. "*Alright!*"

As the Jets took the opening drive down to the Patriots' forty, the brothers heaped insults on the players. Daniel was at a loss for appropriate insults. Third and three on the Patriots' forty, the Jets right in front of him, Daniel hollered himself hoarse, as instructed. *Thwack!* His head bounced. Before he could turn again, *thwack! thwack! thwack!* Three more times.

"What the hell!?"

"Yaas the Helmet Man today. Gotta touch the helmet for good luck."

Thwack! thwack! thwack! Even people in the rows behind him were reaching down to smack the helmet. Dropping back for a pass, the Jets QB held his ground until the pocket collapsed, staggered backward, turned to escape, and was crushed by the blitzing safety for a sack behind the fifty yard line, now out of field goal range.

Thwack! thwack! thwack! With the booze and the thwacking his head bobbled like a doll.

"Yaas lucky, man! Yaas did it! Good job!"

Thwack! thwack! thwack!

Everyone seemed quite pleased with his role. For the rest of the first quarter, pelted with good luck thwacks, he never even felt the cold.

Daniel endured. He was having the time of his life. At least he told himself he was having the time of his life.

At the end of the quarter Lilly appeared, with the others in tow and beers all around.

"Robert!" she protested at once. "Get that silly thing off his head!"

"But he's Helmet Man."

"Take it off!" She ripped it off Daniel's head fiercely enough to make his ears bleed.

"But I'm the Helmet Man," Daniel objected.

"He was doin' good!" Billy complained.

"Daniel, you don't have to wear the helmet for good luck. Just touch it."

Grabbing the helmet by the facemask she lifted it to the crowd. Superstitious hands reaching down from all around tapped the helmet in homage.

"If we lose it's your fault. We were doing fine," Daniel warned.

"You cold?" she laughed.

"No, I don't feel a thing."

"I bet."

The second quarter was a change of fortune indeed, seemingly star-crossed from Lilly's tempting of fate. A blocked Patriots' punt resulted in a game-tying touchdown two minutes later. A field goal at the half put the Jets up by three. Robert complained bitterly.

As they sat, at last, through the halftime show, undistracted by the valor on the field below, the cold set in.

"Brought this." Lilly offered Daniel his sweatshirt.

"What'd ya want to do now? Jinx us?" Robert carped.

"Robert, he's shivering. Daniel, put it on."

"Chief," Daniel said, shaking Robert's hand, "I'm kinda outta practice. Lost my game face."

"Yaa game face is cracking and falling off. Yaa look like a freakin' zombie." Robert laughed heartily and slapped him on the back. His skin sang. "Yaa did good, Helmet Man. Hit the bench."

"Freakin' Jets," said Daniel, pulling on his sweatshirt

"I know. We'll get 'em in the second half. You'll see."

They did. In those years the Pats made your heart stop, your hair fall out, and your head throb. They didn't win big and they didn't win pretty, but when it came right down to it they generally found a way to get the job done. The perfect Boston team. *Faaget the damn Sox.*

ON THE LONG SLOW DRIVE BACK Daniel was hoarse, hung-over, and overloaded on sheer extraverted energy. He couldn't find the strength to hold up his end of a conversation. So he found himself marooned in the back in the RV with Carl.

"Did you remember what I was telling you before? About the missing three minutes?" he was prattling. Daniel fought to keep his eyes open as the late September sky darkened toward an early evening.

"I remember, Carl."

"So, what'd you think?"

"I guess we'll never really know what happened that day."

"Oh, bullshit…" Carl continued angrily, shaking his head. "You gonna let those bastards get away with it too? How can you sleep at night?"

"Which bastards? The terrorists?"

"No, the other bastards. Cheney and the rest. Don't you get it? Three missing minutes on a doctored flight recording. Sounds of the cabin whistling with wind. They shot it down. The bastards shot down Flight 93."

"I don't know, Carl. You worry me. I understand your anger, I guess. I just want you to be alright, and this is…I don't know. I just don't know Carl if this is really gonna help you."

"Anger?" Carl tried to pull himself in, sensing Daniel's discomfort. "You don't know. You don't know nothin' about it."

"I know."

"I had a life. You understand? I had something. Something really good. I had it all. Those bastards took it away from me. And god damn it they are gonna answer for it. They owe me a life. I want my old life back."

"I know, Carl."

"I want my old life back," he whimpered, choking back his tears. "But that's not gonna happen. No. This is gonna go on. It's gonna go on for years and years and years. And not just me. For you. For everybody. I'm gonna wake up every day and I'm gonna be angry cause I just wanted to live my life and be left alone. I never asked for any of this shit coming down. And not just Al Qaeda. Why do they have to come down on us anyway? No. I mean the government too. The Patriot Act. The freakin' F.B.I.. They're investigating us, you know? 9/11 family meetings. All because we're saying crazy shit like this missing three minutes. I mean what the fuck, Daniel? What is with that shit?"

"I don't know."

"You should make a video. Catch the bastards in the act. I'll help you."

"Carl, I'm happy to help you, if I can. Whatever I can do. I guess I just don't know if something like that would really help you or not."

"Well you think about it. Think about getting involved."

"Sure, Carl."

"And what are you two cooking up? Looks like a war council back here," Maureen injected, tottering back down the aisle, hands extended like a subway surfer.

"Solving the problems of the world," Daniel countered, exhaustion taking him. He unbuckled his seat belt and stretched out on the couch.

"Lilly wants to know if everybody wants to get some dinner. Maybe some pizza."

"I couldn't eat another bite. And definitely no more alcohol today for me."

"I'm not up for it, Maureen. I wanna get back to the kids," Carl agreed

"That seems to be the general consensus. God, Daniel…look at your face." She flecked silver scales off his cheek. "Lilly's worried she baked your makeup on your face and you're going to have trouble getting it off."

"Great."

"Why don't you go over to the salon? She's got stuff there. Plus, you need a haircut anyway."

"Too tired, sorry."

Maureen lurched back up the aisle to the others. A few minutes later Lilly wandered back to join them, pushing Daniel upright on the couch to sit between the two men.

"Daniel, I feel bad. I let you do this and now it's gonna be a problem." She wet her finger and slid it down the trough of his face between his nose and cheek. "It's not coming off."

"Great…I just need to go home and go to bed. Then I'll be fine."

"You're gonna spend two hours over the sink before you go to bed." Her eyes met his, apologetic and pleading. "Ten, fifteen minutes in my chair and you can go home. I've got the heavy duty cleansers."

"Fine," he sighed, giving in. "But no hair cut."

"We'll see."

Coming back into town, the *Pat T-Wagon* lumbered past South Station and the financial district, making for Huntington Avenue. Lilly's salon was nestled in the rows of storefronts, block after block, between Symphony Hall and Northeastern University. The football crew, exhausted from their efforts, wished them both well without standing up from their seats. Robert reached a large hand back from the driver's seat.

"Yaas a real Patties fan now, ah'nt ya?"

"Hell yes."

Tommy and Billy slapped him painfully on the back once more. As they pulled away a mighty blast sounded from the *Pat T-Wagon*. Lilly fumbled with her keys, the door, the lights.

"Carl says I should make video," Daniel said as he waited.

"Don't humor him. We've taken to just telling him we don't believe it."

"So, that isn't true about the F.B.I.?"

"Who knows? We never know who all those people at the meeting are."

"And there's nothing really going on?"

"Oh yes, there is definitely something going on. So many things they won't tell us."

"But you're not worried about it?"

"Yes, I am worried about it. We all are. I have to worry about myself first and what I need to do. But not Carl. He doesn't care about himself anymore. Just her."

"Sad."

"It gives him something to make him get up out of bed every morning. But you don't have to humor him. He's a big boy now."

Daniel found himself in Lilly's version of the analytic couch, her place where people let themselves be touched. A wide stone floor absorbed the subtle light from the track lights above. Green plants softened the stone—croton, Chinese evergreen, dracaena, and bamboo—as the sound of gurgling water, like summer rain, washed over the waiting area. Bonsai trees in delicate porcelain trays filled with sand and stone arched from four corners.

"Ah...this is not what I expected. You know? Barbers use more linoleum."

"Barbers? Oh really, Daniel. We were going for a Chinese garden kind of a look. Works pretty well, don't you think?"

"I had no idea. Looks expensive."

"$80.00 to start. We do a lot with the Boston College girls. B.U., Northeastern, Simmons. A good business. The girls need their comforts, you know. Come over here. Let me start you in the wellness area."

In her own space, in her own world, something about her was different. She was as comfortable as he was in his analyst's chair— confident, practiced and skilled, unhurried in a way that spoke of long experience.

"Wellness area?"

"Latest thing in salon design. Chrometherapy and aromatherapy. I'll show you. Sit. This is one of my new backwash chairs."

Daniel found himself settling into an elegant recliner of Italian design, black leather with a zinc-plated sink in black ceramic. At the touch of the arm, it extended beneath him, the leg rest rising to the full sleeper position. The seat warmed beneath his back, vibrating gently but deeply into his muscles.

"Electronic back vibration massage. Relax, Daniel."

"All this to get a haircut?"

"Where have you been? This is state of the art. The Kyoto chair, it's called."

"Out of circulation, I guess."

"I guess. Close your eyes. You need to relax your face or I am never going to get this stuff off of you."

It is little known to this day that Carl Jung played an instrumental role in inventing the lie detector. Something had been stolen in the Burghölzli Clinic. Jung, with his Word Association Test, had already discovered that people's complexes give themselves away in response to a stimulus word, sometimes a very simple word. *Green. Chair. Water.* When he hooked them up to the Galvanometer measuring skin conductivity, pulse, and respiration he soon discovered, with startling clarity, that though the mind can say one thing, the body says another.

Daniel was too tired, too hung over, to notice that while his mind told him to relax, to give into the warm massage and the warm comfort at the end of a trying day, his body with forceful voice said *no.*

"I'm gonna fall asleep."

"Then fall asleep. Just don't move your face."

A spray of warm water washed over his face and hair. Her fingers lingered over the rough patches on his cheeks where the paint was the thickest, eggshell hard and flaking, The muscles in his neck and shoulders hardened, fighting the feel of her fingers.

"Oh Jeez. Now I'm gonna have silver flecks in my sink all week long. I'll have to explain to all the girls how I ended up at the football game with a maniac and a hair dryer. Wait right here."

Eyes closed, he was unprepared for the warm moist towel she carefully draped over his face. Involuntarily he half rose, but her hand guided him gently back down.

"Face towels?" he mumbled inaudibly.

"Yes. We even have towel warmers here. Have to open the pores, Daniel. Makes it a lot easier. Then I will exfoliate your skin. You need a shave anyway."

His mind gave in and he laid back.

"You really know what you're doing with all this, don't you?"

"I've been doing it a long time, Daniel. It's what I love."

"You've never wanted to do anything else?"

"Well…I keep wondering what's next for me. After what I've been through, people keep telling me I should do something different. That I don't have to work here. Maybe they're right. Massage therapy. Something. I saw some classes. Something helping other people." The shaving gel, preheated and silky across his face, quieted him. "But I guess I don't have to work. Doesn't seem real."

"The money?"

"Yes, the Victim's Fund money. Strange, strange feelings. Guilty somehow, to take it, but my family…you know, they try to tell me I'm not thinking clearly. They just want the best for me."

"Your brothers are alright, Lilly."

"Well, they have their problems. I was worried how hard it was going to be for you."

"It was hard."

"You were brave."

"We don't have a lot in common."

"I wondered."

"No more football, I think. For a while."

"For a while?" She paused, hands on his face. "So there's a while? For us?"

"I don't know, Lilly. I don't know. This is difficult for me."

"Hard for me too."

"I don't know what to do."

"I do," she whispered. "Now be very still. Don't talk."

Leaning over him, she took the long steel razor in her left hand and the soft skin under his eyes in her other, pulling in a long, firm stroke. His face tightened under the blade. His fingers clenched. His mind saying one thing, his body another. A razor's edge of balance.

"Daniel," she said softly, her mouth so close to him he could he could feel her warm sweet breath on his cheek. "I have to keep going. I have to keep growing. I tell myself that every day. I have to learn to love again."

She laid the blade aside, still holding his face. Her free hand ran her fingers through his hair.

"I want to break our deal. I want you to kiss me."

Her lips lowered toward his.

But his hands, his treacherous hands reaching out from the deeper part of himself that would not let him go, betrayed him. He could only watch with tears as they embraced her shoulder and pushed her away.

"I have to stop," he heard himself say in a voice he had not heard in many years. He felt his body rise from the chair, like a ghost in a play, a mindless specter doomed to forever walk this earth unfulfilled and unrequited playing an empty scene from the long past over and over again as if to try to find what was missing in its deepest soul before it can ever be free from unwelcomed death and rise to reborn life.

"I'm sorry. I have to go."

CHAPTER EIGHT

THE KEY OF THE GARDEN

HE PROPER DISTANCE BETWEEN THE ANALYST AND THE PATIENT is in direct proportion to the depth of the transference. If the transference is more intense, technically the analyst would virtually disappear behind the mirror of analytic reflection. If the affections are more benign, then the relationship may have a more human scale.

We all have Carl Jung to thank for the invention of face-to-face therapy, which would put the proper distance at about six feet. One body length. Freud preferred his couch. Still six feet, if you measure it in the Freud Museum in London set up precisely as things were at Berggasse 19.

In this way the physical distance approximates the emotional distance. The emotional distance is required because Freud could not help but notice how many times the patient's dependence on the analyst simply replaced the original neurosis with a new one. An unreasonable transference, Freud protested, because it seemed to him that to become so dependent on a simple human relationship was thoroughly unreasonable. And yet it happened all the time. The patient's symptoms returned as soon as they left the office. And so, for some people, psychoanalysis has been interminable ever since.

Ah yes, Jung recounted, although the analyst is entitled to close his door when the symptoms no longer appear, perhaps the unreasonable transference continues even if the patients were freed of their childhood entanglements because as adults they often have no clue as to how to live a human life fully. Perhaps they cling to the analyst not so unreasonably after all, because they hope, if they have been given any reason to hope, that the analyst has some idea of what they should do, how they might live, where they might find a way of living their life that is satisfying.

And the danger of the transference is greatest in that moment, because the analyst only knows but one life. *His own*. He only wrestles with the one set of questions. *His own*. So the hope of the patients, if they are ever to stand on their own two feet, is in their own potential for living. Not the analyst's. That is the risk they must find the courage to undertake if they hope to grow beyond their relationship with the analyst.

WHEN LAUREL APPEARED NEXT at Daniel's office door, ink on the new chapters of her thesis still wet, she was hopeful. Hopeful about her thesis, yes. She felt she had finally broken through the impenetrable oddities of all these introverted analysts, demanding their insights and subtle personal associations. Sometimes girls just like to chat. And men like to feel important and strong. And most people just take the easy way out because most things just aren't all that deep. Women and men dance around each other and flirt because, well, it's fun and entertaining. *Yes*. She was hopeful of finally getting finished.

Yet she was also hopeful about Daniel. She was not so eager to be finished with him. In their last session he had slipped and shown her something of himself, maybe without realizing it. She couldn't tell. Something had broken through his formality. And what she saw, she liked.

There's a certain trick in getting through to introverted men. This knowledge should be in every woman's arsenal. The extraverted men need little encouragement. Catching their eye the wrong way is enough to earn a come on from them. *Fine*. They know how to start a conversation. They know how to yuk it up and make you comfortable, and know when to make their move and close the deal. Nothing complicated about that and sometimes Laurel liked to just relax and let him do all the work. She was worth it.

Introverted men are quite a different species, she had learned. The fumbling conversational skills. The total lack of conversational skills in many cases. You could wait all night and he would never say a word to you. *Strange.* But the thing is, they love to talk. You could never tell it by looking at them, but give them the right circumstances and these guys could talk. Because they wanted to talk. They were dying to talk to someone. And the key difference, of course, was that they actually wanted to talk for talking's sake. They weren't talking just as a way to spend the required number of minutes in conversation just so they could move on to touching and not have to talk anymore. Big difference, if you actually enjoy talking to a man. In different moods Laurel could go either way. There was something exciting about getting the talking out of the way quickly and just getting on with it. *Getting it on.* Like the way you feel in a certain outfit. It puts you in a particular mood.

But change outfits and then it puts you in a different mood. Do something different. Break up the routine a little bit. So he's there at that table by the corner, eating alone. Or maybe there's three guys and he's the one who hangs back while the other two are doing their stuff for you. Just a different mood, that's all. To be patient. To take your time. To make the moves yourself and try to time it so he doesn't run away, like a deer when you've got the apple right there in your hands. Soft nose. Soft fur. Then you're talking, talking, talking, maybe with a little wine. A really nice evening. And then you have to make him kiss you. He always acts surprised, like *wow! I didn't know where this was leading, but sure. That's fine. That would be great.* Just a different mood with these guys. A different pace.

This is the kind of thing any woman should know. And yet she wondered if Carla Greer, her analyst, knew this, frumpy as she was. It was hard to imagine Carla Greer carefully considering the outfits she wore with an eye toward the mood she wanted to be in or a man who might be looking at it. Was Carla concerned with men at all? She didn't seem to be married. Did she have no social life? No love life? Gay? Difficult to interpret. That was the damn thing about psychoanalysis. You couldn't tell. They would never tell you about themselves. You always had to guess.

Except sometimes the occasional glimpse. The mistakes, she was told. But were they really mistakes? Since when did getting to know something about the person who was a very important person in your life, who knew more about you than your best friend…the person with whom you had shared the most intimate conversations in your entire life—she had to give Carla Greer that—since when was knowing who you were talking to such a bad thing? Maybe it ought to be the first thing. An odd relationship, the analytic relationship.

The thing was, Daniel wasn't frumpy. Okay, he was frumpy as far as his clothes went. But he wasn't born frumpy. Not with a body like that. *Well…okay…now wait a minute.* Was it alright to be having these thoughts about her thesis advisor? Daniel was not her analyst. Daniel was unattached. Daniel was kind of cute and kind of tall and if he wasn't wearing those frumpy clothes probably was just good-looking enough. *What is the problem?*

Daniel. Daniel appeared to be the problem. *Why Daniel?* She paused. *Why Daniel indeed?* In the first place Laurel wasn't meeting a lot of men right now. In the university it had been easier, ever so much easier. But in these new analytic circles, frankly, the pickin's weren't as good. And, sad to say, Laurel was hitting that age when it was clear that most of the good men were already taken. Occasionally you might find a suitable guy opening up from a divorce. *And I always go for the quiet and shy ones. My specialty. I like him.*

Honest to god, why did every single simple attraction have to hide some incredible deep penetrating psychoanalytic secret? Carla Greer was relentless with her. *Animus possessed. A father's daughter.* Made her read all the Marion Woodman books about what it was she was secretly doing. When Laurel's father had died in his late sixties, the most obvious reason she started up with Carla, she cried and cried and cried. Laurel couldn't understand why it hit her so hard. What's the big deal? Everybody's father dies.

"You must understand his presence in your life," Carla insisted. "Like a ghost. Remember Lavinia Mannon waiting for her father to return in *Mourning Becomes Electra*. His absence *is* his presence for her."

Oh please no. It's not a recapitulation of childhood trauma. It's a womanly secret, not a Freudian secret. *I am lonely. I miss having a man to talk to. Sometimes I just want to have a little fun.*

What's the problem here? Everyone at the Institute kept expecting that it was a problem. Not that anybody knew anything or said anything, but you just got that feeling about extracurricular relationships. Daniel kept hinting it was a problem. *But what problem? Teacher and student problem? Oh please, give me a break.* This wasn't high school, or college, or even grad school. Everyone was grown up. And it didn't stop teachers and students then anyway, did it?

So what's the problem? Damned if I know. Yes, but Laurel was paying him. Paying him to be her thesis adviser. *Is that the problem?* Money passing between two people? *Hmmm. Fixable problem.* She could stop paying him and he could stop being her thesis adviser. *End of problem.*

End of formal relationship. *Now that's a problem.* Because there was no relationship beyond the formal relationship. *Oh, I see now.* **That** *is the actual problem. Well, well, well…Daniel and I have no basis to be in a relationship outside of our formal relationship.* When the thesis is over the relationship is over.

Gotta change that. But how, when he is so reluctant? The way to do this would be to create a transitional environment—no, not Winnicott, the feminine kind of environment—in which the formal relationship overlaps with an actual relationship so that when the formal relationship is over the actual relationship continues. *Right.*

Maybe she could use a little psychology after all. Find a way to break the therapeutic persona with Daniel. *Get him to do the one thing that he seems always reluctant to do. Talk about himself. Oh! I see it now. Get him out of the office. That's the ticket. But how?*

And in one stunning breakthrough of analytic insight her plan came together. It was simple. So obvious. The one and only thing that would get him out of the office and into himself.

"I THINK I HAVE FOUND THE KEY to *The Secret Garden*," Laurel began confidently as their session opened.

"Have you now?"

"You wanted me to approach it psychologically."

"Yes. I wanted you to use psychological experiences from your own life and from your cases."

"But I have so few cases. So, what about the case of Francis Hodgson Burnett herself? Is that psychological enough for you? Daniel, it's the key to the whole book. She lost a son. She lost her fifteen year-old son Lionel to consumption in December 1890 after he was bed ridden for more than six months. Don't you see? The character of Colin Craven is her son Lionel. Her processing of her grief."

"Perhaps."

"It explains everything, Daniel. The biggest feminist critique of *The Secret Garden* has always been that Colin takes over the book. Mary Lennox is the central character. Mary Lennox finds the key, finds the door, works in the garden, coaxes Colin outside. Mary Lennox does everything and in the end she is forgotten. Given no credit whatsoever for what she has done. In the whole last chapter of the book Mary is barely mentioned at all. Archibald Craven never thanks her. Colin never credits her. Mary Lennox is overlooked, un-rewarded, forgotten. All you have is Colin shouting 'I shall live for ever and ever and ever!'"

"A displacement, then?"

"Yes, Francis Hodgson Burnett's savior complex. That's what overtakes the book. It becomes all about saving the character Colin, in the end; about Colin living when everyone thought he was going to die, which is her own overpowering compensation fantasy that her son Lionel should have lived also. You were right. You had it just right on from the very beginning. It's about grief. *The Secret Garden* is all about grief."

"That's your thesis?"

"You said you wanted it psychological. I even know the title of my thesis now: *The Overlooked Girl: Grief and Compensation in Francis Hodgson Burnett's The Secret Garden*. I don't know, seems quite publishable to me."

"A bit inflated, I think."

"Well, I can tone down the title a bit if you really want me to."

"Not the title, Laurel. You."

Not that again! Not his constant deflecting of her away from the book and toward herself.

"I'll prove it to you, Daniel. I can prove it. In 1884 Francis Hodgson Burnett lived just down the street from Mary Baker Eddy right here in Boston, and a little later in Lynn. They were both in Lynn at the same time, see? She was suffering from nervous exhaustion and she had several treatments from a local mind healer. That's a Christian Science term, Daniel. Francis Hodgson Burnett was a closet Christian Scientist. And that proves it." *Take that! Let him try to dispute it now.*

"I don't remember ever reading anything to suggest that Francis Hodgson Burnett joined the Christian Science Church."

"Read *The Secret Garden*! As you have kept pounding into me all these months. It's right in front of you, Daniel. It's so obvious to me now. I am saying it's the predominant influence, whether Christian Science officially or the New Thought movement in general. That whole late Nineteenth century spiritualist attitude. She's obsessed with replacing negative thoughts with positive thoughts. The negative thoughts she was trying to displace were her guilty thoughts about gallivanting all over Europe while her son Lionel lay dying. This is the complex interfering in her fiction. It's a rock solid argument, Daniel. All the evidence is there."

"Her complex?"

"Don't you get it? Mary Lennox, and Francis Hodgson Burnett herself. Neglected, overlooked girls. The girl whom no one sees. The bitterness of someone who is always striving, hoping for attention, simple love, and is never given it because her parents are too preoccupied or too overwhelmed to give it to her. Call it the neglected feminine. But the feminine principle is the only thing that can bring them back to life…the only thing that can create a family for Mary and Colin and Archibald too. What they need most, the missing Fourth, is the Great Mother feminine. That's the Magic that must be unlocked to save them all. The hidden Quaternity. That Jungian enough for you? That's the Secret Garden. And Mary does it. She finds the key. She opens the door. She saves them all."

She had heard all of this a hundred times. It was simply the way the Jungians talked. He needed to accept it this time because she was reaching the limits of how far she could go with this material.

"But, is this real? Real to you? Have you felt the overlooked girl in yourself and found the key to the neglected feminine?"

"Real to me?" she retorted, a little peeved. "My own femininity is just fine, thank you. Those things didn't happen to me. There never was a girl, Mary Lennox, or a Colin Craven that I have met in real life. There never was a Secret Garden that I discovered. How could there be? These things happened in a book."

"Those things never happened to you? Are you so sure? Nobody ever died on you? You've never felt grief?"

"Of course."

"Who died?"

"My father. What does that have to do with anything?"

"Grief and its compensation," he shook his head. "Grief and its compensation, to use your eloquent title. What's your compensation toward your father's death?"

Interesting. He will not seem to let this go. Laurel's intuition kicked in. Somehow this was what she had been listening for all along. He was talking about himself again but hiding behind the words. Now was her chance to reach him. Her chance to touch him. Time to flush him out.

"You are so infuriating, Daniel. I really don't understand our relationship. You want me to share something quite intimate about myself with you. And yet you will not condescend to share anything intimate with me about your own life. Are you ever going to share yourself? Because if you're not, what kind of a relationship is that?"

"An analytic relationship, my dear. An analytic relationship."

"But you seem to keep forgetting that you are not my analyst, Daniel. You're not. Why do you keep hiding behind it?"

His eyes looked away. Laurel was learning that was one of the signs. When Daniel was on his game his eyes were steady, never wavering. But when she turned the tables on him in the right way, he always looked away, down and to the right.

"Fair enough. Fine…that's a valid comment. I'm conflicted about you Laurel."

"Finally. Are you attacking me because I want to get closer to you?"

"Is that what you think?"

"Is being an analyst your defense? Your defense against entering into a real human relationship?…" Here she hesitated, but fearing this would be her only chance to break through to him, she continued. "A defense against a relationship with a woman?"

Eyes looking away, he pondered a long time. *This is the moment,* she observed. *Either he is interested in me or he isn't.*

"There are truths, Laurel. Partial truths. And by being partial they can lead you astray from the whole truth. Except that the whole truth always lies just out of reach, I suppose."

"An intellectualization?"

"No."

"Then speak plainly, Daniel."

"Fine…yes, I am using my analytic persona as a bit of a defense against relating to you as a woman. All of that is problematic for me."

"Okay."

"I am pestering you because it is my role to help prepare you for the reality of being a psychoanalyst, when you will sit in that chair and have someone else's life in front of you. That's what you are paying me for."

"Maybe…Maybe. You care so much about your role…"

"…as an analyst…"

"…that you would let it get in the way of a relationship?"

"Yes. I care about the training that much."

"Why?"

"Because I know what it has done for me in my life."

"Daniel, if the analysis has done so much for you in your life then why are relationships with women still so problematic for you? Why hasn't it saved you?"

"Why am I not cured, do you mean? Because analysis does not cure. Analysis does not save."

"How can you say that? Analysis has saved many people."

"I wouldn't say that. Not at all. A cure, such as it is, is always one step at a time. That's what I am trying to get you to see, Laurel. Mary Lennox doesn't save anybody. The power is in the garden, not the girl. The feminine power, the Great Mother to be sure, as you said, but it is the garden itself, Laurel. Nature itself."

"I'm not talking about *The Secret Garden*, Daniel. I am talking about you and why you have such problems being in a relationship."

"Because I am not yet healed. I am still in process."

"Maybe I can cure you. But to do that we would have to have a relationship."

"What kind of a relationship?"

"I don't know. Normal. That's the kind of relationship that comes to mind. You talk to me. I talk to you. The usual stuff …hmmm, I almost believed that you were not enjoying our conversations."

"No. I find them stimulating."

Once you had the deer so close that he could smell the apple in your hand, you had to be very, very still. You had to let the desire for apple win the fight over the instinctual fear of contact.

"And you would be open to more …stimulating … conversations?"

"You are an interesting person, Laurel. Yes. I guess."

"And you're not so angry with me you just want to see me go away when I am not paying you to be my thesis advisor?"

"No. I'm not."

"Because I don't think I want to go away. I think you are an interesting, stimulating person too, Daniel. Friends. You and me. You know, have a drink and talk about our lives."

"Not a physical relationship, Laurel. That is not possible."

"Have you tried?"

"I beg your pardon?"

"Just asking, Daniel. In a friendly way. How long has it been?"

"No. I haven't tried. In a long time."

"If you haven't tried in as long as you say, then how can you know?"

"I know. Trust me."

"For all that you know, and you are a brilliant analyst Daniel, you are still alone. Just a little friendly advice, between friends."

That was as directly as she could put. There really was no point in going on with this if he wasn't going to take the apple right in front of his nose. If he really wasn't going to give in on her thesis either, then she would just have to move on and find another advisor. Life is too short to linger with a losing proposition.

"Yes. I could use a friend," he said at last. "It's time I shared a little. Call it a scientific experiment. Like Colin's."

"Then, being friends, what if you and I went on a little educational outing? Got out of the office for a bit. A field experiment?"

"*Educational?*"

"*Educational.* Did you know that *The Secret Garden* was made into a play? A Broadway musical, in fact. Music by Lucy Simon, Carly Simon's sister, if you can believe that. It's opening in revival at the Colonial Theatre next week. I think we should go see it together for my education. And then we can have some stimulating conversation."

"Only if you promise to learn what I am trying to teach you. Because you're not ready to graduate yet, Laurel. I say that as a friend," he tried the word on for size, "not in any official capacity at the Institute. But you're not ready."

"Fine. So you'll go with me, then? To the play?"

"As a friend," he said the word again.

"And you'll enjoy it? You'll have fun? You have to promise."

"Oh, I enjoy going to the theater."

"You see, we are making progress. I didn't know that about you."

"Oh yes. The theater has been a part of my cure."

"Your cure that isn't a cure."

"Precisely. Still in process, I would say."

CHAPTER NINE

IN THE GARDEN

WHAT IS THE HEART AND HOW ARE HEARTS BROKEN? A psychoanalyst must know these basic facts. The heart is the way a person engages the world, sometimes trusting and sometimes fearful. Winnicott, perhaps, has said it best—that what the human heart knows most deeply it knows only from before memory or words or even thought itself. That we reach out for the Other from deepest reflexive instinct, from the inner image of someone out there to be grasped. And in that reaching moment a lifetime is on the line because everything depends upon the profound satisfaction or profound frustration of the hungry touch; whether, in the end, our reaching heart is nourished or in the unfortunate moment deprived of what it seeks. The secret heart of love, then, is always a mother's love. You risk your heart to reach and share the most intimate hungry thing and it is rightly held.

Or sometimes not. The heart is broken by love's failed dream, by love's imagination splintered on the rocks of a merciless shore. Why? Because we inhabit love's imagination almost against our will, inspired by the beauty of it and in an instant we are already aboard her and casting off the lines, and setting the sails in the bracing wind and off we go at once without chart or compass.

Why all this, then? Because love is a dream.

DANIEL OSGOOD SAT ALONE IN HIS OFFICE. His chair was uncomfortable today for some reason. Sitting to the left or to the right, he could not find a comfortable position.

Before him on the desk sat his summons before the Complaint Committee of the Board of Registration of Medicine. The final date was two weeks hence. He knew he should be wrestling with the truth of what he wanted for himself. Or didn't want. Calling for the third or fourth time last week, his lawyer had pushed him to settle yet again. "Settle and be done with it, Daniel," he urged him. And Daniel knew he was probably right.

But he couldn't think about that right now. He was distracted. Giving up on finding a way to be comfortable in the chair, Daniel stood and paced. There are a thousand reasons, he thought to himself, prowling the office. A thousand reasons why he should not put himself in a position to disappoint Lilly. Lilly of all people. How could he do that? *I can't let her down.*

But how could he have ever avoided letting her down? What hope did he have? What was this all about anyway? How could he have put himself in this position when he knew with a kind of despairing certainty that he couldn't, well, go through with it. Not all the way.

A psychoanalyst should be able to figure this out, if he still wanted to be a psychoanalyst. There was Laurel to consider too. She wanted to be, was demanding to be, a psychoanalyst and also a friend. Sometimes it crossed his mind to simply ask her *Why?* Why do you want so desperate to look into people's lives and see them for what they are? Why do you want to get to know me and see my private pain?

He was startled by a knock at the door.

"You make DVD's, right?" said Maureen, trundling past him with an arm-load of video tapes that she splashed across his desk.

"Maureen!" He waved her away. "I'm not going to take your money."

"Hey! You want my business or not?"

"No. I know why you're here."

"Fine. So are you going to call her?"

"I've been thinking about it."

"You've been thinking?"

"I can't call her till I get this all worked out in my head."

"Are you nuts?"

"A little."

"Word to the wise. Call first. Think later."

"I don't know what I want to say to her."

"Did it ever occur to you that if you want to be in a relationship you're going to have to work things out together, not by yourself? Or don't you get that yet?"

"I don't think I get it, no."

"Just talk to her, Daniel. Open your mouth. Words fall out. You'll see."

"It's not that easy. Maureen."

"Yes, it is, Daniel. It really is. Here's her number."

"I have her number."

"So call her. She's too good a woman for somebody to mess around with. I am not going to let you screw this up. The only way you could understand what that woman is going through is to have lost somebody yourself."

"Who appointed you?"

"At my age, dearie, I can appoint myself to whatever I want. You needed a push. So I'm pushing."

"Fine." He turned his back to her, retreating behind the desk. She stood immovable in the door. "Well?"

"I can be persistent."

"No kidding. Maureen, I am not going to call her while you are standing there. So here, take your videos and go on."

"I'm leaving the videos."

"You really want me to make your DVD's?"

"I'm leaving the videos so if I don't hear what I like, I'm coming back for them tomorrow!"

"Great. Good-bye Maureen!"

"I'll be seeing you, Daniel."

Introverts and telephones do not mix well. Obviously the telephone was invented by an extravert who wanted to keep talking to his friends. In the first place, when you are lost in thought a ringing telephone seems like the most god-awful disruption, a clanging fire-bell over your head at three o'clock in the morning. In the second place it is such an output of energy to have to move all of that thought from the left cerebral cortex down the back of the spine, out along the arm to the fingers to dial the number. Finally, Daniel had noticed other people seem to get nervous with long introverted pauses on the telephone just when you need the time to think. They're always jumping in and shouting "Are you there? Did I lose you?" *Yes. Yes you did, in a way.*

In spite of these things he needed to call Lilly. It was the right thing to do. *Fine,* but there are going to be some long pauses.

"Hi," he offered. "No, that's stupid. I mean, it's Daniel."

"I know."

"Maureen said I should call you."

"Maureen is a noodge who should mind her own business."

"I know. But she reminded me of something I always tell me clients."

"The customer is always right?"

"No. My other clients. Psychoanalysands."

"That's a big word."

"It means…well. Forget it. I tell them it only works if they stop trying to censor themselves and just say the first thing that comes to their mind."

"So what's on your mind?"

"You."

"Oh really."

"Night and day."

"And how long were you planning on waiting to tell me?"

"And I don't like it. It's kind of strange. Obsessive, really. Ruminating thoughts."

"Is that good?"

"No. Not a good sign."

"You don't think it's good when people think about other people?"

"I don't think it's good when you can't stop thinking about something, when you can't focus on what you're supposed to be doing without these others thoughts intruding all of the time. It bugs me. This has never happened to me before."

"Sounds bad."

"So I have to figure this out. See? That's why I haven't called you. I haven't figured it out yet. I don't know what to say."

"You could start by telling me what happened the other night."

His heart sank. Long pause. Just say the first thing that comes to your mind without censoring your thoughts.

"Lilly, I'm sorry. My feelings got the better of me."

"No. I made a mistake, Daniel. I was pushing myself too hard."

"It's not how I wanted the day to end. Things had been going so well."

"Going so well? You had paint baked on your face."

"And it took two days for me to get the rest of it off," he laughed. Laughing helped. Laughing helped a lot. Then a long pause from her, long enough that it made Daniel uncomfortable. "Hello? You still there? Hello?"

"I broke the deal," she said at last.

"I know."

"And now I'm a little confused." She paused again. "You don't like me?"

"I like you, Lilly."

"So what's the problem?"

"The problem is with me." He stopped. He thought a long time. She was patient and didn't interrupt him. "Have you ever been in a situation where the only thing that ever mattered to you, even if you didn't know it at the time, was so close you could taste it?"

"Yes…Daniel."

"But you lost it. You had it. You lost it. And now you can't live without it anymore?"

"Yes."

"So what do you do?"

"Don't you think I'm trying to figure that out every single day?"

"Yes, Lilly, I know. I am too. But sometimes I get stuck."

"Like the other night."

"And I can't go on."

"I see," she said slowly.

"No, Lilly. That's not what I mean."

"I understand."

"I mean it gets in the way. It gets in the way of me having what I want in my life. The past. The things that happened. I don't know if I can get over it."

Long pause. And yet, even on the telephone, a comfortable silence.

"You know what I think, Daniel?" she began. "It was a woman, right? Someone you can't live without?"

"Yes."

"Don't you think what's more important is that you felt something? Lost or found, it means you're still alive. At least that's what I tell myself."

"I'm trying to believe that. Trying to stay engaged and not retreat back into my cave. So here's the deal." *Open your mouth. Words fall out.*

"New deal?"

"New deal. I just figured something out about myself. I really appreciate that you showed me a part of your life last week. I learned a lot about you. And a little about football. Now I want to show you a part of my life. There's a show, a musical, at the Colonial Theatre. I want you to go with me."

"Do I have to paint my face?"

"No. No face painting allowed."

"It only seems fair somehow."

"No face painting. No brothers. No alcohol. Well, maybe a little wine. And no kissing either."

"Oh…that's the deal, then?"

"And no blue jeans. Dress up. You have a dress, right?"

"Strangely enough, I even have a dress."

"I just mean, well, I've never seen you wear a dress."

"I think there's quite a few things you don't know about me."

IT WAS AN INDIAN SUMMER NIGHT ON A SUNDAY, tauntingly warm as the New England autumn sometimes offers when it hesitates to plunge into the changing tide of winter's coming as even sturdy New England children will often hesitate at the cold water's edge that time of year.

Laurel also hesitated at Daniel's office door, checking her hair. *Now that I have him out of the office I wonder whether I will like him or not?* She said to herself. *He hasn't ever shown any hint of being a literary man. I don't even know if he likes poetry or is the kind of man who can be moved by art and beauty. Maybe outside of his consulting room he's going to turn out to be as boring as the other analysts?*

On the other hand, when he shows those glimpses of himself things get interesting. The office door sprung open at last and Daniel turned to greet her in his best black tux. He seemed taller than she remembered, reminding her how a well-cut tuxedo can make any man seem somehow larger than he is.

Okay, this is interesting. I knew he wasn't born frumpy. Good thing I wore the heels. She smiled at him approvingly. And the thought sneaked in faster than she could block it out of her conscious mind—*I wonder if he'll kiss me tonight? No, it would be too soon. And yet, with guys like this you can't wait for them to make the first move.*

"You've been to the theater before, I see."

"The theater. The symphony. Things I enjoy," he said.

"Shall we go?"

Daniel held the elevator door for her as she brushed by him with the long line of her shoulder rounded in the backless dress. In spite of himself he sighed, turning away.

"You look different, tonight. Lovely. Let me pay you for the tickets."

"My treat, Daniel. You should get out more. Introverts forget that having a little fun can do wonders."

"No. I insist. Let me pay you. This is an educational experience, after all. A scientific experiment." He fished in his wallet for the cash.

"No. Maybe you can buy me a drink later." She decided she needed to give him a little time to get used to the idea.

When the elevator door opened, she stepped beside him on the sidewalk. *If he takes my arm, I'll know he's softening a little.*

"What a wonderful evening," he said, inhaling deeply and looking to the skyline. He brushed past her two steps on a brisk pace. "I love to walk this time of year."

"Daniel," she hollered after him in frustration, "I'm in heels!"

"But it's only four or five blocks," he began, already knowing it was a mistake. "I'm sorry. I forget these things. I'll call a cab."

She sighed. *He's hopeless!* Standing on one leg at a time, Laurel stepped down from her long heels. "A gentleman would take the lady's arm, lest she fall, and furthermore not comment on her soon-to-be torn stockings."

With a sweep of his hand, he offered his arm.

"I didn't think ahead, I'm sorry," he said thoughtfully. They turned the corner on Arlington Street toward Boylston and the theater district. "I'm realizing I've never done this before."

"But you've been to the theater?"

"Not with…a guest. How's the feet?"

"Fine. A little slower, please. I remember you had said you suffered from a libido attachment one time," she said with mischief in her eyes. "She did not like the theater?"

"I suppose I don't really know what she liked or didn't like."

"You don't know what she liked? For an analyst, I get the impression sometimes you don't know a lot about love relationships."

"That's a little bold," he said, smiling slightly. "I think I know quite a lot about it from the things other people tell me, in great detail."

"I see. Don't you think an analyst should know the most universal human experience from the inside?"

"Ah! There I would argue with you on your diploma examination."

"That an analyst should know about love?"

"That a sexual relationship is the most universal human experience. If that's what you mean…and it is. I would think the relationship with the mother is the most universal human experience, for men and for women too."

"I suppose."

"And then the father."

"Yes. Yes, the father too. But you have to know about love. Surely you don't disagree with that?"

"I know about love. And loving. And losing. I know that as well as any man."

She looked to his face. "I read your thesis. The death anima."

"That old thing? Why would anybody want to read that?"

"To understand something about you."

"About me? Not very interesting, I would think."

"That's a little defended."

"Well, fine. I think if you want to understand something about me, *The Secret Garden* will show you just about anything you want to know. Shall we go in?"

Laurel dragged at his arm long enough to totter on one leg and slip her heels on under the marquee, etched in gold, at the Colonial Theatre. *I don't understand,* she thought to herself. Who is the death anima character in *The Secret Garden?*

LILLY DIDN'T TELL HIM SHE NEEDED TO BUY A NEW DRESS for the theater. Evening apparel was not in her wardrobe. There was simply never the occasion for anything like that to have ever come into Tim and Lilly's life. It had been hard enough to get him to wear a suit and tie to his own wedding. She hadn't been to a play since high school and had never seen the magic that a Broadway crew, lives dedicated over the course of decades to a single art, could bring to life.

Her emergency call went out like a siren to the other widows, and fortunately since she had the weekend to prepare for the Monday night show, they all had the time to huddle in Filene's Basement on a Saturday morning and find the right equipment. Time enough also to design her plays. Carl opted for the better part of valor on this expedition and begged off.

Maureen wanted to dress her in red. "God, girl, what about something like an Alfred Shaheen Quant dress? See? Fits you perfectly."

"Maureen!" Paula lampooned. "Honestly. You'd look good in it, but this girl is still young. She can go with something a little tighter."

"Try the Georgette Wrap dress." Lilly dutifully tried it on, squeezing in, flaunting her shoulders in the sheer lavender chiffon.

"Oh! Oh my!" said Donna. "Look at this. It has a button-close draped wrap back."

"And these wonderful appliqués, sequins and Swarovski crystals. Stand back."

They scrutinized her with intense womanly assessment.

Lilly smiled, then pouted.

"I don't know."

"Hmmm," said Paula, taking the fabric in her fingers. "It's not a wedding, girls. It's a play."

Maureen sighed, still disappointed she could not make any ground on her attachment to red dresses. "When in doubt, all black and all back."

"I guess."

Donna trolled out a Gabardine Little Black Dress, cut with a side vent in the asymmetrical hemline. The bateau neckline flattered Lilly's long neck.

"But she's gonna need the right purse."

And they all flew off happily and spent the rest of the morning fitting her out like a little sister on her first date.

When the evening came, still warm enough that she was having trouble deciding whether or not to wear the jacket the widows had argued over for an hour, Lilly finished her appointments early and dressed at the salon without going home. Without eating dinner. *Odd, he didn't say anything about dinner.* She was too nervous to eat anyway. It struck her, too late, that she had better meet him outside or the girls in the salon were going to give her grief for weeks to come. On the other hand, they would find a way to see him inside or outside, and, for that matter, she wanted them to see him. Still, thinking now of Daniel, after what had happened she decided perhaps it was better not to embarrass him any further.

Ten minutes early he breezed through the door in his Marks and Spencer black tux. Without a doubt, he was the only man who had walked through that door in ten years wearing such an elegant tuxedo.

Every eye, every one of them feminine, turned toward him. Water from rinsed hair splashed on the floor as heads were raised and turned. Daniel stopped dead in his tracks, unsure what to do with his hands. Finally he unbuttoned his jacket and fingered his suspenders nervously.

"Is Lilly Summers here?"

"Daniel!" she whispered too loudly from behind the wall in the employees lounge. "You're early."

He glanced at his watch, bewildered. "Maybe I'll wait outside then."

"No. Just a sec." She shuffled through the makeup on the counter looking for her purse and just left everything where it was. "All set."

When he saw her in the black dress—shoulders, back, and legs new to him, coming out from under jeans and blouses she had always worn—he instantly mistook her for a lady who had graced a thousand dinner parties all her life. She could see it his eyes, but couldn't decide if she wanted him to say it out loud in front of all of them or not. All the women sighed silently.

"You look lovely, Lilly," he said as they passed through the door. The women heard it nevertheless. They were listening for it.

The chauffeur opened the door to the limo for her gracefully.

"You got a limo?"

"Well, normally I'd walk or take the T. Don't own a car. But I thought you might have heels, or something."

"Heels. A dress. A little jewelry. The obvious. Honestly, Daniel."

"Good thing I got the limo then."

"No car?"

"Don't need it. I have access to an old Lincoln if I wanted to get out of town."

She tried not to look at him in the limo. It was hard enough to keep her mind off of herself—the dress, the purse, the shoes—so that she wouldn't think about what she was actually doing. *No.* She couldn't think about it. She had only to act, to be doing this, willing herself forward without once looking back to contemplate what it meant. *No, Lilly. Don't stop to think. Just keep moving. Just keep breathing. Just keep going.*

In the swirl of lights at the theater she took a deep breath. One quick step out the door of the limo and she found herself surrounded in shining elegance she had only seen on television. Couples chatted amiably, arm in arm, laughing through the open doors.

"Are you ready for this?" Daniel asked, smiling.

"It's a little overwhelming."

"I have to admit, this is a little more daunting than I had thought it would be. I'm usually alone, you see."

"So am I, Daniel."

"Well, aren't we a pair, then?"

"I'm ready if you are."

He took her arm and guided her along into the crowded foyer, a bright lively party sparkling in the gilded golden ceiling work and sconces. High above, the massive crystal chandelier, a holdover from another century, seemed to Lilly like a star-burst holiday display trickling down out of the sky in delicate fingers of color. She clung to his arm, passing into the boxes, her breath stopping as the wide hall leaped above her in turrets and arches and carved Grecian lintels. As the houselights went down, she turned to him, still clutching his arm.

"Thank you, Daniel." He smiled, looking away.

Lilly, enfolded in sound, relaxed. Everything about the stage was larger than life—the lights, the music so large and surrounding, the voices and costumes. She could not help but think now of what she had labored so hard this evening not to think. That her life as she had known it had been so small and somehow she had always strained against it, like clothes and shoes and worn-out jackets that she had long outgrown; as if her heart, too large and too strong for the clinging body that had for so long contained it, was finally finding its place in the world.

THE THEATER IS DARK, AS THE MIND IS DARK. There exists therein only form and possibility. So one must remove oneself from daylight things and retire into sleepy silence undistracted by chattering thoughts and swirling crowds and dazzling clothes for these things only show the outer appearance of people's lives, only the way in which they wish to present themselves.

But the theater, the dreaming dream as it dreams itself to life alive and present, shows the inner aspect. The theater, like a dream, shows the deeper situation in its timeless form. Half-thought, yawning, we tell ourselves that we live what we live in our lives by choice. That we make our own way. That our actions are unscripted, our paths unmapped, each and every encounter unrehearsed. This is a pleasant fiction.

The truth is more dramatic. We play ourselves, in character, more or less. We find ourselves in scenes that we did not ourselves create. We speak our lines as from another's mouth without even knowing the meaning of the plot that unfolds from the hands of an unseen director.

And so it is well to sit in the theater and watch ourselves as from above on the stage below because it is only from that perspective that our grave and constant sadness can be seen for the tragedy that it truly is; and, being seen, ennobled by that very act of awareness because it joins our little lives with that larger life that also plays in us and goes on playing itself out from age to age, audience to audience, and never dims or loses its essential meaning, but springs fresh from the dark stage once more.

It helps to see ourselves on stage. Theater is the original therapy, a healing ceremony of mythic figures showing us who we really are. Frau Delarosa had hoped that Daniel would see that picture of himself and recognize it as an image of what ailed him.

In the dark, a sound. An opening theme plays in chords that are already sad, but somehow also sweet, sweet as the white summer dress with lace and frills that flows from the pretty young mother as she swings from a long rope swing in the June, blossoming garden while the stage lights come up. She is a ghost, dead these many years from her fall upon that very swing. She watches over her garden, now long abandoned; over her husband, also long abandoned, and over her son, whom she will never abandon.

And soon another ghost, outlandish and foreign, in the garb of his native India, sings an odd song with exotic intervals. He is the Fakir, a Holy Man, weaving his strange maya over the scene and dancing as the Shiva, destroyer and renewer of the world. He conjures a memory, an image from the past of a party in the British East Indies in 1906 where a little girl waits alone. And waits some more. And waits alone.

For they are dead. All of them. Lily, the young mother on her swing back in Yorkshire, and Rose her sister, off in India with her military husband. All dead from the cholera. All dead, but one. Mistress Mary Lenox, quite contrary, found by herself alone in her room the night of the party.

Odd, to see the truth of it dressed in white and following the actors on stage like a Greek chorus, crowding every moment, singing gloomy songs in a way that Frances Hodgson Burnett would not have imagined. Or perhaps she did, transposing her novels for the stage herself as quickly as she finished them. But no, she would have found the dead too fearful. And yet Marsha Norman, writing the libretto, insisted that while adults try not to talk about it children are curious about death and don't want to be lied to.

And neither did Daniel. He liked the ghosts the best. Every time he saw them they walked straight out of his imagination with arms extended, old friends and his lover, beckoning him like the figures in his sandtray with Frau Delarosa long ago.

She had been right to make him see the play. Right to make him confront his ghosts. But Frau Delarosa could never have known how his heart leapt to see her on stage, to see her restored, alive and vital, in the character of a lovely and engaging woman with a sweet siren's voice. His mother. Lily, as Marsha Norman had created her and given shape to a mother's love.

He couldn't stop himself. Not from the first time he saw the play. Not for the twentieth time. It was his mother's voice he heard when Lily sang, her touch he felt nestled secretly in her arms in that faraway garden safe and untouchable behind those stone walls. It was the only way he could be touched. The sound of her ghostly voice was the warmest feeling he could feel, wet on his cheeks, and if any woman could have ever seen this in him she would have observed him waltzing alone, hands outstretched, like Archibald Craven in Scene Two of the first act dancing with the circling ghosts.

Daniel did not fight the tears anymore. That scene was always his undoing. Archie is remembering his Lily, a girl in the garden, the day they first met. And though they are separated by the wide length of the stage, they sing of each other and their love. Happy memories of flowers and picnics together, as it once had been. They circle, never touching, weaving in and out among the waltzing ghosts, until Archie joins them, partners spinning from gentleman to gentleman until at last he almost holds her, just at the moment when Mary Lennox interrupts him, tearing him away from his revelry with empty arms alone in an empty ballroom on a lonely night. It was a feeling Daniel knew very well.

"But I want to know what happens to dead people," Mary Lennox demands. "Do all dead people turn into ghosts?"

Laurel contemplated this tortured man. In the dim light, she saw Daniel's wet eyes, his face so sad it broke her heart, and yet that same sad face lifted up to the stage in joy, in the seeking of joy so close he might have raised a finger reaching out to touch it. Torn, then, in nearness and separation, she watched him struggle with the weight of it.

How could one man be so sad? In a way that she had never seen before his lonely heart was opened to her. She had never seen how a man could be so lost. It made her want to touch him, because in touching him she could somehow save him.

Laurel touched his hand, in spite of herself, drawn by his pain. His hand was hot, feverishly hot, as though he were himself on the stage below under the fierce hot lights. He did not acknowledge her, would not pull himself away. He only sat as if in a trance until the scene ended as Archie walked away and the little girl scolded him. At the scene change Daniel gently withdrew his hand, fumbling in his jacket for a handkerchief he always brought just for the occasion, and dried his tears.

Ten year-old Mary Lennox stood on the stage directly below Laurel, her long hair covering her face in the same way Laurel's hair often covered her pain. *Why won't the man see her?* Laurel thought. *It's all the girl really needs from him.* In spite of herself, she was touched by the magic of the theater.

In a way she had never apprehended before, Laurel finally grasped her deepest connection to *The Secret Garden*. She could see it standing now right in front of her in the form of Mary Lennox with her Pinafore dress, hands clasped shyly behind her back, ten years-old and starring up at her gloomy Uncle Archie. He is tall, towering and remote like a misty mountain wrapping itself in clouds too thick to ever penetrate, while she, so impossibly small and insignificant at his feet, only wants the simplest questions answered and can only shake her head at these adults all around her who for reasons she cannot even contemplate make themselves so oblivious and so distant.

As Mary Lennox pleads her case on the stage below at last Laurel can understand her own inscrutable father. Laurel stands before her father, just as Mary Lennox stands before Archie. *Don't send me away. See me. Notice me. Acknowledge my existence.* It's all she wants.

Atya. Apa. Pater! Because she could imagine him happy again. Happy with her. She has learned, long ago, that what a sad man needs most, a man like her father, is to forget his troubles. Atva lives in the past, clings to the past, because he has seen nothing better to live for. *Atva watch me. Atva embrace me. Let me play for you and you shall be whole again. Whole and warm and loving and tender as I have seen in you even when you can no longer see it in yourself. This I can do. For you, Atva. Let me help you.*

She would be like an opening door for him, a light descending into his dark cave to show him the way home. Unlocking him. Turning his life around. Saving him from himself, from Hungary and the Russians.

And what then, Mary Lennox? What then, Laurel Wolff? What will you have achieved when you have reached down there deep in his darkest heart and willed him back to life with the cost of your own?

Because if I could be his opening angel then he would surely love me. Love me forever. Love me with the fierce strength of a once-damned man who has been brought back from the edge to live again. How could he not love me after so great a gift as I would make for him?

But she was not wanted. Her gift, denied. Archie turns his back to her and leaves her silent on the stage.

And that wound, that aching longing spilled there on the floor and left, unheeded, was more real to her in that moment under the stage lights than it had ever been before. So it was Laurel who found her own bitter tears now, turning away from Daniel so that he would not see her cry. So that he could not see her unbearable bitterness, like little Mary Lennox. The unwanted child, left to play by herself alone. Unseen. Unremembered. And undone. Unbearably, bitterly alone.

AT THE INTERMISSION, DANIEL WAS LOST INSIDE HIMSELF. His usual habit was to silently take his place in the line at the wine bar, hiding himself, not engaging anyone, and sip a dark Merlot in the quietest corner he could find. Blindly following his ritual, Laurel followed him, needing to order her wine for herself when he walked away.

This was certainly not what she had expected, expected from a staged *Secret Garden* or expected from Daniel. He was, if anything, more inaccessible than she found him in his office. And at the same time more available emotionally than she had ever seen. Surely he knew that she had been watching him, watching his sad entrancement and his wet eager eyes, always on the stage.

Joining him finally, wine at hand, she approached carefully.

"There are ghosts?"

"Yes, in the play there are ghosts."

"That's quite a change from the story. The play is different than the book."

"Artistic license, I guess."

"It's not a children's story any more. The leads are Archie and Lily, a man and wife and their love."

"Yes. In the play it's about adult problems."

"And Mary's problems with these adults." She sipped her wine, contemplating how to say this to him. "Daniel, what happened to you? It seems to make you very sad."

"My mother died. I was eighteen."

"I'm sorry to hear that." She hesitated. "And this show makes you think of her?"

"Yes. Doesn't this play make you think of someone you have known?"

"Yes." She paused, thinking of Atva. "I get the sense you've seen this play before. You've known it all along."

"I was trying to find the right time to tell you. Yes. *The Secret Garden* is very important to me. This is my experiment, sharing myself, letting you see me when I am like this."

"I know. Part of your process."

"But Laurel, you have to give me some space. It's not something I can talk about right now. Maybe after. Or maybe not."

Daniel found it very strange to be sharing something so intimate, so private. Only the smallest part of himself could observe himself crying gently there in his seat and being seen by another person. The intricacies of remembering another person sitting beside him were unknown and untried, because he had not risked showing himself since that day, that very last day with his mother laughing and talking on the bed so long ago.

He had hidden himself even from Frau Delarosa and the closest he had come to pulling back the curtain to his inner treasure was that day with her in the consulting room with his sandtray figures. The day she had the wisdom not to speak. It was as close as he could get, as close as he would let her come to that part of himself that was most himself.

People say that the risk of sexual intimacy is the closest two hearts may come, soul pressed close to soul as aching flesh allows. But closer still is not the act of sex, but the fantasy of what might be shared. Closer because it is more vulnerable. More vulnerable because it is closer to the truth. This is what it means to be naked.

And Daniel was risking it now because even after all the wounding he had suffered that minute part of himself still flickered with the tiniest of hope that perhaps just once more in his life he could be truly known, and in that knowing, no longer alone. After so many years alone, sharing his private play had been a gamble all along. Laurel had put the question. *Are you ever going to share yourself?*

And perhaps that was the meaning of their relationship to him, the risk he had accepted on that first night back at the Institute party, that Laurel would actually succeed in prying him open as she meant to do, as she was born to do for men like him, because he knew it meant the time had come to let himself become a man, not a doctor, and see if there was anything still there after all these years.

Now Lilly was quite a different problem. By the strangest of coincidences, the crisis had been forced upon him seemingly from the outside when he lost his medical license, suspending the doctor in him long enough for him to be just a man.

The crisis was simply Life saying *I will take this away from you now.* And his reaction to it was simply *Fine, I will find something else then.* And lo and behold that something was Lilly Summers out of the blue, never knowing him as a doctor with all its hang-ups and presumptions.

So the question with Lilly was more basic, and by being so basic left him no room to wiggle out of it. *Did he want her? Did she want him? What next then?*

What next was the play. The play, the limo, the tux, and the dress. Two people sharing life and getting to know each other. *Does it work?* Forget the complexes. Forget what they are each struggling with in their own way. Doesn't matter. *A man. A woman. Does it work?* Only one way to find out. Hence, the risk.

"It's so sad," Lilly said, standing with him at the same wine bar the following evening.

"Yes, a sad play. A sad story. But there is hope."

Lilly was still caught in the magic of the show, touched by the music more than anything else. Music had always given her a vocabulary for all the words she did not know.

Sometimes when she played her guitar the chords were words. The harmonies could speak of lifting up and triumphant joy, or sometimes of deep dark valleys that had no other name. The music was her way. The music was her voice when she did not have a voice.

And did the music move Daniel too? Could he possibly feel the same landscape it was painting that she felt, like a moving picture? When they stood in the corner with their drinks he was very quiet. As the lights flickered for the second act, she looked up. He finally spoke.

"That means it's time for us to return to our seats. The second act will begin soon." As they shuffled through the rows, she asked him,

"Daniel, why did you bring me to the show?"

"Because something happened to me, Lilly."

"Something sad? Like the show?"

"My mother died. I was eighteen."

"Oh…I am so sorry…So this play must be difficult for you."

"Yes, close to home." He paused. "But I like it that way."

"It makes you sad?"

"The play makes me sad. And happy…Strange, I guess." He took his seat.

"And she was the woman you lost, the person you mentioned on the phone?"

"Yes, Lilly. I loved her very much."

"And her name is Lily too. The mother in the show. Is that why you wanted me to see the show with you?"

"In a way." Daniel looked away from her. "I just wanted you to know why things are so hard for me sometimes. I don't know how else to tell you."

LILLY COULD NOT HAVE KNOWN UNTIL THAT NIGHT just how much the live music added to the experience. The actors, living people close enough that she could see their iris eyes and breath on their cheeks, were so much more real than characters in movies. The magic of the theater is that it is so fully human. And as the curtain rose on the second act and Lilly saw the little girl on stage, so real, so vulnerable, her voice quivering with a heart fully open, Lilly was transported as if she herself were also singing on that stage, alone, surrounded by the ghosts that would not let her be.

There's something about seeing the ghosts on stage. Something very real. We too are crowded by ghosts. If we could only see them streaming by like holiday crowds on a busy street in Boston bunched together at the corner waiting for a light, jostling and bumping, we might just once start to see our life as it really is — that we are so easily crowded by the past, somehow taller than we are, so that it becomes difficult to see the way forward.

Lilly saw the ghosts, watching Mary Lennox stand alone and sing, but not alone. She could not help but see herself as she had been these last three years, alone and surrounded, seeking a place inside herself to somehow become herself amidst this crowd of ghosts who would not go away. She could not believe or understand how it was possible that a girl like Mary Lennox, forlorn and lost, could hold herself against their crowding, to see portrayed on the stage her own lonely struggle. It's so difficult to wrestle with something other people do not understand. You try to tell them sometimes, because of the loneliness of it all. Try to break out of the shell of silence.

And if Lilly could sing as Mary Lennox was singing, if she could write a song like this song and put herself on stage there, head down, with nothing but her guitar and her voice in a single spotlight that melted away all the inessentials so that the only song and the only voice was a song of pure desire, white hot, sung in a voice as naked as a soul, what would her soul sing?

I shall not be defeated. I refuse defeat. I shall not be stopped in my assent up from the confinement of my birth. Not by 9/11. Not by people and worlds and habits that are too small for me. I shall with unrelenting drive break every chain and shackle and rise up from this place until I reach the full expression of myself that shall not be denied.

She did not, could not, know these things, too deep for words. She only felt it in the music, washing over her unexpectedly in the theater seat like her tears; and there had been so many tears, and yet, the tears that night did not belong to the past or to the ghosts, because all the other tears on all the other nights had been tears for what was lost. These new tears flowed from a cleaner place, the clear spring bubbling up from the ground of herself flowing outward and away down a path that was the place where she must go.

Lilly, head in her hands, looked up. In the soft, reflected light of the corner sconces, she saw Daniel lost in his trance. *So that's what it is,* she realized. *That's what is it about him I recognized the day I first met him. He's lost someone, like me, and hasn't found a way to move on. I wonder if he'll ever get over it? I wonder if I will myself?*

Below her, Archibald Craven sits in a rocking chair deep in the night beside his invalid and sleeping son Colin reading from a story book. He loves the boy but in the strange logic of his grief his love is only a nighttime presence, unacknowledged and un-acknowledgeable in the daylight hours.

In this scene Daniel always thinks of his own father and the gulf that was always between them; tenderness and love Daniel always felt from him somewhere, but only like a dream, and an unremembered dream at that, because he would only wake in the morning with a certain feeling, a taste in his mouth that vanished when he opened his eyes to find his unknown father already gone.

Only in the second act could Daniel identify with a boy hidden away in a room from the rest of the household, crying alone in the night. Because of his absent father.

And now, coming quickly in another dream on that dark stage, another revenant appeared. Her coming to his bed filled Daniel with dread he could almost not endure. Colin's absent mother. Lily in her terrible ghostly presence, all the more terrible because she came lovingly, sweetly, tenderly to beckon her son. The first time he had seen the play, before he knew what was coming, he was unprepared. When she entered the room it was as real to him as if he were back in his bed on Beacon Hill and she had materialized through the closed door, arms outstretched, so that his heart raced so wildly he could have died right there in panic and fear.

But now, now for the twentieth time entering fully into this moment, in enduring her presence and facing his fear, he could talk to her. He could say what he had to say, needed desperately to say to her, and know that he had been heard. That was why he came to the play, time after time, his private confession with her after so many years. He came for this very scene so that he could talk to her.

Arms outstretched, the ghost mother in her white dress calls to him, her beneficent intent reaching out from beyond death to heal him and to help him, willing him to health. *Rise. Rise and walk my son!* This was the moment. This was the miracle. *For all that you have lost, I wish you well. For all that you have suffered, you must rise again and walk and grow and love.*

This was the devastating insight of his healing. Her telling him not to linger. Her releasing him from her own spell. A dangerous and necessary illusion, as Frau Delarosa had seen it even back then, of conversations with the dead, and of having-it-out. "*Doch*, Herr Doctor, *eine Auseinandersetzung!* This is the only way," she insisted. But he couldn't do it. Not in his analysis. He couldn't have that imaginary and necessary conversion. Only here. Only here in the theater with the right lighting and the props and the costumes, and most of all the living presence of a woman who beckoned him with her song.

Mother, he cried, but I have been so long in this bed. I do not know how to walk again, how to love again. *I will help you*, she whispered. But how, Mother? How can I go on without you? There is nothing left to live for.

You will love again, my son, when you feel joy. You must seek joy. When you feel held again, the joy will be the miracle. But you must get up out of your bed. You must stand on your own two feet and seek it.

And what is joy? I have not known joy in so, so long. I have forgotten the taste of it. I have known only pain and sorrow.

Joy, my son, is the reunion of things large and small. Mother and son. The birth of a child. The reunion of something that was once one. Something from the inside that has come into being and now greets you smiling. This is my wish for you, that after all your long suffering you will find the world still full of grace.

The nearness of grace. This was Daniel's only prayer. That the world, like a mother, might still smile and bless what is given and what is suffered. The smell of blessing like a window that opens unexpectedly on a dark day, and the sun shines in. And fresh, spring air fills the winter's gloom. There is no other prayer.

WHEN AT FIFTY-NINE YEARS-OF-AGE FRANCIS HODGSON BURNETT wrote *The Secret Garden* in the spring of 1909, she could not have known when she began that she would discover, in her own story, the presence of her dead son. So from the very beginning *The Secret Garden* has always been about the dream of a conversation between the living and the dead. Yes, yes it was her Christian Science and New Thought and the comfort it gave her, it is true, but in the spiritualism of those times the living can speak to the dead.

The only mention of it in the book is ten pages from the end, when Archibald Craven finds himself, having wandered all of Europe, at a valley in the Austrian Tyrol beside a little clear stream. Almost asleep, he finds himself, quite without thinking about it, noticing "things growing at its edge." Blue forget-me-nots. And now, you see, somehow touched by "the wonderfulness of undiscovered things," as Burnett writes, he has a dream—the "real-real dream" in which he heard a voice calling "Archie! Archie! Archie!" seeming very far away, but so distinctly it could have been by his side. And he answers her, "Lilias! Where are you?"

"In the garden," She clearly said. "In the garden."

In the magic of Broadway, this reunion is too important to overlook. And so it is staged to have Archie crying out in his torment as he sings "Where in the world can I live without your love?" just as Lily appears. And in this one searing emotional climax of the whole play, each and every time the director must decide whether, for the first time in the show, Archie and Lily may embrace during their duet. Many directors seem to want to keep the tension of the almost-touching, the forever distance of the living and the dead. But most directors, giving the audience what they really want, after all, allow the pair this one reunion, this one kiss, this last reconciliation.

Lily sings on stage what the heart of grief yearns most passionately to hear: forgiveness, release, and blessing. And inevitably, in a most private way and yet without fail, there are always people in the audience having conversations of their own, saying what they must say to their own dead. You can hear it in the aisles.

And now Laurel too, through her tears, was seeing her own father, whom she had missed so terribly without ever realizing what ailed her. *Why wouldn't you let me get close to you, Atva?* she said, like a prayer. *Why do you keep me from you when I need you so much?*

Because I failed you, little lanya.

How Atva? How could you ever have failed me?

Because I took away your birthright. I lost it to the Russians. You might have had art and music and honor.

But I have had all of those things, Atva. You gave them to me.

My lanya, we were so poor. We were so lost. I have always feared the refugee camps had ruined you.

No Atva. I have survived. The only thing that I have ever wanted that I did not have is you.

But I loved you! I would have thrown my life away to annoy the Russians but I could not leave you, my lanya. It was for you. I left all that I loved for you to have your chance.

And I did, Atva. I did. You succeeded.

But do you love me now?

I love you, Atva. I have always loved you.

Then you must return, my little lanya. For my sake. You must return to Hungary and reclaim the life that I have sacrificed.

I will, Atva. I will. I will go home and be with you.

Laurel did not see the rest of the play. She was lost and far away in her own thoughts. She even missed what had been her chief concern and complaint with Frances Hodgson Burnett—that Mary Lennox was forgotten in the end, swallowed up in the complex of Frances Hodgson Burnett's obsession with her son. For on the stage the playwright set it right and has Archie on his knee finally remembering Mary Lennox and promising her the Secret Garden forever.

WHEN LILLY'S TURN TO FACE HER OWN GHOSTS came the following evening, she was lost in the magic of the play and of the music, utterly unaware of Daniel. Archie's song undid her. *Where in the world, tell me*

where in the world, can I live without your love now that you are gone? Every feeling of that blue September day came rushing back to her. Every day after was September 12, as Maureen had told her. It was more than she could bear.

Until Lily appeared. *Until Lilly appeared.* The music, aching, cut straight into her soul, building, swelling as she sang reaching for him, always reaching and for the first time touching him, taking him in her arms at last, reunited. The dead and the living, reunited in the magic of the dark stage and having that one last chance, in spite of everything, to say what needed to be said.

Tim? Her heart pounded, afraid and overjoyed. His eyes blue, as they were always blue. His shoulders strong, a head above hers, and holding her tight against his chest with such a deep love that she had never doubted. No. Not his love for her. Even with everything that had bothered her in her moments of fighting his embrace she had never doubted, even once, that it was she, Lilly, who needed to find herself apart from him because he had always from the very beginning found himself in her.

Tim. Don't you have anything to say to me now that we're apart?

He smiles. He smiles his great smile, unchanged by anything. His blue eyes hold her as tight as his strong arms and looking there, soul across soul, she sees that he is complete. He is still complete and whole and unbroken. He is a man who had everything he ever wanted, in her, and 9/11 cannot take that away from him, did not take that away from him, and now in this final moment he has no regrets. Only love. There is nothing to say, but thanks. There is only what she has to say to him.

Tim, you surround my every breath. Every memory. Every day. You are more of a presence in my life today than you were on the day I married you. All my tears have given you a depth that you would never have had if you were still coming in the door for dinner. You've become the inescapable fact of my life. They say the living hold the dead in their hearts and yet I can't help but feel just how fiercely you cling to me, how much you moan when I change our lives as they might have been, or even disturb the picture, still gathering dust in an unchanged room, of how things were when we were together.

But Tim, you have to let me go. I can't breathe. I'm suffocating in this cocoon of sacred widowhood, this halo of your sainthood descending like a steel band to imprison me in your unknowing sacrifice. How can you possibly understand what it has been like for me? I've become your better half, half dead with you, and buried in the ground with you up to my waist at the foot of your grave facing your headstone. That is not a life, Tim. That is half a life.

I think you fear you would dissolve away to nothing if I gave your things away, sold the house, and bought new furniture. Some other family would walk your halls, watch TV in your chair, and sleep in your bed. And they would never know who you were, how you lived, what you had done in your life. There would be no trace left of the life you and I once shared. Not even the children we might have had. I know, Tim. I know because I fear it too. Every day.

I understand what love is now, Tim. I understand it in a deeper way through your death than I could ever have understood it living a life with you. When we were together I thought that love was sacrifice, the way I had to sacrifice myself to be with you. I thought it made me happy to give myself away for you. But now I see that love is gratitude. Now that you are gone I am grateful for every single day you spent with me in a life we never dreamed would be so short and it fills me with such great love.

I was not grateful enough, Tim. I felt too cheated. I felt like you were taking something away from me and when you died I felt the greatest thing had been taken away from me. And I couldn't love you that way.

I guess this is the other side of my grief, because I could be a widow forever if I hold on to what I lost that day. No more. I saw how to turn it all over. I love you more today than I have ever loved you and I will light a candle for you every year on our wedding day and I will remember the little time we had together and I will be filled with gratitude and love you all over again. Always.

And wherever you are, you must light a candle for me too. If you love me, Tim, if you love me as much as I love you now, you will let go of what we have lost and you will light a candle and feel a deep, joyous appreciation for what my life was, and for what it is still beating in my breast. Then I will honor that. Then I will wake up every morning and sing.

CHAPTER TEN

It Has Come

SYCHOANALYSIS IS AN ATTITUDE OF THE MIND. IT IS A commitment to accept the truth of a human life for all that is it, wholly and completely. And it is always dark, dark with what we push away and hide when truth disturbs the way in which we wish to see ourselves, and darker still when the truth is too deep for words and thoughts that do not even have a name. Can we remember this? Can we endure the truth of our whole selves?

Psychoanalysis remembers that every single great idea that ever changed our history, men and women of courage pulling us forward, owes its debt to the life of the single struggling individual—each little life bearing the weight of loss and struggle and doubt, of inward pain, of the inner wounds of childhood, of love risked, of illnesses endured, of private hopes and dreams laid down on the line and suffered. Not a one of them escaped life's demands. Many perished, swept away by larger forces both without themselves and within, that they did not understand. Little lives taking their place in larger patterns.

"YOU'RE A MESS," DANIEL SAID, Laurel clinging on his arm in the flow of the crowd out from the dark theater into the too bright foyer. She fumbled through her purse to find something to touch up her face, her mascara, her red eyes.

"So are you," Laurel replied. "You didn't warn me this was going to be so intense. Daniel, I need to talk. I need to go somewhere where we can talk about this."

"You found it intense, did you?" he said, calling a taxi as they waited.

"Yes, of course. How can you say that?"

"I don't know, Laurel. I've never discussed it with anyone else. I thought perhaps it was only me." The taxi was taking impossibly long. He shrugged, looking at her red face. "I'm sorry, I should have thought ahead. I usually walk, you know."

"I think I'm going to cry. We need to find a place where it's safe enough for me to cry. Take me to O'Reilly's. They have booths in the back behind the bar. I can put myself back together." A taxi finally opened up, and they rode the length of Chinatown over to the financial district, Laurel clutching his arm all the way. "Why don't you order while I clean my face up a bit."

"Wine then? Red or white?"

"I think I need something a little stronger. Jack Daniels. On the rocks. Straight up." She retreated to the Ladies Room.

Sitting in the booth with time to think, Daniel didn't like that all of this was so out of context for him. He did not know it, did not think ahead, but after the play it was clear to him for the first time what he needed to do for Laurel.

Ordering her Jack Daniels and a little Merlot for himself, he realized he could never have talked to her this way in the office.

Returning to the table Laurel found him alone with his wine, looking rather sad, still, and retreating into frumpiness, his tie undone and hanging loose, jacket laid aside.

"I didn't know you had this other side," she began carefully. "A passionate side."

"Passionate?"

"The play. The way it moved you."

Daniel sipped his drink. "I find it very interior and very private. I have never shared it with anyone else…but I'm beginning to think it's time I shared it."

"I couldn't tell what was going on with you."

"Wrestling with the ghosts, I guess."

"Daniel, I am so pleased you let me see you. I think I understand you now. But it pains me to see you so sad." The next phase, as she had learned in her long study of introverted men, was to get him talking about himself. The long soliloquy. "I hope you would feel like sometimes you can share your burden."

He caught her eye, looking up from his drink.

"Laurel, have you ever lost a patient?" he began, very slowly. "I've been thinking about this a lot lately. David. His name was David. You know what one of the best things about psychoanalysis is? It's how close you get to people. What they're up against in life. What ails them. And sometimes, in the best patients, I guess…not all of them…you can see them, really see them, feel the weight on their shoulders. And they see you seeing them…maybe in a way it's all you really want, to be seen so clearly under the weight that you bear, and then to know somehow that another person sitting over there in that chair across from you has been penetrated by that weight too. You can see it gets to him. The analyst suffering with you.

"…and when it's like that I sometimes get a glimpse of my analysand's courage. I don't know what else to call it. I don't know how to describe it. It's like those runners at the Boston Marathon. Not the professionals. The regular folks. The average runners. It's like the end of the race, a mile out or something, when you see them out there on Commonwealth Avenue staggering. You know, a leg muscle cramps and they're crying out, swearing, dragging that leg behind them. Sweating. Stumbling. Eyes fading. God, I have seen people like that struggling so hard.

"They won't quit, you know? They don't quit. Their body already gave out back on Heartbreak Hill…they reached that limit of endurance…limit of human endurance and, you know, still they don't stop. God, I've seen them fall down right there, right on the asphalt and then…and then they're crawling, they're howling…and the people on the side of the street are bending over them, you know…words of encouragement from strangers…*don't stop. You can do it. So close now. You're so close.*

"That's me, Laurel. Their analyst. I'm their running partner, you know, one of those guys who jumps in five miles from the finish of the race and who's already dying there way before the finish line, because he can't really run, not like that, not like they can…but I stay with them. I stay right there with them, down on my hands and knees too if I have to. I'm crawling right beside them, head to head, eye to eye.

"And you know why I do that? Why I really do it? To see that look in their eyes. To see them looking ahead, eyes straight ahead, like they're already there. Like they're already on Boylston Street and that finish line is right in front them. They're there. They're right there…it's just that their damn body won't believe it…won't follow fast enough where their spirits have already gone.

"That's courage, Laurel. That's the courage of my patients. It's amazing. It's the most amazing thing I know.

"And when I see that courage…when I see that fight in them, I have hope. That's what it is. I have hope I maybe could have courage like that too. Even just a little. To do what I have to do. I don't know…I don't know if I have or if I don't have it, maybe not like that…but it gives me hope anyway…and I keep going too then. Do you understand me? Do you understand me now?"

His eyes, full of tears and far, far away like runner's eyes on the distant finish line, would not look at her but clouded themselves in white fog.

"I understand," she said through her own tears, feeling his compassion, moving closer to him on the vinyl bench. She reached for him, gently…carefully, with comforting arms to take him to her like a mother. But he pushed away from her, turning his head to hide his face so that he could say what he had to say.

"And they want to take that away from me now." He could not speak to her, but only to the wall. "They have taken my license."

"Don't let them, Daniel. Don't let them do it," she said.

"All this time, I have been thinking. I keep trying to get my head straight about David. What I did. What I could have done. He was one of those young bipolar patients. Did you ever have a patient like that? Smart. Harvard smart. Editor of the literary journal. A young man with such great promise. It's so sad…these illnesses that hit just when a young person is taking off in life. The worst. Better if they took us somehow…only not him. Not him, Laurel."

"But you tried, Daniel. You tried to save him."

"Save him? No…don't know how to save him. That's just it, Laurel. That's what I have to get straight about him. You know nowadays it's all about brain chemistry and blood levels. Lithium levels and Depakote. No room for psychoanalysis. Laurel, it was his brain, yes. His genes.

"But it's also the stress. The life he lives. The way things are. Do you know the burden that young man carried? Sent off to Harvard, sent off to do well…sent off to be the golden goose and keep his parents in money for the rest of their lives. He was that good. But at home, he was their slave…locked up in the house, literally, Laurel. Literally locked in. Not allowed to play with other children. Home-schooled. Kept to be a slave…I am not exaggerating. No. You really don't want to know how other people live. You really don't. You don't want these glimpses of what is possible. That's why they're suing me, you know. Crazy bastards. They're so pissed off because I killed their golden goose.

"Laurel, he was getting better. Clinically. And he hated that. He hated it for good reasons. His mania was his only defense. His defense against them. Against who they were, what they wanted, what they demanded of him. In his crazy mania he could shout them down and make them back away. It was the only power, the only weapon he had in that fight.

"So when we took that away from him…when I took that away from him with the lithium and we put him on that bus back home stabilized, but having to miss the rest of the semester at Harvard…he said NO. He screamed NO. Not back to them. Not defenseless. NO. He would rather die than face that kind of life.

"You know why he went to Memphis to do it? Because his mother worshiped Elvis. Filled the living room with Elvis paraphernalia. I think he wanted her to sit in that room for the rest of her life and think about him dead at Graceland.

"You know why he did it with the lithium? That was for me, I think. Sure, he was smart enough to know what it could do to him. But, it's more than that. He wanted me to know that the stuff that I was giving him was killing him."

Daniel bowed his head now, in full whimpers of pain, in full confession of what he knew. Laurel wanted so desperately in that moment to take his head in her hands, hold him close, and wipe away his tears, but he would not let her. She could see that he would not allow it, and that he never would.

"None of that comes out, you see," he continued when he could talk again. "None of that comes out at a hearing. It's not in the notes. It's not in the blood tests. It's not written down anywhere that anybody could read because nobody cares about the inner situation. Not in that context."

"It's not your fault, Daniel."

"No. It's not my fault in any legal sense. But here's the thing. I made a mistake. I made a mistake that's easy to make, and I know better. I got caught up in the race, Laurel. I got caught up in the finish line. Because he was so smart and so young and so beautiful I let myself give in to the cheering crowd and the thrill of victory and the power of the medical profession to change the circumstances of someone's life so that they can go on."

Her mind reeled. She instinctively backed away as if she might somehow make her ears close so that she would not hear him, would not think, would not see what she did not want to see, and had been refusing to see all these years in her training.

"I forgot, Laurel. I forgot the basic principle because I needed so badly to believe that you don't give up, you don't give in, you don't stop the lifetime of struggle. I need that for myself. I live by that myself. But it is not mine to impose on any other person. That is my life, but it was not his life. I forgot his basic freedom to opt out of the entire equation, Laurel. And because I was his doctor I had the power to enforce my need on him against his will and leave him no other options but the one he took."

"No, Daniel. That's too harsh."

"Oh yes. You have to see this part of it. I know you don't want to. You've fought me every step of the way and I think I realize now that you are not ever going to accept this. And as much as I would rather that somebody else...your analyst, your supervisor, your training committee...anybody but me...demand this of you, there doesn't seem to be any choice. It's not going happen unless I do it. Laurel, do you know why I am telling this story?"

She refused to answer, her whole body tightening against him.

"You are not ready to be a psychoanalyst."

"Damn you!" She burst into furious tears, hiding her face in her hair.

"There are many hang-ups an analyst can have. Lots of different wounds and pain and burdens. It doesn't have to get in the way, as long as you know it. As long as you know what ails you and understand that blind spot in your own psyche. Your weakness for a particular set of circumstances that will always make you useless, or even dangerous to other people with the same circumstances.

"But Laurel, what you suffer from and have yet to get worked out is exactly the wrong kind of motivation for this work. I can't just overlook it."

"I have worked, god damn it! You have no idea."

"You can't save them, Laurel. You can't save the patients. People can only save themselves! If they are saved at all. Sometimes the illness takes them. If it is illness. You cannot stop it. You remember what I told you? When you're down on your hands and knees with them, eye to eye, you must allow them the choice in that moment when their burden is the greatest. Because it's not your burden, Laurel. It's not your life. It's not your choice. They have to see in your eyes that you do not judge, you do not impose, you do not inflict your own disappointment when they reach the letting go. When they collapse. When they give up and never rise again."

"Damn you, Daniel. I will go around you. I will find somebody else. I will not let you get in the way."

"Sure. It's easy enough to do. I'm just one man. And people do it all the time. They slip right through the training because they're smart enough to do it. I can't do anything about that. I'm not a political type and I'm not going to go whispering to your committee or your analyst or anything like that. It's not the way I work.

"But you're going to sit here and hear me out, Laurel. Just so I know you've heard it this once. People are lost sometimes, Laurel. And sometimes Life takes them. Something happens. It is too big. And they are lost. Life is bigger than you are, Laurel. Life is bigger than us all. Some are lost. And they never recover."

"How do you know?" she said bitterly.

"I know because I have lived it. How else?"

"So they're all like you! Aren't they?"

"Fine. Say what you will. But this is only Life as it is. If you cannot accept that reality then you cannot be a psychoanalyst. No. If you live to save your patients then what will you do when they resolutely refuse to be saved? Will you berate them, as you berate me? Will you drown them in your own bitterness because of what they will not do for you?"

She still didn't want to hear it. In her fear and grief and pain she only wanted to tear him apart. A quick reflex. A cat-like instinct to finish him now that she had toyed with him long enough. She had only to extend one long claw toward his weakest spot.

"You are not my analyst!" She cried. "You are not my analyst."

"No. I'm not. I'm just reading your thesis and making comments. You have more work to do. More work on yourself. A big piece of work. So you are not finished yet."

"And what about your thesis? How good is that, then?" She tried to hurt him, wanted to hurt him. "Did you really finish it? Huh? You never answered the question. If a man is in love with his dead mother, then what does he have to live for?"

"There is left only the will to live, to struggle on. Or the death instinct. The choice of release. Of letting go. The patient cannot decide to live or to die. Something deeper weighs the balance of going on, or maybe never going on. It decides, in the end, and we have to wait for its judgment. There is no more to be done."

"And that's it?"

"That's all."

"Oh, but that's bleak, Daniel."

"No. Not really. Not to me. It's actually reassuring somehow. A greatness to it. Awful, yes. Yet, very large."

"I don't know if I can live with that."

She pushed herself back from the table, standing as she gathered her purse.

"Fair enough…But Laurel, what are you going to do? About the Institute, I mean. About the training?"

"I don't know. Why do you care, if you are so disappointed in me?"

Look at yourself, Laurel. Little Ianya, look what you are doing! She heard the voice as clearly as if he were standing beside her.

"You've been a great help to me, Laurel. Working with you has made me realize that I do love this work, difficult as it is. I miss it. I miss working with people like you. I miss all this trouble and pain, I guess, of getting to the truth. I couldn't decide what to do about the damn review board hearing. I was almost thinking that I maybe didn't have it in me anymore to be an analyst."

Look at how your own disappointment is making you hate him. You're ready to kill him. You're ready to lie about him. You're ready to inflict pain because he will not give you what you want. Because you love him.

"I know this is hard. But our time together has helped me remember what I love about being an analyst and I think maybe I am ready to fight for it now."

Laurel, stop fighting this. You know they've all been trying to tell you in one way or another for a long time and it's just that he's the only one who took the trouble to put it so plainly and was man enough to be honest with you, for once.

"So I am sincerely grateful. I was afraid, in the beginning, that you were going to just run away from it when you realized I wasn't going to take your thesis at face value. I really thought you might leave and find an easier analyst. It happens. But, to your credit you have stuck right in there. You can run away now, of course. There isn't anything else I know how to do for you. I just wanted you to know that I do care about what happens to you."

Still in tears, she turned toward the door, brushing past the waiter. Unsure of himself and how to handle this situation, he thought perhaps he needed to call a cab and see her safely home, but it struck him as a fatherly way of tending to her needs.

He needed to let her decide what she was going to do and wait for the judgment. There was no more to be done. He let her go.

ON THE FOLLOWING EVENING AFTER A LONG SLEEP, exhausted from his time with Laurel, Daniel strolled with Lilly through the noisy lobby of the Colonial Theatre out to Boylston Street where they waited by the curb for the limo in silence, both lost in their thoughts. During the long play a cold front had moved in from the northeast, as it often does in the New England autumn, pushing the summer air to the south most likely for the duration of the season. The familiar chill was bright and clean as Lilly hunched against it, arms wrapped, awkwardly enough that even Daniel noticed. He draped his jacket over her shoulders as the limo, finding its turn in the line of taxis, pulled in.

"I'm grateful, Daniel," said Lilly, smiling at long last. He held the door for her. "Thank you so much. I think I'll always remember tonight and the play."

"My pleasure."

"But I don't want to talk about it right now. I just can't talk yet. I need a few minutes."

"Yes, me too." He closed the door with a flourish and hurried to the other side.

The limo stopped at the light on Tremont Street, still busy at this hour. College students in groups passed them on the crowded sidewalks. They sat in silence as the driver continued on through Chinatown.

"Let me have the driver take you home, Lilly."

"I don't think I'm ready to go home. The play has got me all stirred up…" Daniel leaned forward to say something to the driver. They turned toward Southie. He settled into the leather seat, his eyes out the window away from her.

"You can chitchat, Daniel. I just meant nothing serious right now."

"Okay." Daniel was trying to remember how to chitchat.

Finally she had to say it herself out loud. "I'm hungry, Daniel. Aren't you?"

"I ate…" He turned to see the look on her face. "But that's a good idea. What kind of food?"

"You're the man, Daniel."

"Yes? I am the man…"

"The gentleman handles the arrangements."

"Oh…sure. Makes sense, I guess. Sea food then." He leaned forward to the driver again. "Legal Sea Foods."

The limo turned again, toward the harbor and the Aquarium. Daniel was only now realizing his mistake. He had been so focused on the play, he had forgotten about all the little things he might have done. Flowers. He should have brought flowers. He had seen movies, of course, and listened to endless hours of dating successes and fiascoes from his patients. But it was all so new to him. Daniel found himself wondering if his mother might have seen this shortcoming in his character and found a way to tell him what he needed to do, if she had been there when the time came.

Unfortunately the timing was all wrong. They could already see halfway down the block that the lights were off at the restaurant.

"Daniel, you know the way it works, you're supposed to think ahead and make reservations," she said. "That's Rule Number Two of dating."

"Ah…well actually I don't know how it works. But thanks for the tip. What's Rule Number One, by the way? Just so I'll know."

"Rule Number One: The woman is always first."

"Oh…I could have guessed that one. My mother taught me that."

"Good for her. There may be hope for you after all."

"Hmmm…I'm not really such a good date, am I? Not knowing the rules and all."

"It helps if you're teachable."

"I'm a fast learner."

"We'll see…well? I'm waiting."

"Waiting for what?"

"Back to Rule Number Two…but you better hurry."

"Thinking…Thinking…I guess this is harder than it looks. Okay, I know this one. Think ahead and make reservations."

"Think ahead, Daniel. Just simply think ahead."

"Thanks. You're very patient with me."

"Not for much longer. Think ahead…as in *right now*."

"Right…I am having trouble trying to decide how to make reservations when the restaurant is already closed. Having some difficulty there."

"Daniel. Rule Number Three...just for you...DO NOT, under any circumstances let the lady get hungry."

"Oh...That rule. Right. It's kind of late, Lilly."

"Do better."

"I mean, right, that is to say, it's kind of late but Boston is such a happening city...um, driver, Marriott Long Wharf."

"You're taking me to a hotel?"

"It's one block away, and it has a good restaurant. And if the restaurant is closed, the bar serves food 'till closing."

"Yes, but it's a hotel. On our third date? Not likely."

"Second date, but who's counting."

"I am. Third date. The Coffee House..."

"...which wasn't a Coffee House with actual coffee, as I remember. Nor was it a date, as far as I could tell."

"...The Pats game. And the play tonight. Three dates. And I invoke Rule Number One."

"The woman is always first. Right. Three dates."

"That still doesn't get you any closer to a hotel with me."

"I wasn't thinking of a hotel at all. I was only thinking of you and of Rule Number Three. The fact that the food is in a hotel has nothing to do with it. Honest to God."

"Good!"

"Right, then. Shall we eat?"

On a Monday night in early October, the restaurant at the Marriott Long Wharf was closed well before the theater crowds exited. Daniel sheepishly hurried Lilly to the bar, on a Monday night after tourist season quite empty except for the drone of Monday Night Football and a few businessmen, and found a quiet table with quick food. Daniel picked at a plate of nachos, red peppers and cheese, no meat, and tried to watch the football game with feigned interest while Lilly ate her Polynesian Chicken Wings with hot mushrooms, the only Hors d'Oeuvres available. In spite of the food, she felt better after eating, well enough to laugh out loud at the disaster.

"This is awful."

"I know. I feel so bad. I'm sorry. I'm hopeless."

"You are really gonna have to do better next time."

"There's a next time?"

"The play was fine. Better than fine. Wonderful."

"I'm glad you liked the play, Lilly. I'm going to run out of plays pretty fast though, I guess."

"Oh, I think not a play. Next time dancing."

"Dancing?" he said, looking nervous. "Only if you promise to wear that dress again and go easy on me."

"You liked the dress?"

"Yes, Lilly. I think you should wear it every night." She laughed again. "I really should talk to you about the play. Explain myself. If you feel ready?"

"I feel better now."

"How to say this?" he said, leaning back, arms above his head. "That play is very special to me. It's been like a friend, maybe, or at least a comfort to me for the last ten years. It has to do with when my mother died, as I said. Sometimes it seems like the only way I can still feel close to her. After all these years...I only have a few pictures, you know...I'm afraid I won't be able to remember her face, if I can even now...Lilly, I asked you to go to the play with me because I wanted you to know that the two of us have something in common. We've both lost someone. Of course, my loss is nothing like yours. I wouldn't say that. But it's still on my mind. You know how it is. It's every day, even after all this time."

He stopped, head dropping.

"Tell me about your mother, Daniel."

"Oh, she was a wonderful mother. Funny, you know..." And so he told her, only the third person in his life—after Dr. Marcowitz and Frau Delarosa—with whom he had ever shared the story of his mother. He had never let any one else get close enough to him, even Anna, he realized later. She had never asked him. It slowly sunk in that he and Anna had not really been close at all.

He didn't tell her the whole story, not that night. There was so much to tell and it had been so long inside of him untold, building up like a long novel, that like a true introvert he could have talked in a long soliloquy hour after hour, day after day, emptying himself of years of reflection. And Lilly would have let him. But for that night, feeling exhausted, he was content just to tell her of the happy times. The fun he had in the television studio. The one brief time she came back from Vietnam and they had the house to themselves. It was enough.

"It feels good to talk about it, doesn't it?" she said when he was finished.

"Yes. It does."

"You should talk about it when you need to then."

"Maybe I will. Was that what it was like in the widows group for you, Lilly?"

"Not at first, Daniel. Nowadays, yes. But not in the beginning. That's the thing. Couple months after...you know, it happened... they encouraged us to go down to New York for that National Day of Mourning. The counselors wanted us to see it, I think, maybe to help us all really see that it was real. Still smoldering, you know? But it wasn't such a good thing to do that. I think it was a mistake for me to go. But I went. And they started up the grief group and it didn't feel right to talk. It felt like I was betraying something. Betraying him, I guess. Because it wasn't real yet. That's what I mean. Talking about it felt like that was going to make it real and I didn't want it to be real. I think you understand that."

"Yes. Yes, I do."

"But it does get to be real. Every day, a little bit more. In the beginning it was like the reality was a nightmare and I wanted to wake up and be back where I started. But now, it's different. It's better. Now, it seems like that life was a dream. And sometimes I want to go back to sleep."

"I'm glad you can talk about it like this, Lilly."

"That play, Daniel. You said it made you think of your mother. It made me think of Tim. That scene in the end, where he sees his wife and they sing."

"I know. Gets to me every time."

"It made me cry for the first time in a while."

"I'm sorry, Lilly. That's what I wanted to talk about. I think I was being selfish. I was thinking about me, about myself. I don't think I really stopped long enough to consider what it might be like for you…And that's not right. I just wanted you to be there with me and I am sorry if it hurt you."

"Daniel, it's all right," she sighed, eyes filling up again. She wiped them, smiling. "We just had a little talk. Tim and I. That's all. Just a minute…okay now…I meant it when I said I was grateful. I think I need to try to be more grateful in my life right now. So, thank you. I haven't seen a lot of plays, you know. Not like that. That…That was something…so beautiful. The music was wonderful. I don't listen to music like that. Maybe I should. I like it. I just had one question though."

"Yes?"

"Are all plays like that?"

"Like *The Secret Garden*?"

"All so sad?"

"No, Lilly." He laughed. "Some plays are even funny. Make you fall right out of your chair. I promise to take you to a funny play next time."

"I think I need a little walk right now," she said, wiping her eyes. "Then you can take me home."

"Sure thing."

When they came out of the south door of the Marriott, Daniel told the driver to give them a few minutes and, taking Lilly by the arm, guided her toward the sea out to the point on Long Wharf. She buttoned up his jacket against the chill of the sea breeze. Daniel braved it stoically. At the end of the pier a pavilion, strung with lights, looked out over Boston Harbor. The city twinkled brightly on two sides and the lights of Charlestown across the harbor floated on gentle waves. They sat on a stone bench.

"Lilly, this has been a wonderful evening."

"Except for the food."

"My mistake. I'll do better next time. But I'm worried, Lilly. I have to be honest with you. I like you. I think we can understand each other." Her face was clear in the reflected light. "Lilly, I need to know, what do you want?"

She stood, understanding him, but more than that, understanding herself and where she was in her life and what she needed to do and where she needed to go.

"I just want people in my life who make me think," she began, speaking to the sea. "And to try new things, and go out to see the world. People who make me laugh. I want to learn about things that have always made me curious. I want to know what it's like not to live in the city. What it's like to see green all around, and water, big water. Like this. And rocks and mountains and music too. Is that so much to want? I wanted it when Tim was around and I still want it. I can't let what happened take that away from me. And I won't. I will not for one minute give into fear. I will not be defeated by it. Is that what you want too, Daniel?"

"Lilly, I am quieter than you are." He stood, joining her. "I am happy enough to sit by the fire with a book. But I want someone else to sit with me. I am tired of being alone. Lilly, I don't know how to explain it to you. You have brothers, family, friends. I see that. For ten years or so I had to pay an analyst to sit by the fire with me, and those were the best ten years of my life. Not because of what I learned. Not really. It was more that I just needed someone to sit with me and not feel so alone.

"I used to fool myself, Lilly. I told myself I preferred to be alone. I guess a lot of hurt people do. I just got used to it. The habit of just being around the house without needing to say anything to anybody. Or making a decision without having to work it out with someone else. Just a habit. But, on nights like this, which is only the second time I've ever shared something that I love so much with another person, it makes me realize maybe it's not enough to live just inside my head. I want somebody to share it with."

"So," she said, turning to face him. "You want to be my boyfriend?"

"I don't know how, Lilly. Honestly I don't."

"I know. That part is clear. But, somebody is going to have to teach you how to do it right and it may as well be me."

"That's not what I mean."

"I know, Daniel. I know." She closed her eyes. "I'll just say it. What about sex?"

"That's a problem."

"What's the problem?"

"It's been a long time, and even then there was a big problem. I'm willing to risk it. Try again. But I have to tell you, I don't know. I really don't know what's going to happen."

Lilly moved closer to him, standing face to face. "Daniel, I don't have time to wait. I'm moving on. Are you moving on or not?"

"I am trying, Lilly. God knows I am trying."

"Then kiss me."

"Are you serious?"

"Right now."

He leaned into her shoulder, raising his hand to her long hair to brush it away from her face. His lips found her lips slowly, halting, then proceeding. After so long a time the feel of a woman was new. He had forgotten the sheer physical reality of the closeness of another being; how the whole world collapses into the nearness of two and no other reality intrudes and there is only attentiveness and reaction to the minute movement of lips firming, softening, opening, and closing. What she withholds. What she allows. What she invites. All with the slightest flutter of a breath and the delicate caress of tiny muscles.

"I think you remember how to kiss," she said.

"Not really."

"It's a start." She took his hand.

THREE WEEKS LATER Daniel stood in the familiar elevator, holding the door, holding the door forever as his father labored painfully in the direction of the dining hall. The white back of his neck was wrinkled and furled under white laps of hair that needed a trim. Daniel made a mental note to talk to the staff about a barber, and then smiled. Maybe Lilly would enjoy coming out to the nursing home to cut The Old Man's hair. Or maybe not. He still found it hard to believe that anybody else would enjoy coming out to visit The Old Man.

"They're serving spaghetti tonight, Dad. Your favorite."

"Not if it's cold by the time they put it on the tables. It was last time."

"Well, if it's cold, we'll send it back. Or I'll take you out to eat."

"It'll be alright."

Daniel couldn't tell as he watched his father whether it was just his imagination or a clinical insight. Paul Osgood's shuffle seemed slower. His gait more unsteady. Geriatrics was not Daniel's specialty. He'd have to ask around to get someone to look into it.

"Looks to me like you lost a step or two, Dad," he said as they finally sat. "I thought you were working with the physical therapist?"

"Not for a while."

"Why not?"

"Getting to be too much of a bother. He's gonna break my legs."

"Maybe I should have somebody look at your legs then."

"Hell no."

"I'm just saying if I got you a good doc, maybe he could do something for you."

"I know what they're going to say. They're going to want to put me in a wheelchair. Mentioned it last week."

"Well? Might be for the best, Dad."

"No. The day they put me in that wheelchair is going to be the last day that I walk. And I'm not gonna give it up, see?"

"You're not going to give up?"

"No. I may be slow, but they can just wait a while, can't they?"

"Good for you, Dad. Good for you." Daniel laughed.

"Look, here's the spaghetti and it's steaming hot. Not so bad."

Even though only the two of them sat at a table set for eight, the staff brought the full course—prawns, fillets of fish, scallops, mussels, calamari rings, and the marinara sauce with fresh tomatoes. Daniel arranged the plates for both of them.

"Prawns again, Dad? I think I'll stick to the scallops."

"I'll take those prawns if you don't like them."

Daniel fed his father while his own plate went cold. It didn't bother him. It happened every time.

"Hey Dad, can I borrow the Lincoln? I want to take a little trip."

"Sounds alright to me. I don't think I'll be needing it this week."
Paul Osgood hadn't driven in ten years, but it was a game they played.
"But you better get the timing checked."

"What's wrong with the timing?"

"That Lincoln is finicky, you know. Doesn't want to run right if
you don't get it just perfect. That's why I always keep it in tip-top
shape. Nothing like a Lincoln for the open road."

"Smooth as silk. Floats like a boat."

"Not if the timing is off."

"I'll check it."

"You getting some time off from the hospital?"

"I don't work at the hospital anymore, Dad. Got my medical license
reinstated though. Guess I could work there if I wanted to."

"You lose your license?"

"That patient I lost. You remember. We were talking about it."

"I…remember. Yeah."

"Won the case. Civil suit too. My malpractice insurance went up
though, even when I won."

"What you gonna do? They get you coming and going. Just like the
damn Democrats. Taxes. Even a good doctor can't make a living any
more…You'll be back though?" Paul Osgood looked up at his son,
spaghetti on his lips, with genuine concern.

"I'll be back, Dad. Just going for the weekend. See you on Tuesday,
maybe. If I don't have patients. Friday night for sure. Like always. Don't
worry about it."

That same week, back at his office, Daniel packed his 8 millimeter
projector in the same box he had used to bring it home from the garage
sale. He had thought about selling it, winding down from the DVD
business, but decided to take it back to Beacon Hill. When you find an
old friend, something that brings you pleasure, he had learned that
you needed to keep a piece of it in your life because not a one of us is
only this or that, but a multitude of selves; old selves, becoming selves
not yet fully lived, and more importantly unlived selves that have only
been dreamed and even though they only live in fantasy, they live a life
of their own undiscovered and merely wait for the day when they might
have their chance to blossom. Daniel needed the feel of film through
his fingers to connect him to that part of himself.

A postcard lay on the desk. From Budapest. It pictured Buda
Castle, Heroes' Square, Parliament, Liberty Statue, the Roman
Aquincum and a striking architecture that Daniel did not recognize.
Hungarian Art Nouveau. Hungarian folk motifs mixed with other
Secessionist decorative elements. Distinctive Hungarian features

with not hint of an American influence. On the back of the card, Laurel had written simply:

```
Funny, there seem to be people
who appreciate literature living
here. Guess I'll be teaching in
the University. Imagine that! You
could visit, you know. Love,

Laurel
```

It was enough.

ON A FINE CLEAR SATURDAY MORNING in the first week of November, Daniel pulled up in front of Lilly's house in Brockton with a mighty blast from the gold-on-gold 1988 Lincoln Towncar, all nineteen feet of it, loud enough to challenge the *Pat T-Wagon* for bragging rights in the neighborhood.

"You gotta be kidding me!" Lilly protested, hands on her hips.

"What?!" said Daniel, a little disappointed. "Got no sense of style?"

"They gave you the limo?"

"No. But they made limos from these babies 'cause they knew a good thing when they saw it. You ready?"

"I am not getting in that thing until I know that you made reservations. And, when I do get in, no way in hell I am gonna drive it."

"I thought ahead. I planned everything, including food. I promise not to screw up…for a while…due to unforeseen circumstances that…I can't foresee. Madam."

"Like traffic on 128?" she said, getting in and running her hands over the blue leather.

"No. The Tobin Bridge, up Route 1 and then 128 all the way to Gloucester."

"God."

"Why is it that South Shore people have an innate fear of the North Shore? You've never been to Rockport in your whole life?"

"No."

"Amazing. Scoot on over, Lil, full bench seats. Fully reclining too."

In grand style, one arm out the open window and the other arm over Lilly's shoulders, Daniel guided the Lincoln out on the highway where its best qualities could be appreciated. It floated like a yacht over the asphalt, steady as an operating table. Lilly rested her head on his shoulder.

"Eighth date."

"Seventh, I still say, but who's counting. You like the drive, Lil? Do you feel that? Nothing like a Lincoln for the open road."

"I like it now. Let's go somewhere."

"We are going somewhere."

"No, I mean somewhere big."

"Where you wanna go, Lilly?"

"Out west. New Mexico. I want to see Taos. And Santa Fe. And then Arizona."

"Painted Desert."

"And the crater thing."

"Meteor Crater. Winslow."

"Saw that in a movie once. *Starman*. Good movie."

"Jeff Bridges, Karen Allen. 1984. You were young then."

"Ha-Ha. And Sedona. Northern Arizona Massage Therapy Institute. One week course. Just to try it. I'm serious. Let's go."

"I know you are." He kissed her forehead. "We can go. But first, Rockport. And if you still like me after this weekend, then we'll get out there."

"One step at a time, Daniel."

"I know."

The New England color was already past peak, but here and there stands of maple were vibrant reds and oranges among the darker greens on pines and spruce and Eastern hemlock. In Rockport, the streets narrowed, winding up the hill, and the gray and weathered cottages and white Colonials spoke of centuries by the sea. Only a few sailboats, halyards clanking on the masts, were still in the water so late in the season. Over the water the lowering sun cast a Winslow Homer light up over the rocks to turn the sea spray yellow and gold. Daniel wound the Lincoln up the narrow road to Annisquam Village and out to Halibut Point.

"I want to show you something," he said, taking her hand.

They walked briefly through the cool and crunching leaves under the trees, out as far as the lighthouse, and then turning up a gravel path angling they continued past the deep pits of granite, their fresh water clear as mountain streams thirty feet below the sheer cliff walls.

"It's beautiful," she began.

"No. Not yet. There's more."

Up a steeper path now, they could hear, but could not see the ocean, far below, crashing on smooth granite ledges carved a hundred years ago for buildings in Boston, New York, Philadelphia. With the last ten yards the blue sky, bluer than the sea, opened to the water, bigger than the sky, green in the shallows, and a darker green fading outward, and dark unfathomable blue at the horizon circling wider than their eyes could take in at the tip of Halibut Point.

In a joy she had seldom felt, Lilly clutched him. He felt it too, unfamiliar, because it had been what seemed a lifetime ago since he had last felt that flutter in his heart of something open and unrestricted without any holding back on account of fear or longing or sadness. Was this what joy felt like? He could not remember. And the miracle of it was that it could be shared.

"You done good," she whispered.

"You said you wanted rocks and mountains and green and big water. Best I could do, for now. And there's a fireplace back in the room, for me. And a book or two. So I thought maybe this time we had the bases covered."

"It's beautiful. It's perfect."

"It's always been one of my favorite places. We used to come up here when I was a kid."

She kissed him. "I want to go back to the room now."

"You don't want to walk on the rocks?" He said, finding himself more nervous than he liked.

"You have to trust me, Daniel." She took his hand.

The fire was already lit in the early afternoon. Daniel had thought ahead. The mantel was laid with enough wood for the weekend and the little oak table was set with flowers, an Italian white wine in the silver bucket, sharp cheese, French bread, and fresh grapes.

"I thought a little wine would help. So I ordered this crisp Italian Pinot Grigio. I should let it breathe." He popped the cork and poured two glasses. In the time it took him to finish and set them on the tray, she was already out of her clothes, except for a single strap on her white dress, which she gently pushed from her shoulder as he turned.

"Later, Daniel."

She wanted him to see her, to witness her undressing; to witness the first fact of her new life—that she was unafraid. She wanted him to see her heart still beating and still open after all that had happened so that in his eyes she would see it herself and believe. She would know it from his quickening breath. She would know it from the basic assent of a man to a woman's body.

She was not disappointed. His eyes met hers, at first, then wandered to her body. Head bowing slightly, Lilly looked away only once. And quickly up again, arching, turning toward him unafraid. He sighed, a shudder slowly rolling down from his eyes as his body awoke to her body. His hands took in her hands. His chest took in her chest. His hips took in her hips.

Absorbing the warm light of his regard, Lilly felt the shudder herself. To be so respectfully regarded, at last, was the only healing she really needed. Because she was already herself again.

"Now you."

"I'll need help."

"I can help you."

He had to close his eyes. Her hands unbuttoned his shirt, lingering on his shoulders. It fell away softly. Then his belt, his shoes, his pants. He was not embarrassed, only fragile.

"Kiss me now."

She embraced him, straining toward him on her toes. His arms steadied her. When she had had enough of kisses, she turned, guiding his hands with hers, to explore her, receiving him and teaching him in the same moment.

A woman is such a beautiful thing. Beautiful in line and form and curve. Essential. Like a fine charcoal drawing of the archetypal form. Complete in itself with nothing more needed. Beautiful in receiving all that yearning desire can imagine and beyond the imagining offer to her out of its deepest heart, fully given, without fear, without any holding back at all, but unrestrained empty itself in living as it is only meant to do. Life spending itself entirely to create more life. This is life fully lived. There is nothing more essential.

www.ingramcontent.com/pod-product-compliance
Lightning Source LLC
Chambersburg PA
CBHW030542030726
47495CB00004B/1098